The Twilight Zone

Book 1
SHADES OF NIGHT, FALLING

JOHN J. MILLER

ibooks

new york
www.ibooks.net
DISTRIBUTED BY SIMON & SCHUSTER, INC.

With love and thanks for
Bob and Dorothy Gerstner
for their support over the years, and
also for their collaborative effort on who became
the single most important part of my life.

An Original Publication of ibooks, inc.

The Twilight Zone
TM and © 2003 CBS Broadcasting, Inc.
ALL RIGHTS RESERVED.

An ibooks, inc. Book

All rights reserved, including the right to reproduce this book
or portions thereof in any form whatsoever.
Distributed by Simon & Schuster, Inc.
1230 Avenue of the Americas, New York, NY 10020

ibooks, inc.
24 West 25th Street
New York, NY 10010

The ibooks World Wide Web Site Address is:
http://www.ibooks.net

ISBN 0-7434-5858-3
First ibooks, inc. printing May 2003
10 9 8 7 6 5 4 3 2 1

Edited by Karen Haber

Special thanks to John Van Citters

Cover design by Mike Rivilis
Printed in the U.S.A.

There is a fifth dimension
beyond that which is known to man.

It is a dimension as vast as space,
and as timeless as infinity.
It is the middle ground between
light and shadow, between
science and superstition, and
it lies between the pit of man's fears
and the summit of his knowledge.

This is the dimension of imagination.
It is an area which we call...

The Twilight Zone

"Certain it is, the place still continues under the sway of some bewitching power, that holds a spell over the minds of the good people, causing them to...[be] subject to trances and visions; and frequently see strange sights, and hear music and voices in the air. The whole neighborhood abounds with...haunted spots, and twilight superstitions...and the nightmare...seems to make it the favorite scene of her gambols."

—Washington Irving
The Sketch Book

PROLOGUE

June 21, 1821, dawned like many of the other first days of summer that had come to Geiststadt, a small village nestled between hill-ridge and marsh in Kings County, New York, on the west end of Long Island. It was bright and sunny, pleasantly warm with the mildness of spring surrendering to the promise of sultry summer in the air. But before day's end cold wind and snow would lash the village, terrifying its inhabitants and setting in motion a chain of events that would take more than three hundred years to resolve.

Captain Benjamin Noir paced restlessly all afternoon outside the birthing chamber occupied by his wife Gretchen, the midwife, and Callie, the housekeeper who'd been with Noir for decades. Noir was sixty-four and a retired seafarer, but he was still handsome, dark-haired, and strong as a man of half his years.

He'd met, wooed, and married his young wife in the eleven months he'd lived in Geiststadt. She carried two infants in her womb. The Captain prayed fervently that at least one would be a boy. The odds seemed to favor that possibility. Benjamin Noir had fathered seventeen children—nine were still alive—on three previous wives. None on paramours, mistresses, whores, or passing fancies. He had been very careful about that. Of the seventeen children, twelve had been boys. It seemed likely that at least one of the two Gretchen now carried would be a boy. One had better be. Benjamin Noir was impatient for another son. He wasn't getting any younger and he needed a thirteenth son. This was also an auspicious day, one of the ancient calendar's most auspicious. It was the first day of the New Year. It was a good day for children to be born.

Only the infants would not come from his wife's womb.

Gretchen Noir had gone into labor at noon. Her water had broken almost immediately. The nearest doctor was in Brooklyn, a day's journey to the west. Geiststadt's midwife had presided over most of the births in the village for over two decades. She could undoubtedly bring wife and child safely through the birthing process as long as there were no complications.

But afternoon turned to evening with only strangled groans and occasional shrieks coming from behind the closed door of the birthing room, as well as murmurs of encouragement from the midwife, and constant mumbled prayers from Callie in a language that only Noir and Callie, in all of Geiststadt, knew was not Spanish.

As the moon rose the night air suddenly turned cold.

The temperature plummeted fifty degrees in less than ten minutes. The summer wind turned to an arctic blast. Rain froze to hail and then to snow as thunder crashed and lightning split the sky.

The Geiststadt simple farmers and small merchants looked up at the sky, dumbfounded. The inexplicable temperature drop was bad enough, but the hail threw the livestock into frenzied panic as chunks of ice larger than any anyone had ever seen thudded to the ground. Some hailstones crashed through barn and manor roofs,

THE TWILIGHT ZONE

braining half a score of unfortunate animals as well as old Victor Derlicht as he tried to drag himself on his stroke-crippled leg to the safe haven of The Hanged Hessian.

The snow that followed on the heels of the hail was even worse, skirling down the lightning-stricken sky in ragged sheets, promising disaster at harvest time if it enshrouded the tender crop for too long.

Benjamin Noir felt the sudden spear of cold air strike inside the three-story house he'd built upon coming to Geiststadt and halted his metronomic pacing. He smiled. It must be time.

A scream burst out of the birthing chamber. Noir wondered if he should go in, but ultimately restrained himself. It was not his place. The midwife was in attendance, as was Callie, who had presided over the birth of all his children. None had died before, during, or soon after their birth. None yet, anyway.

Inside the chamber Gretchen Noir screamed again, and gritted her teeth in pain. She hadn't thought that it was going to be like this. Like most of the villagers she was of German stock. Unlike most of them she was lean, almost ethereal in build, not a stolid, wide-hipped baby machine. It was her beauty and grace that had first interested Captain Noir. And she'd certainly been attracted to him, despite forty years difference in age. She'd been fascinated by the air of strangeness about the sea captain who had traveled the world. And there was also his gold, of course.

She clenched her teeth, choking back another scream while the midwife, stationed between her spread legs, urged her on and the old housekeeper murmured incessant prayers over her in a strange language. Spanish, her wandering mind said, trying to fasten on something other than the excruciating pain wracking her abdomen and spreading in waves throughout her body. Callie was from Cuba, Benjamin had told her, the daughter of a noble Spanish family fallen on hard times. Benjamin. I'll never let him near me again, Gretchen promised herself, as her empty birth canal contracted, and the pain cut through her.

"Push, girl, push," the midwife told her. "Send them on their way."

"I'm. *Trying*," Gretchen Noir clenched her teeth as Callie wiped the sweat from her forehead, murmuring over her.

She spoke softly, she spoke quickly, words that were not Spanish but were heard and dimly understood, almost by instinct, by those in the womb who didn't know their meaning, but somehow did understand the promise in them.

The bigger, younger one moved, positioning himself in the warm darkness, feeling with tiny, clumsy hands, for what he could not see. He found his brother's body and pushed against it, heading instinctively where the murmured words told him to go. His tiny fist closed around something and his muscles stretched and swelled, shaking under the unaccustomed strain, as he wrapped the cord around his brother who was also straining foreward. He slipped ahead. He pushed off him, adding impetus to his descent, as powerful muscle caught and pulled him from his sanctuary.

THE TWILIGHT ZONE

He was born screaming into the bright, cold world. No one had to slap him to get his lungs working. He hated this awful new place. He had been tricked by the murmuring words that had come into his gently sleeping, nearly quiescent brain. He had no concepts to define this place except fright and hate as the words in his brain turned from a cajoling whisper to a triumphant shout.

"A male child!" Callie screamed in English.

She snatched the baby from the midwife's hands as soon as she'd cut the umbilical cord, and raced with it toward the door of the birthing room.

"A male child!" she shouted again.

Captain Noir flung the door wide, a look of profound joy and anticipation on his face.

"My son," he said, enraptured, reaching out for the red, wriggling, blood- and fluid-smeared infant.

The midwife looked at them as if they were slightly mad.

"The other child— " she began, and fell silent when Captain Noir turned cold eyes upon her.

"What of it?"

"There is trouble—"

"Do what you have to," he said brusquely.

Callie wrapped the squalling newborn in a length of cotton swaddling, wiping the birth-remnant off his tiny face. She handed the bundle to the Captain and they both made to leave the room.

"You don't understand," the midwife said desperately. "Your wife's in great danger. The other child—"

The Captain turned to her and fixed her with a gaze that had served him well during many a crisis at sea.

"It's your job," he said. "Take care of it."

The midwife turned back helplessly to the groaning Gretchen Noir as Callie followed Captain Noir from the room.

"My son," the midwife heard the Captain murmur. "My thirteenth son."

Twenty years,
eleven months,
three weeks,
and
two days later...

1.

Thursday, June 16th: The First Intercalary Day

Unlike the rest of his family, Jonathan Noir was an early riser.

He woke as the sun broke the horizon and shone warmly into his east-facing bedroom window. He was eager to get up and into the day. There were always many things to be done about the manor and on those rare occasions when the work load was light, there was always someplace interesting to explore around Geiststadt or the surrounding fields and hills.

He dressed quickly in brown trousers, almost white linen shirt, and rough leather boots well suited for farm work or hiking, whichever would occupy his day. After chores Jon hoped to steal a few hours in the afternoon to explore the meadows of HangedMan's Hill, which was more a long, rough, rocky ridge way than a gently sloping hillside. Summer would arrive in five days—along with his twenty-first birthday. The upland meadows were in their first bloom with a wealth of colorful and interesting wildflowers and butterflies. As far as Jon Noir knew, no one had yet done a systematic study of the *lepidoptera* of Kings County. It would be an interesting subject to occupy his idle hours for the next few months.

He went down the steps quietly, making little noise. Jon had ten siblings. All, even his twin brother, Thomas, were older than him. Only he, Seth, and James still lived with their father, Benjamin Noir, at Noir Manor where

THE TWILIGHT ZONE

Jon now enjoyed the privacy of his own bedroom. He could rise as early as he wanted without disturbing a roommate, and clutter the chamber with books, papers, and specimens of insects, plant life, and the local fauna without anyone complaining. But he did miss the hubbub and hustle of his younger years when the house had been full of his brothers and sisters. They were a varied group, fathered by Benjamin Noir on a succession of four wives. As the baby of the family Jon had garnered a lot of attention from them, particularly from his four sisters.

But his sisters were now all married. Sarah and Emily still lived in Geiststadt. Jane was in Brooklyn, a short day's journey to the West, and Catherine in faraway Massachusetts. His brothers Thomas—who boarded in Manhattan while attending Columbia University—Daniel, Alijah, Matthew, and Reuben also lived away from Geiststadt. Thomas spent his summers at Noir Manor. In fact, he was due any day, as Columbia's spring term had recently ended.

Jon envied Thomas's education. It was only one of a long list of grievances between them, dating back to Jon's earliest memories. Thomas had always had the finest of everything. Jon had to be satisfied with leftovers. He'd had only the scant local schooling, supplemented by occasional tutors somewhat grudgingly provided by his father. But Jon had learned a lot from books, as well as from simply observing his surroundings. Ultimately, though, he knew college wasn't for him. He could never go away to school. He loved Geiststadt far too much to leave it for long.

He took the back stairway down to the ground floor,

stopping in the kitchen where Callie sat in her rocking chair before the roaring fire in the open fireplace. As usual, she wore flowing skirts, apron, and cloth bonnet. Though it was nearly summer, she rocked before the blazing fire soaking up the warmth like an old beetle worshiping the morning sun.

No matter how early Jon rose, Callie was always already in the kitchen. A small, bird-like woman with a deeply lined and darkly tanned face, she'd been with Benjamin Noir for nearly forty years before he'd moved to Geiststadt, and the twenty years since. Captain Noir had never again married after Gretchen, his fourth wife, had died giving birth to Thomas and Jonathan. Callie was the woman of the house. Officially she was the Noir housekeeper, but basically she bossed the other servants and performed what few domestic tasks she felt like doing. Most often she sat in the kitchen warming her gaunt frame before the roaring fire. She could never get enough heat. She was from the Caribbean—Cuba, the story went—and though Geiststadt had a relatively mild climate, it couldn't compare to the tropical balminess of the islands of her long-gone youth.

She shot Jon a glance from her dark, hard eyes, sunken deep in a thin face wrinkled by years spent in that tropical sun. She wore a calico kerchief that hid her thin white hair. Her tiny, frail body was enveloped in her thick, voluminous skirts.

"Up already, boy?" she asked. She stood, and slapped some bacon in a pan and put some day-old bread to toast on the edge of the hearth. "You gone get some work done today, or waste your time crawling round the marsh?"

THE TWILIGHT ZONE

Jon smiled to himself. The marsh that lay west and south of Geiststadt was also one of his favorite hiking grounds.

"Not today," he said. "Thought I might poke around HangedMan's Hill some."

She turned and fixed him with her brilliant stare.

"Stay away from that place, boy. Stay away. Bad things happened there, long before we come to Geiststadt, when the Dutch was here."

"I know."

Callie was a fountain of tales, whether of strange happenings in the Carribean, or Key West, the island off the Florida coast where Benjamin Noir had last plied his seaman's trade before moving north. Or even the history of the Dutch village called Dunkelstad, which had once stood on the very land where Geiststadt was now.

There were even stories concerning strange happenings in Geiststadt itself—tales of ghostly sightings and mysteriously disappearing farm animals. Even people. Strange mists sometimes arose from the marshes, or crept down from the heights of HangedMan's Hill whose crest and higher slopes were still covered by virgin forest. There was even an odd tale connected with Jon's birthday. Callie solemnly swore that it had snowed on the night Jonathan and Thomas had been born, though they had come into the world on the first day of summer. Fortunately, that frigid episode had been brief. Normal temperatures had returned before the crops were ruined. Otherwise, Jon's and Thomas's reputations in the village might have forever been tarnished, though clearly the strange weather couldn't have been the fault of the newborn babes.

Callie liked nothing more than spooking a roomful of servants and children on a cold winter night with her tall tales. Sadly, though, Jon thought, there were no more children in the house. Seth and James had no interest in Callie's yarns. He was the only Noir left who did.

He sat at the wooden kitchen table. Callie brought him a platter of food and a mug of strong gunpowder tea that had come all the way from China. It was his father's favorite. Jon liked it as much as his father did, though they had little else in common.

Jon had inherited the features of Gretchen Noir, the mother he'd never seen. He was only of moderate height, and lean. Clean-shaven, with thick, unruly blond hair, blue eyes, and delicate cheekbones, nose, and mouth. He wondered if Callie—and his father—saw his mother's face in his. They never spoke of her. They never would say what she'd been like, and Jon had stopped asking a long time ago. Callie wasn't a tender woman, but, besides his older sisters, now all gone away, she was the closest thing to a parent Jon had ever had. His mother had died giving him birth and his father, at best, simply ignored him. When he and Thomas were growing up his father had given Thomas all his attention. But even Thomas, Jon realized, hadn't gotten their father's affection, for Benjamin Noir didn't have much affection to give.

Jon sopped a hunk of toasted bread in bacon grease and chewed it thoughtfully. His father was a big, strong, distant man. Still fit and vital though now in his eighties, he was educated, too. Not only about the sea, but about history and languages and astronomy and botany and many strange, odd things. He'd let Jon borrow his books and watched as Jon taught himself Greek and Latin with minimal help from occasional tutors, but he'd had no interest in educating the boy himself.

Jon had made himself useful on the manor from an early age, purely from an innate love of the house, the land, and the people and animals who lived on it. Benjamin Noir took advantage of Jon's talents, enabling him to turn his attention to his own arcane studies. He let Jon have more and more say in running the farm as Jon grew older and more knowledgeable. But what his father spent long days and nights studying, Jon couldn't exactly say. Benjamin Noir had shut him out entirely from that part of his life. Though he had some curiosity regarding his father's studies, Jon had found interests of his own to occupy his time and attention. Most of them centered about the land, its flora and fauna, even its imperfectly known history. There was more than enough in all that to occupy Jon's time and energy.

Jon finished the bacon, bread, and tea, and pushed away from the table, calling out a farewell to Callie, which she acknowledged with a wave of her wrinkled hand from her accustomed place in front of the fireplace.

Outside the sun was shining. Its rays blazed in glory upon the *uraeus* symbol made of gold leaf, blue and red enamel, and jet inlay set above the main entrance to Noir Manor on the east-facing side. The *uraeus* was a kind of Noir family crest. It consisted of a winged sun disk with a snake said to be a cobra writhing under it. Jon had seen similar insignia in travel books about Egypt. Some of the villagers—especially the Derlichts and their client families—proclaimed the *uraeus* pagan and sacrilegious, but it always made Jon feel safe and protected as it shone like a golden beacon in the rays of the sun.

There were probably twenty things that needed doing about the farm, but first Jon headed for the Glass House.

The villagers had called it Noir's Folly when Benjamin Noir had begun building it. Noir had lived for three months in a hut that barely had room for him and Callie and the children, erecting the Glass House before he built a barn for his livestock or even Noir Manor for himself and his family. Set in a slight depression that protected it from wind and storm but left it exposed on all sides to the sun, it was a hundred feet long, sixty wide, three stories tall, and was by far the biggest building in Geiststadt.

It was constructed of glass windows embedded in a web of wooden frames oriented north-south, with the main entrance in the south wall. Part of the north wall was brick and stone. An adjacent furnace room abutted this wall, designed, Jon had discovered, like those in ancient Roman bathhouses. The furnace heated water, which was then transported in ceramic pipes—also built on the Roman model—that ran under the conservatory's floor.

When it had been completed the plants began to arrive.

Orange and lemon and lime trees from Florida. Orchids of every size and color and description from a thousand islands of the far west. Herbs and medicinal shrubs from China. Insect-eating oddities from the jungles of the New

THE TWILIGHT ZONE

and Old world. Water lotuses and lilies from Egypt and the Amazon.

Benjamin Noir made a fortune—on top of the rumored fortune he'd brought to Geiststadt with him—supplying fresh fruit to the growing metropolis of Manhattan even in the dead of winter, as well as exotic flowers to society ladies and medicinal potions to doctors and quacks of every persuasion.

No one laughed at the Glass House now.

Jon went through the antechamber—the entrance was double-doored to conserve heat during the winter months—and entered the House proper. He wrinkled up his nose at the stench that suddenly assailed him and waved a hand at the swarm of flies whose buzzing was an annoyingly audible hum.

After twenty years his father's Corpse Flower was finally blooming.

It had started to flower two weeks ago. The previous season's single-leafed stalk, nearly twenty feet high, had collapsed and given way, as always, to a new bud growing out of the soil inside the giant tub in which the Corpse Flower resided. But this bud was different than the one that usually appeared. It grew ferociously fast, sometimes a preposterous foot a day, developing into what was technically called the spadix, a fleshy central column that bore an uncomfortable resemblance to a phallus. A bell-like structure called the spathe was now unfurling around the base of the spadix, reaching perhaps halfway up its eleven foot length. This spathe resembled a frilly-edged, upside down skirt. Its outside surface was dull green speckled with creamy spots. Its interior was vivid crimson, as if it had been painted with blood. As the spathe continued to slowly unfurl to its four-foot diameter, the plant's odor grew more and more potent. Its stench attracted swarms of insects, mostly flies by day and certain species of moths at night, which entered the Glass House through its ventilation panels.

This smell of rotting flesh gave the unusual plant its name of Corpse Flower. Benjamin Noir had brought its seed from the South Sea island of Sumatra. Jon could find no reference to it in any of his botany books. It was clearly related to the little Jack-In-The-Pulpit that Jon often came across during his rambles through the woodlands, but when this plant was compared to the homey little native it stood out like an oak to a shrub. Jon had been observing it with growing excitement over the last few weeks, visiting it early in the day and late at night and whenever he could in between, measuring and jotting down notes and drawings in his journal.

Even his father seemed entranced by the plant's transformation. Jon would find him standing before it nearly every day. Benjamin Noir took no notes or observations concerning it, but the rare flowering had clearly captivated him in his own way.

Jon had just finished his initial notes—the spadix had gained another six inches of height during the last twenty fours—when he was interrupted by a young field hand who came running breathlessly into the Glass House.

"Jon—" Isaac had been with for the Noirs for nearly five years. He and Jon were fast friends and companions. Probably several years younger than Jon, Isaac was an escaped slave from one of the larger plantation-style farms up the Hudson River, or, considering his accent, perhaps from somewhere far to the south. No one in Geiststadt particularly cared. Benjamin Noir owned no slaves because he thought they generally caused more problems than they were worth. He only cared that Isaac, who was bigger and stronger than most fully-grown men, did the work of two for the wages of one. Jon only cared that he was an ideal companion on his rambles through the countryside.

"What's all the excitement?" Jon asked.

"Old Erich says the cows broke through the fence again and got into the marsh. We gotta get them back before we lose any in the sinkholes."

Jon sighed. This was sure to take up most of the morning, which in turn would push his regular chores back to the afternoon. So much, he thought, for a quiet ramble up HangedMan's Hill.

"Let's get out of here," Isaac said. "The swamp smells better than that ugly old plant."

Thomas Noir rose earlier than usual. Much earlier. While he saw nothing wrong with languishing in a warm, comfortable bed, he knew that he had a busy day ahead of himself and he had better get going.

His once cozy rented room was no longer cozy. It was bare and sullen-looking in the early morning light. The things that made it bearable—his few pieces of furniture, his fine rugs, his books and manuscripts—were all gone. He'd packed them yesterday with the help of his servant, Tully McCool. Well, he thought of McCool as his servant. He knew that McCool had a different interpretation of their relationship. But that was all right. McCool could think what he thought. He—Thomas—knew the truth of the matter.

McCool had left the previous afternoon to get a head-start in the slow-moving furniture wagon. There was nothing left in Thomas's room but the bed and the chamber pot under it, a change of clothing from underwear out, and a small satchel that held the few necessities he'd need on the way to Geiststadt. Even his copper bathing basin, which he'd kept in a closet-sized room just down the hall, had been carted away by McCool and was already on the way to the bucolic little hamlet that Thomas had the misfortune to call home.

Thomas sighed as he relieved his bladder, rather inaccurately, in the direction of the chamber pot. He didn't care. He was leaving this room forever and when he returned to the metropolis of Manhattan—which he would, as soon as possible—he would have achieved his majority, his birthright, and his inheritance.

There would be no more hired rooms. He was tired of living on the Captain's parsimonious handouts. He wasn't ready to build a house yet, so he'd take a suite in a fine hotel. In fact, come to think of it, he wasn't ready to tie himself to a single place, even as fine a place as Manhattan. The whole world—Boston, London, Paris, Vienna—was out there, ready for him to explore. Perhaps he wouldn't return to Manhattan after all, but book passage to the Continent. He had a year more to finish his degree, but what did he need with a piece of paper proclaiming him a college graduate? He would finish his more important studies this summer. Then perhaps a year on the Continent would suit him more than a year in college cramming his head full of worthless scraps of knowledge that were no use in the real world.

Thomas dressed carefully, fastidiously, as he mused about his future. He was a big man. He had inherited the Captain's size as well as his dark good looks. That was, he realized, one of the reasons why the Captain favored him over his brothers. With his thick black hair, dark eyes, sharp features, imposing height, and evident physical strength he looked more like a muleskinner or stevedore than a gentleman. That was why he always dressed like a gentleman. So people would know who he was. Not a fop, with excessive perfume and a high-combed pompadour. Not a dandy, with too-high collars and too-lacy cuffs and too many accessories cluttering his appearance. But a gentleman, like Beau Brummel, the man who'd defined masculine fashion on the Continent for the last thirty years.

His friends thought him excessive to change his underwear every day and take a water bath two or even three times a week. But besides being a disciple of Brummel, Thomas also liked the sensation of cleanliness. He enjoyed the scent of freshly washed skin and the soft caress of newly laundered linen.

His best clothes were already packed and on their way to Geiststadt. He didn't care to waste them on a seven or eight hour carriage ride over dusty roads. His second best—even his third best—were quite sufficient to bedazzle any observers on the road home.

He put on clean linen drawers and undershirt and a fresh pair of cotton socks. Then his Wellington boots. It was difficult to pull on the knee-high, calf-hugging brown leather boots without the assistance of a valet, but Thomas persevered. Then he shimmied into his dark blue trousers with the buttoned side panel. Skin tight to the knee, they were cut looser below with enough slack in them to fit over his boots. Thomas buckled the straps that fit under the Wellington's insteps tight to ensure unwrinkled perfection over his muscular thighs. He shrugged into his white linen shirt and struggled with the cravat for a moment, seeking that elegant drape which only an experienced valet seemed capable of producing. He decided in the end not to waste too much effort on its meticulous folds. He was going to spend the day in a stage and then a hired carriage, not in a fashionable dining establishment.

The waistcoat came next, ribbed wool and silk, a somewhat lighter blue than his trousers, then the double-breasted riding coat that matched the trousers perfectly. It hugged his broad chest and narrow hips, its faultless construction declaiming Thomas's faultless taste as a gentleman of refined elegance.

He checked his pocket watch, giving it the customary morning wind before arranging it on its golden chain in his waistcoat pocket. It was not a terribly old watch, dating from the closing years of the previous century, but nevertheless it positively emanated *heka*. It had been one of the Captain's prize possessions. Thomas had been thrilled and amazed when the Captain had given it to him last year on his twentieth birthday.

It was French. It kept exquisite time, even having an insert face that ticked off the seconds. Its gold outcast

THE TWILIGHT ZONE

was decorated with an Egyptian scene done in *repousse*—dating it to sometime soon after Napoleon's invasion of that country in 1798. It showed a sphinx with an outsized *uraeus* figure hovering in the air above it. When the Captain had given Thomas the watch he'd told him with more than a little satisfaction that once it had belonged to Napoleon himself.

All antique, odd, and beautiful objects had *heka*. Or so the Captain said. The fact that this object had once been owned by the most powerful man in the world increased its *heka* considerably. Thomas, who had inherited the Captain's inclinations and talents as well as his looks, could feel the watch's *heka* when he held it in his hands. It was warm in his waistcoat pocket. Its ticking was like heartbeat of a hidden familiar, secret, cunning, waiting to spring into action to enforce Thomas's slightest whim.

It was good, Thomas thought, to have power.

He sighed. Someday he might really discover how good it was. Meanwhile, it was a waste of time to muse upon the future and what it might bring when the present had to occupy his full attention. First he had to take the stagecoach to Brooklyn. There he'd hire a carriage to Geiststadt. The regular stage service between Brooklyn and Flatbush—with a stop at Geiststadt—was too sporadic to suit Thomas's needs. He hated wasting his time waiting on schedules arranged by others.

He sighed again. He anticipated three, maybe four months in Geiststadt. Well, it couldn't be helped. He had to be careful. He had to make sure that the transfer of power and wealth went smoothly. He couldn't afford any mistakes. He had a long and prosperous life waiting ahead of him. If his plans worked. And why wouldn't they?

Jon Noir stood in dark unmoving water up to his calves, the mud sucking greedily at his boots. Slogging through the marsh that spread out for miles southwest of Geiststadt took effort, but Jon had tireless legs and a deceptively strong back and arms he'd developed in a lifetime of hiking, working the farm, and wandering the surrounding countryside.

It was a warm day. Jon and Isaac and old Erich, at times separately and at times together, had been chasing their runaway milk cows all morning. They had found all but the one named Elsa, leading them in turn to safer pastures than the unfenced marshland with its infrequent but deadly sinkholes. As it approached noon, the three searched different areas of the undulating landscape calling for her.

Jon took a breather, sitting on a grass hummock and wiping the sweat from his brow with his forearm. He could use a cool wind for a momentary respite from the heat, like the one that had blown on his birth night. Callie used to hold the entire Noir household spellbound telling of it, but none more so than Jon and his twin Thomas. For Jon the stories were enough to quench his thirst for the faraway. Thomas, though, was as different from Jon in this as he was different in so many other ways. Callie's stories only seemed to fire his desire to see everything, experience everything, and somehow maybe someday even come to own everything.

When Thomas graduated from Columbia, Jon expected

THE TWILIGHT ZONE

his father would send him on the Grand Tour. A year in Europe. England. France. Germany. Spain. Italy. Greece. Jon did envy Thomas that. A year abroad would be something to remember and talk about all the rest of his life in Geiststadt. But it seemed unlikely that Jon would get the opportunity to take such a trip. His father would never pay for it.

"Jon!!! JON-A-THAN!!!"

Isaac's deep shout carried strongly over the open marshland. Jon turned and saw the large, dark figure waving strenuously. He waved back across the rolling marshland and started to slog towards him, avoiding the open water and overly lush regions of vegetation that indicated sink pits which could very well be bottomless.

"I found Elsa!" Isaac bellowed unnecessarily, as Jon could see the black and white spotted bovine standing placidly at Isaac's side.

"Fine!" Jon said as he approached. He happily thumped the cow on the side of the neck. "Just in time for lunch." He turned around in a circle, scanning the expanse of marsh that surrounded them. "If we can find Erich, we can head for home."

There was no sign of the old cowherd. He could, Jon realized, be almost anywhere in the marshes. The bog land was relatively flat, but did slope in rolling waves to the south. Fed by a stream running off Skumring Kill, the marsh covered hundreds of acres south and west of Geiststadt. Although mostly a grassy plain, it was also dotted with copses of willow, elm, and oak as well as bramble thickets too dense and thorny to penetrate.

Isaac mopped the sweat from his face with a rag and tucked it in the back pocket of his breeches.

"Maybe Erich got tired of looking. Maybe he already headed off to the Hanged Hessian."

"Maybe." Jon smiled to himself. Old Erich had been with the Noirs for longer than Jon had been alive. He was inclined to take advantage of his age, as well as Jon's good will. Jon frequently covered the cowherd's lapses with his father. Erich was a good man, loyal and knowledgeable, but he was getting up in years and lately took more rest than Benjamin Noir might approve of. "All right. We're not too far from The Hessian. Let's go see if he's there."

"I could do with a drink of cool water," Isaac said, leading Elsie by a rope he'd looped around her neck.

Jon squinted up at the sun riding high in the middle of the sky.

"I could do with a pint of cider and a bite of ploughman's." He stuck his hand in his pocket and jangled the change therein. "And fortunately I think I've got enough for both of us."

Isaac grinned. "All right."

Together they picked a path through the marsh, trying to stick to the higher, drier ground. Isaac led the cow. Jon watched for butterflies and unusual flowering plants. They both kept an eye out for Erich, though truthfully both were thinking more of the cool pints waiting for them at the inn on the Brooklyn-Flatbush road.

But life in Geiststadt was not all butterflies and cider.

Jon stopped so suddenly that Isaac, trudging at his

heels as he led Elsa by the rope around her neck, almost blundered right into him.

"What is it?" the ex-slave asked as his friend stood rooted to the ground.

Jon Noir had a number of small, but useful talents that he accepted as his lot in the everyday scheme of things. One was his talent for finding lost things. He was so good at finding lost things, he'd often find things that no one actually realized were lost.

Like old Erich's body floating face down in a patch of scummy bog water, flies already buzzing around him looking for places to lay their eggs on a warm spring morning.

"Sweet Jesus," Isaac whispered, catching sight of the body over Jon's shoulder.

Though they could see only the back of the head, neither doubted that it was Erich. The body was dressed in the old cowman's clothes. It was tall, lean, and stringy. The hair that floated like a dirty halo on the scummy marsh water was long and grey.

Jon, finally compelled to action, ran forward, splashing through the standing water that had accumulated in a slight hollow. It came up to Jon's thighs as he reached Erich's side and knelt beside him. He turned the body over.

Isaac, who had followed him, cried out wordlessly.

Erich's expression was one of utmost horror, as if he realized his impending doom. As if he knew it would be horrible and painful beyond endurance. A wound gaped in the old man's chest where his heart had once been. The organ had been messily excised, it seemed, by a sharp blade that had hacked through Erich's sternum and ribcage.

But that wasn't all. As if to make up in some fantastic measure for the removal of Erich's heart, a childishly crude cupid's heart had been incised on Erich's wrinkled forehead. Words had been cut in block letters in his right and left cheeks. They were hard to read in the stubble that covered Erich's hollow, seamed cheeks like a salt and pepper snowfall. They were in German, which was not Jon's native tongue. But Jon was good with languages and he'd lived in a German-dominated community all his life. He'd picked up enough Deutch to decipher the legend "I AM" on the old stockman's right cheek. His left bore the word "RETURNED," spilling over past his jawline and onto his leathery neck.

Jon and Isaac looked at each other in baffled horror as Elsa chewed her cud in bovine contentment.

2.

The limp corpse almost seemed to squirm out of their grip when they tried to carry it by its arms and legs. Jon decided to carry the burden alone. Isaac helped him heft the body over his shoulders, but Jon was staggering under its awful weight after only a few steps. He soon acquiesed to the inevitable and allowed Isaac to bear the corpse most of the way to the village.

They were in the northern part of the marsh, so they headed—as best as they could figure—toward the northernmost of the three bridges that crossed Skumring Kill and led to Geiststadt and solid land.

The heat got worse, as did their thirst, but Jon ignored as best he could both the harsh sun and his dry throat. His thoughts centered on who in Geiststadt could possibly want Erich dead and on who had the savagery to kill him in such a terrible manner. But there was no one whom Jon could think of who'd be the answer to those questions.

The rickety old North Bridge was the oldest across Skumring Kill. It had been built by the Derlichts when they'd settled the village over a hundred and twenty years ago. Isaac carried Erich's body like a baby in his brawny arms, though even he was obviously struggling by the time they reached Johann Schmidt's cooperage on the village outskirts. Isaac set the corpse down gently on the thick grass in the cooper's yard and collapsed in the shade of the spreading oak which had become the gathering place for those who wanted to talk business with Schmidt.

Schmidt, a recent arrival to the village who'd opened shop a few weeks previously, was not present. Agatha Derlicht, who'd been inspecting the cooper's stock of wooden barrels, casks, tubs, and buckets, watched with her hawk-like eyes as Isaac and Jon approached, body and cow both in tow. She was in her eighties, but still spare and straight. The hair pinned under her cap was snow white, but still as thick as it had been nearly seventy years before when she'd been not only the richest but also the most beautiful girl in Geiststadt. Agatha had gone lean with age. Her face and broad forehead was lined with creases, but she still had the elegant cheekbones of her youth and her clear blue eyes were still sharp with intelligence. The age-induced leanness of her face made her blade of a nose seem even more prominent, and her lost teeth gave an unsightly pucker to a generous mouth that once had been inviting but was now drawn in a perpetual grimace of distaste. Wiry veins stood out in the thin column of her neck and pulsed rhythmically in the hallows beside her forehead with every breath she took. She shook with a constant tremor that made her seem like a lean tree trembling in an unseen wind. Sometimes the tremor extended to her voice, making her stutter.

Another woman, much younger and much prettier, was with her. Jon hadn't yet met her, but like everyone else in the small community he knew that she was the cooper's daughter. She'd been extolling the virtues of

THE TWILIGHT ZONE

her father's workmanship to Frau Derlicht. The expression on her lovely young face changed from polite inquiry, to puzzlement, to outright horror as she realized the nature of Isaac's burden.

"Pardon...ladies," Isaac said, panting for breath. "I need...to rest...a moment."

The two women, one the oldest inhabitant of Geiststadt and probably the wealthiest, the other, along with her father, the newest, looked at Erich's body with uncertainty and horror.

"E-E-Erich." That Agatha Derlicht realized immediately who it was was unsurprising in a community of three hundred. Nor did the old woman fail to notice the blood splashed on his jersey. "What happened to him? What kind of acci-ci-ci-dent—"

She fell silent as Jon Noir shook his head.

"No accident, Frau Derlicht. Someone—" He hesitated. He had no wish to shock either Agatha Derlicht or the beautiful young woman, but he had no other words to describe it. "Someone took his heart."

"Took?" Agatha leaned over creakily. "L-l-looks more l-l-like it was cut out. B-b-butchered."

"Oh." The cooper's daughter made a faint sound of distress as Jon bobbed his head meekly, acknowledging the truth of Agatha Derlicht's words. He wasn't afraid of Agatha Derlicht. Not exactly. Before Benjamin Noir's arrival she'd controlled Geiststadt with an iron first rarely softened by a brocade glove. Her father's older brother had founded the village in 1710 on the remnants of an abandoned Dutch settlement, and the Derlichts had controlled the community ever since. Only Benjamin Noir disputed their leadership, and had actually succeeded in making some inroads upon it in the last twenty years. The matriarch of the founding clan was the only Derlicht left from the second generation of settlers. She and her younger sister Katja, purportedly bedridden in her dark bedroom in the attic of Derlicht Haus, purportedly mad. But no one ever talked of Katja.

Agatha Derlicht settled her disquieting gaze on the girl. The matriarch had little use for the faint-hearted. Even, or perhaps especially, among women.

"You act like you've never seen a b-b-body," she sniffed.

"Not one like this," the girl said.

"Forgive us," Jon said, turning towards her. "If we'd known you were here, we'd have avoided your yard. But we couldn't carry him farther without a rest—"

Jon looked into her eyes and found himself captivated. He had seen her a few times before at a distance. Never close enough to talk to. Her eyes were blue like Agatha Derlicht's, but where the Frau's eyes were like ice on a frozen pond in the dead of winter, hers were like a summer sky on a warm afternoon. Soft and soothing and somehow infinite. Jon thought he could get lost in those eyes. Her face was heart-shaped, her cheeks plump, her thick golden hair, uncontainable, slipping away from the pins that tried to hold it in place under her cloth cap.

"Perhaps I could prevail upon your father for the loan of a barrow, so we can get poor Erich home as quickly and, um, in as dignified a fashion as possible."

"Father's resting now," she said. Her voice was music.

"But, certainly, please feel free to take a barrow. I'll fetch a cloth to cover your friend."

Jon bowed. "Thank you."

She turned and hastened to their living quarters in the loft above the cooper's workshop.

Jon turned to look again at Agatha Derlicht. She was observing him with a disapproving expression. But that was not unusual. He cleared his throat.

"What do we do now, Frau?" Crimes of a serious nature were rare in the village. There hadn't been a killing in Geiststadt in all of Jon's life, as far as he knew. Any disputes that occurred were usually settled through appeal to Agatha Derlicht, though in recent years some villagers had come to Benjamin Noir to settle their grievances.

"We must send a messenger to the magistrate in Brooklyn." Brooklyn was the county seat, the source of law and government in Kings County. "They will send someone to investigate this hideous crime."

Jon and Isaac exchanged glances, nodding. Yes, that was the natural first step to take in finding the murderer. But who, Jon wondered again, who in Geiststadt could have done such a terrible thing? And furthermore, why? Erich had been a grumpy old man with a temper, but he was harmless. He owned nothing worthy of stealing. He had no personal enemies that Jon knew of, and Jon was pretty sure that he'd know if the old man did. Erich had been garrulous to a fault. But no one would kill an old man in such a savage manner because he could be ill tempered and sometimes talked too much. Would they?

Jon chewed on his lower lip thoughtfully.

"What," he asked Agatha Derlicht, "do you make of those words and signs carved on his cheeks and forehead?"

"Eh?" The old lady seemed a little startled by Jon's question. The incised words weren't obvious. They hadn't bled much and, as Jon had noted himself, they were almost hidden by Erich's facial stubble. Also, Frau Agatha's eyesight wasn't what it had been. She bent down limberly for one her age, and looked closely at Erich's face, grasping his cheeks almost absent-mindedly and turning his head on his stiffening neck to get a good look at both. "I AM RETURNED," she read aloud.

She looked back at Jon Noir, and he was surprised to see a suggestion of surprise on her face.

"I don't know," she said. "I don't know what it means."

"And the heart on his forehead? At least, I think it's a heart."

She took another close look at the dead man's face and shook her head, obviously baffled, as the cooper's daughter approached with a length of linen cloth to cover the body. Agatha Derlicht lowered her head and said softly, "There's no sense in bandying this about town. No sense in scaring people. This is something for the magistrate's investigator. Perhaps the priest as well. Not for idle gossip in the tavern and stables. Understand?"

Both Jon and Isaac nodded. The tone in her voice had turned her words from suggestion to command. "Yes, Frau Agatha," they said in unison.

THE TWILIGHT ZONE

She nodded back at them. "Good boys. Now take him home."

Thomas drowsed, despite the stifling heat and the clouds of dust swirling about the coach as it jostled down the rutted dirt road to Brooklyn. At least the coach wasn't crowded. Thomas had one bench all to himself. The other was occupied by a couple of cloddish farmer types who seemed bound for an even more distant—and pitiful—destination than Geiststadt. Thankfully, for some reason they seemed suspicious of Thomas. Other than eyeing him distrustfully and whispering to each other in an unfamiliar language, they left him alone. There was no attempt at travelers' camaraderie, for which Thomas was grateful. He stretched out his long legs, achieving a certain amount of comfort as the coach bounced along. He closed his eyes. Perhaps even slept. His inchoate thoughts were part dream, part reminiscence, part desire, as the coach clattered down the road.

There was nothing to look forward to in Geiststadt . The place itself was a tedious sinkhole that smelled mostly of cows and pigs. He liked no one in his family. He had active contempt for the three brothers who still resided in Noir Manor. As to the Captain—he was more of an impediment to Thomas's ultimate goal than a revered parent. He respected, in his own manner, the old witch, Callie. Perhaps even feared her. A little, at least. She'd almost been like the mother he'd never known and scarcely missed. More importantly, she'd been his first teacher. She'd laid down the foundations of his real education, which, once he'd understood the basics of reading and writing and manipulating human nature, had then been taken up by the Captain.

He'd spent hours with the Captain, cooped up in that big gloomy room on the second floor that was Benjamin Noir's study. And in what the Captain had called his "work room," a claustrophobic underground chamber in a crypt below Noir Manor's basement. It was an elaborate chamber where the Captain stored and experimented with dangerous materials, chemical and otherwise.

It was there that Benjamin Noir had taught Thomas his first lessons about the nature of *heka* and how it could be used to transform base materials. They couldn't create gold from lead. Not yet, anyway, though the Captain was exploring some very promising avenues along that line. They'd had some very tantalizing near-successes. Near-successes that would have astonished Thomas's oh-so-learned superiors at Columbia, if he'd been foolish enough to mention them.

Thomas was well aware that those experiments were only for the Captain and himself. And perhaps Callie, though her talents were more visceral than intellectual. The clay she preferred to work with was more basic. Closer to nature. Fire and water. Animals. People, even, were the elements that Callie knew how to mold best. From her and the Captain Thomas had obtained the knowledge he valued most highly. The rest, the book learning he'd received from the limited intellects at Columbia, was mostly polish. He needed the proper veneer to fit in comfortably with high society. To make the proper contacts in the proper world in which he really wanted to live.

THE TWILIGHT ZONE

The Captain seemed unaccountably happy living in Geiststadt. So did his cloddish twin brother, Jonathan, whose idea of a good time was chasing butterflies through the swamp. *His* world would be considerably wider, Thomas promised himself.

Thomas almost smiled when he thought of his twin brother. Jonathan was useful in his own limited way. Someone had to milk the cows and butcher the hogs. That was his rightful place.

As she did in so many circumstances, nature favored the strong. The brave. The decisive. He'd been so favored since before his birth. Thomas had no conscious memories of that event, but he'd retained murky visions of it in his brain. Dreams, perhaps. They were vague and inchoate, probably much like the primeval chaos that the Captain liked to go on and on and on about. Somehow Thomas knew that even in the womb he'd bested Jonathan, and so became the Captain's favorite son. He would inherit. That wasn't conjecture. It was knowledge. He'd seen the will the Captain had thought was securely locked in his desk.

While Jonathan remained the fourteenth son. In Geiststadt. With cow shit on his boots.

By the time Jon and Isaac returned bearing Erich's body, the entire Noir household had been stirred up by another recent arrival. A young, red-haired man was directing some of the field hands as they unloaded trunks of clothing, furniture, and odd bric-a-brac that Jon immediately recognized as belonging to his brother Thomas. Automatically his hand went to the base of his throat where his tightly buttoned collar hid what he euphemistically thought of as his "birthmark." Actually only he and Thomas sensed its real significance from cloudy memories that barely reached the level of consciousness but had always had fueled the intensely antagonistic relationship that existed between them. Thomas had tried to kill him once. They both knew it. Neither was ever likely to forget it.

The sudden appearance of Thomas's possessions, Jon knew, meant that his brother was almost home for the summer. He frowned. He'd hoped that the insufferable fop was going to fritter away a few more weeks in Manhattan, wasting life, time, and money at his usual prodigious rate.

"What in name of the good Lord is this durn thing?" one of the fieldhands asked wonderingly as he and a companion manhandled a large copper basin out of the wagon, carefully setting it on the ground. It looked like some kind of cooking vessel, only it was large enough to stew a whole calf.

"Oh, that." The red-haired man spoke with a lilt that Jon recognized as coming from Ireland. He was probably, Jon thought, a recent arrival from the old country, perhaps right off the boat. "That's His Honor's bathing basin, isn't it."

The farmhand scratched his head.

"Bathing basin?" he asked.

"Yep," the Irishman said with a grin. "Master Thomas fills it with hot water, climbs into it, and washes himself."

"Washes himself?" the field hand exclaimed in disbelief. "You mean, all of him? He washes all of himself?"

The Irishman nodded, grinning. "With soap. Sometimes two, three times a week."

The two farmhands looked at each other and shook their heads.

"Someone should tell him that ain't healthy." The hired man shivered. "All that water. Why, you could drown in it."

"Mebbe," the Irishman said, "but His Honor thinks it's very progressive." He leaned forward and said, confidentially, "He gets his ideas from an Englishman, he does. Beau Bumfull. Or something like that."

The hired man shrugged, as if it was all beyond him. Like all normal people, he submitted to soap and water maybe once a month in the summer and much less often during the cooler months. He motioned to his fellow worker and together they lifted the bathing basin, carrying it towards the manor.

Like everyone else in the vicinity, they stopped and stared at Jon and Isaac as they approached. Isaac was leading the cow while Jon pushed the barrow with Erich's body. The workmen's eyes widened and they just managed not to drop the bathing basin as they recognized Erich's corpse.

"Master Jon!" the loquacious one exclaimed. "What happened?"

"We don't know for sure, Will," Jon said seriously.

"Some one did for Erich!" Will said, spotting and accurately interpreting Erich's blood-soaked clothing.

It was only moments before most of the Noir household assembled around Jon and Isaac and the sad burden that they bore. Foremost among the observers was the redheaded Irishman, whom Jon assumed was Thomas's servant. He looked over Erich's corpse with a cool eye and unmoved expression. Others of the household were less stoic.

A babble of voices broke out, excited, confused, angry, and frightened.

"Erich! Lord Jesus, what happened?"

"Who did it?"

"What killed him?"

"Is he dead—he's dead, isn't he?"

Jon tried to hush them, but the torrent of exclamations continued until a deep, guttural voice accustomed to command roared up and over them all, drowning out the clamor.

"QUIET, you fools! Let me through!"

The crowd of chattering servants and field hands mobbing Jon and Isaac suddenly parted and like Moses himself, Captain Benjamin Noir strode through the ensuing gap. He was indeed a man of Biblical proportions. None of Benjamin Noir's sons had reached his height of four inches over six feet, though Thomas came closest. Even in his eighty-fifth year he was unstooped. He had the bearing of an eagle. His mane of hair was thick, still mostly black, though streaked with white, as was the beard that fell in generous waves to his chest. A dozen small stone trinkets, red, green, and blue, were entwined in his beard, half a dozen rings shone on his long, strong fingers. He was lean rather than broad, but only a fool would think his spare build indicated weakness. His muscles were whipcord strong. Veins and tendons stood out on the backs of his large hands like twine. He looked as though he'd been chopped out of a block of hardwood, weathered and knotty, salted by the sea and baked by the sun. His eyes had the confidence of a man who knew he was physically powerfully and mentally tough. His bearing was regal, even arrogant.

He stopped before the barrow and looked at Erich's body for what seemed to be a long time, but was probably no more than three seconds. Then he looked up at Jon, his face unchanged though knots of muscle jumped at his temples as he clenched and unclenched his jaw.

"Where did you find him?" he asked in a level voice.

"The marsh, sir," Jon said. "We were rounding up some stray cows."

Captain Noir nodded once, then looked down again at the corpse. He frowned, bent closer, and took Erich's chin, twisting the dead man's head to get a clearer look at his cheeks. He looked back at Jon. From long experience, Jon could see the sudden anger in his father's eyes as they became even colder than usual.

"What does this mean?" Benjamin Noir asked in a quiet voice. That tone, Jon knew, meant that he was furious, raging as he stared at the words carved on Erich's cheeks and the symbol incised into his forehead, presumably by his murderer.

"I don't know, sir."

Captain Noir nodded, studying the corpse, Jon thought, as he himself might study a particularly interesting, previously unknown species of butterfly.

"Frau Agatha said that we should send a messenger to the magistrate in Brooklyn. And perhaps also, the priest." Jon wasn't sure why he repeated Agatha Derlicht suggestions. Perhaps, he thought, to annoy his father. He respected him tremendously and probably even loved him in a distant way, like one might love a god who metes out punishment far more often than he answers prayers. But for reasons he never really understood, he also constantly tested him, pushing the ill-defined boundaries that stretched between them.

Again anger shot through Benjamin Noir, but Jon carefully kept his grin to himself, knowing better than to smile in public at his father. Impudence like that was sure to bring a reaction. If not immediately then later, in private. Noir clamped down upon his anger so quickly that Jon realized he was probably the only one in the crowd who had recognized it. Another point, he told himself, adding it to the tally in the private game that he played daily with the man who had sired, then for all practical purposes, lost interest in him.

"She did, did she?" Agatha Derlicht was his father's bitter enemy. They competed for money, status, and prestige, in every big—and little—thing that happened in Geiststadt. Clearly, he wouldn't like her dictating to the Noirs. Even when her suggestion made good sense. "Well," Benjamin Noir said, "for once she's right."

He turned away from Jon, and looked back at the assembled household, which, as always, was hushed in his presence.

"SETH!" he bellowed.

There was a stirring in the rear of the crowd, and a small, mousy-looking man pushed through. It was Seth Noir, the oldest of the Noir brothers. He was thirty years Jon's senior. For all of Jon's life he'd been Benjamin

THE TWILIGHT ZONE

Noir's private secretary. He lived at Noir Manor, jumping at the sound of Benjamin Noir's voice, scurrying to do his bidding. He existed in the shadow of the man more as a servant than as a son.

"Yes, Father." Jon could hear the capital letter that Seth placed at the beginning of the word "father" as clearly as if he'd seen it on the printed page. Seth spoke as if he were addressing a distant but feared priest rather than the man who'd sired him.

"You heard Frau Derlicht's suggestion," Benjamin Noir said, "conveyed so ably by the boy here."

Seth's head bobbed in a servile bow.

"Yes, Father."

"Off to Brooklyn with you then, to the magistrate's office."

"Yes, Father. And the priest?"

Benjamin Noir scowled. "Piss on the priest. He comes here once a week to gather money in his collection plate and then scurries back to his comfortable parish in Brooklyn." He looked at Erich's body. "I suppose he'll be needed for the funeral. We'll summon him then. Not sooner. I'll not put him up at Noir Manor to eat our food and guzzle our brandy any longer then absolutely necessary."

Seth nodded and turned to go.

"Wait a moment!" The tone of command in Benjamin Noir's voice stopped Seth in his tracks. "Don't forget to give them the killer's message."

Seth turned, puzzled as well as cowed. "Message?"

"Open your eyes," Benjamin Noir said with a hint of disappointment. "Do I have to tell you everything?"

"No, Father," Seth said, even more puzzled. Even more cowed. "But—what message?"

"I AM RETURNED," Jon intoned, and a flash of satisfaction ran through him at the hint of approval he detected in his father's eyes.

3.

The prodigal son returns, Thomas thought, *but not a fatted calf in sight.*

He carefully picked a meandering path around the piles of cow dung as he approached the front entrance to Noir Manor. It was a silly, pretentious name, he thought, but he did have a bit of fondness for the old homestead. The manor itself, though twenty years old, looked as if it'd been built just that spring. The Captain ran a tight ship. Painting, minor carpentry repair, washing, and waxing were constant activities inside and outside the house. It shone under a fresh coat of whitewash. The *uraeus* sign above the lintel gleamed like the sun.

Thomas liked the house's cleanliness. He was quite neat himself and he liked living in neat places. That's why at times it seemed a relief to leave the crowded, noisy, palpably *dirty* city, and return to Noir Manor where everything smelled faintly of fresh paint, soap, and wood oil.

Too bad, Thomas thought, as he noticed his brother James reclining on the front porch, *that tiny bit of charm evaporated so rapidly.*

"Ah," James said. He was apparently the entire welcoming committee. "The prodigal son returns."

"How original," Thomas sniffed.

James was, as usual, drunk as a lord, though only someone like Thomas, who had known him all his life, would realize it. James was handsome with black hair and the dark, brooding eyes of a spaniel dog. He'd inherited a somewhat swarthy complexion from his Hawaiian mother, who had been the second of the Captain's four wives. He was as lean as the Captain and nearly as tall as Thomas, but he carried himself in an inelegant slouch. He slouched even while reclining, which he was now doing on the cushioned wooden bench on the Manor's front porch. His clothes looked lived in. Indeed, they probably were. Thomas's practiced eye told him that it had been several days since James had changed them.

Intolerable, Thomas thought. *How does the man stand it?*

Sloppy, drunk, and handsome. Four words that described his brother to a jot. There was no more to him, nor less. He wondered how the Captain had tolerated his mooching about the Manor for so many years. All the other Noir brothers—but for Seth and Jon, of course—had gotten married, or at least moved out and started their own lives away from Geiststadt. But it seemed that James was a permanent fixture. A leech good for nothing but draining the wine cellar on a regular basis.

Well, Thomas thought, *that would change.*

He mounted the porch's short, wide stairway and regarded his brother, who indeed did have a glass of brandy resting on a small table within easy reach.

"Where is everyone?" he asked.

James waved briefly. "Busy. Jon with the cows, or something agrarian. Father in his study. Of course." He reached for and took a healthy sip of brandy.

"Seth?"

"Ah, Seth." He put the glass down and looked closely

THE TWILIGHT ZONE

at Thomas. "You've come too late. Missed all the excitement."

"Have I?"

James nodded. "Murder. Foul murder. Father has sent Seth to Brooklyn to report it to the magistrate."

"Not – " Thomas paused. "Not anyone from the Noir household?"

James made a negligent gesture. "Just the old cowherd, Erich. You remember old Erich, don't you?"

"Vaguely," Thomas said, thinking, *So. It begins.*

He went by his brother, passing him as he reclined on the settee.

"Don't get up," he said, glancing down at James' twisted, clubbed left foot that was housed in a clumsy-seeming leather boot.

James flushed, pulling his lanky leg back towards his body, unconsciously hiding the ungainly boot as best he could behind the normal one as Thomas went by into the house, smiling to himself.

The cooper's yard was empty as Jon Noir pushed the barrow he'd borrowed back to the great oak tree and the wooden table that sat under its spreading branches. The cloth that had served as Erich's temporary shroud was folded in a neat bundle under his arm. Callie had cleaned it—she was marvelous at getting bloodstains out of clothing—laundered, and dried it so that it was as white, soft, and stainless as it'd been when he'd borrowed it. It was only right, Jon thought, to return the items as soon as possible. As much as Erich's death pained him, for he'd been genuinely fond of the old man, he didn't want to dwell on it. Or on the implication: there was a mad killer loose in Geiststadt.

The only thing, he thought, that just might take his mind entirely off such dark ruminations was the girl he'd met earlier today. She could take the minds of the damned off the torments of Hell.

As he approached the cooper's yard he could see someone sitting at the table under the oak, drinking desultorily from a pewter mug as he planed some long, narrow wooden planks with an adze. He was a moderate-sized man, stout and red of face, with a bald head under a straw hat, sweat-stained shirt, dirty trousers, and a leather work-apron that was spattered with wood chips, sawdust, and other unidentifiable stains.

"Hello," Jon said uncertainly.

The man looked up suspiciously from his work. He looked from Jon to the barrow.

"Is that my barrow?" he asked, the suspicion suggested by his face clearly present in his voice.

"Uh, yes. Your daughter, was kind enough to lend it to me earlier today when I, uh, had need of it." The cooper continued to look at him suspiciously. "So, I'm, uh, returning it now."

"Yes," the cooper said. "I remember. She told me. Something about a body."

"Yes—"

The man took a long pull from his pewter mug and plunked it down heavily on the table. "You've returned it. Now you can go," he said, turning his attention back to the stave he was planing.

"Yes." Jon was nonplused. "This too. A bolt of linen."

"Put it in the barrow," the cooper said, without looking up.

"Yes." Jon looked over to their shop, but there was no trace of the girl. She was probably inside, cleaning, or cooking, or—

Suddenly he saw her, peering out at him from a second floor window. At least he thought it was she. He could see the gleam of sunlight striking her glorious hair. He resisted a temptation to wave, and turned to cooper, who was still engrossed in his task.

"I know you're new to Geiststadt. We haven't really had a chance to meet yet. I'm Jon Noir."

The cooper finally stopped running the razor-sharp blade over the wooden stave when Jon said his name. He put his tool down and rubbed his hands together, as if he were washing them without water or soap.

"Noir?" Johann Schmidt said. "One of them Noir boys? One of them sea captain's boys I heard tell of?"

"Why, yes," Jon said. "I suppose so."

A new look came into the cooper's watery eyes, calculating and servile, at the same time.

"Why'n't you tell me you're a member of such a prominent family?" he asked, continuing on forcefully. "Come, sit a spell. Have some brandy. My name is Schmidt. Johann Schmidt." He turned to face his shop and raised his voice in a shout that would wake the dead buried on the lower slopes of HangedMan's Hill. "Trudi! Bring more brandy. And another mug for Master Noir!"

"Take your hobnails off the furniture, McCool," said Thomas Noir as he entered his bedroom and found the

Irishman sprawled out in his comfortable chair, hands behind his head and his feet upon the small inlaid table between the bed and chair.

Tully McCool complied, but with his usual deliberate pace and the half-derisive grin he wore whenever Thomas issued an order. Thomas acknowledged the grin with a smile and slow nod of his own, saying to himself, *Wait my lad, just wait. Revelation will come to you like all the rest.* McCool stood in his usual slouch.

"Hope you approve of your quarters. *Sorr,*" he said in an exaggerated brogue.

Thomas looked around and nodded. It wasn't the same bedroom he'd shared with a brace of brothers while growing up. Noir Manor was well-near deserted now, compared to its crowded condition when a swarm of brats fought for their father's attention as they fought for the food on the table. Most of the third floor bedrooms were empty. McCool had chosen the most spacious of the unused chambers for him. Thomas approved. His trunks of clothes and boxes of books and manuscripts were still packed, but that was all right. Unpacking and storing his clothes was not a task he trusted McCool with. The bog-trotter didn't know how to handle and care for fine clothing. And the books...Thomas didn't know if the Irishman could even read. If he could, there were some volumes in Thomas's collection that it was best McCool remained unaware of.

But something was missing...

"My bathing basin?" Thomas asked, after he'd looked around the room and taken a mental inventory of the furniture, trunks, and boxes McCool had brought up.

"Ah, yes," the Irishman said. "I've put it in the small room down the hall, haven't I? *Sorr.*"

"Satisfactory," Thomas said. He was well aware that McCool looked at him with scarcely concealed derision. That was all right. Visionaries were always mocked.

"Young master," a voice said from the bedroom's doorway, "welcome home."

It was Callie. McCool looked at her with his usual expression of amused interest, Thomas with the uncertain caution he always felt around the tiny old woman. He was, well, not afraid, exactly, of her cold gaze. Wary of it, more like. He remembered the time he'd poked around her room and found her collection of dried, shriveled heads. After that he always was sure to be at least outwardly respectful to her. He could sense the *heka* in her. Before he'd reached his later adolescence, she was the one who'd assisted the Captain in his studies. Even now, he hadn't really taken her place. There was a strong bond between Callie and Benjamin Noir. Thomas sensed that in the early years of their relationship they'd been closer than master and servant. Closer even than savant and apprentice. Much closer.

"Thank you, Callie," he said, after a silent moment. He gestured at McCool. "This is my man, Turlough McCool. I'd like him to have a room on the third floor."

"Servants live out back," she said in a flat voice, referring to the unmarried farmhands' quarters adjacent to the barn.

"You don't," Thomas said bluntly. He challenged her consciously if cautiously, wondering how she would react.

Callie puckered her thin lips. Humor more than anger shone in her cold eyes, but a bit of both was present.

"The Captain requires my presence," she said.

"I require McCool's," Thomas replied.

"All right." He was surprised at her quick acquiescence. "He can take the room next to this."

Thomas glanced at McCool, pleased with his success in overriding Callie's orders. The Irishman seemed unimpressed.

"The Captain wants you in his study," Callie said.

"I haven't even had a chance to unpack," Thomas protested, "Or even refresh myself—"

"At once, young master," Callie said in a dry voice. Thomas recognized that voice. It meant that she was serious. There was no denying, even questioning her, when she used that tone. His sense of triumph quickly dissipated.

"Very well." He turned to McCool, who didn't even struggle to keep the smile off his face. "You may take your things to your room." He looked around his own chamber, reaffirming his previous hesitance about McCool handling his books and clothing. "I'll unpack my things once I've spoken with the Captain."

McCool bowed, but somehow the gesture didn't seem at all deferential.

"As you say. *Sorr.*"

Thomas brushed past Callie with a nod. She didn't acknowledge him. Instead, she looked at McCool with unspoken questions in her dark eyes.

Thomas went down the stairs to the second floor study, thinking that this abrupt summons was typical of the

THE TWILIGHT ZONE

Captain. The man was utterly self-absorbed. He never had a single thought for others. He was only concerned with himself and his own needs. In the long run, Thomas thought, that self-absorption would prove his downfall.

He stopped for a moment at the closed door, engulfed in sudden memory. The Captain's study was the largest room in Noir Manor. Even so, it was a cramped place crammed with shelves and stacks and piles of books and pieces of bric-a-brac that the Captain had picked up in the course of his worldwide wanderings.

There were marble busts of forgotten Romans and granite statues of even more ancient and even more forgotten Egyptians. An ancient wooden sarcophagus sat in one corner, converted into a file bin for rolled scrolls and tattered papyri. Some of the artifacts were less identifiable, but the Captain had taught Thomas all about the Polynesian Tiki heads and the other idols he'd brought back from other faraway seas. Some were carved from wood, some from bone. Some were hacked from a soapy stone that was almost repellent to the touch. With somewhat human faces and multiple tentacles that seemed to squirm in the uncertain light they were certainly repellent to look at.

Thomas had spent many hours here in close study with the Captain. The subjects he'd studied were more formal than the lessons he'd taken from Callie. First he'd learned the basics. Latin and Greek and other languages, many of which were no longer spoken in the living world. Mathematics and chemistry. Astronomy and astrology. Theology and demonology. Collegiate academics had been simple after years of the Captain's tutelage. In fact,

Thomas had to be careful not to reveal too much of what he'd learned from the Captain's ancient tomes. They hadn't burned a witch in the colonies for almost two hundred years and Thomas didn't want to start a new trend.

He rapped sharply on the dark wooden door, once. That single knock was almost a private signal between him and the Captain. From inside the deep, familiar voice called, "Enter."

Thomas opened the door. For the briefest moment the well-remembered scene was before him. The chaos of books and manuscripts crowding shelves, listing in piles on furniture, floor, and mantle. Dark wood chairs and the Captain's great desk. The sarcophagus in the corner, the various statues and icons scattered about, most gazing impersonally into the distance—some disturbingly focused. The Captain himself behind the desk, as hale and hearty as always.

And then it changed.

Thomas blinked. He couldn't believe it. His right hand went up to massage his eyes, then dropped back to his side. He knew that it would all still be changed no matter how hard or long he rubbed.

He was suddenly facing a long, dark hallway built of stone like those in an ancient temple or tomb. It was lit by open torches guttering in the dense, unmoving air. The walls themselves were covered with intricate pictographic writing that he recognized immediately as Egyptian hieroglyphics. Along one of the walls, as if they were an audience, crouched a line of men dressed in the clothes of Egypt's long gone past. At the far end of the corridor a man sat on a throne. He was wrapped in funeral garments and his arms were crossed over his chest. His unbandaged hands held the crook and flail of royalty. On his head was the crown of pharaoh. Behind him stood two women whom Thomas knew must be his sister and sister-wife.

Between Thomas and the enthroned figure was a large scale. A creature stood by it, bearing papyrus and stylus. It was a man with the long-beaked head of a bird. Another creature crouched nearby. This being was even more horrible to see. It was an amalgamation of beasts, with the head and terrible snout of a crocodile, the body of a lion, and the thick hindquarters of a rhino. From where he stood Thomas could see slavering anticipation on its face as it regarded him intently with cold reptilian eyes that reminded him, oddly, of Callie's.

"Are you ready?" a voice growled at Thomas from the shadowy area beside him in the corridor's mouth.

Thomas barely contained his impulse to flinch. Standing there, previously unseen, his dark-furred features blending into the darkness, was another man wearing an Egyptian kilt. His head was that of a dog, or jackal, complete with long, lolling red tongue. The words he'd spoken hadn't been in English, though Thomas understood them perfectly.

It wasn't a jackal-headed man who stood before him. It was a jackal-headed god. It was Anubis himself.

Thomas suddenly knew where he was and what was happening. He was in a dream world, a construct, sprung from the mind of the Captain, and the bloody bastard was testing him. Again.

It was just like the Captain, Thomas thought. Don't even give me a chance to get my breath. Catch me off-guard. Throw me into a frightening, possibly hazardous situation, and see how I react. See how well I've remembered my lessons about reality in general, and *this* reality in particular.

Thomas smiled. I remember them pretty damn well.

He looked at Anubis, who was grinning a dog-like grin, his tongue hanging out of one side of his mouth. He'd spoken a few words in the language of ancient Kemet, which was what the Egyptians themselves had called their land. Thomas called them back to mind. The few words were little to go on, so he quickly scanned the hieroglyphics painted in bright red, deep blue, and shining gold upon the corridor walls.

Champillon and his rival, Young, had only twenty years ago published their first papers on their theories for translating hieroglyphics. They'd managed to decipher fifteen or twenty of the signs. Scholars were still arguing about the basic underpinnings of the language, whether it was syllabic, ideographic, or alphabetical in nature, among other things. But the Captain had taught Thomas how to read hieroglyphics fluently when he was twelve.

The only question in Thomas's mind, at this time, was what dialect to use in reply. Language had evolved over the three thousand years Egypt had been in existence. The few words that Anubis had spoken, along with indications from the written gylphs on the walls, indicated a mid-period form, around the time of Ramesses the Second, when the power and might of ancient Kemet was at its peak. One could call it Kemet's Classical Age.

THE TWILIGHT ZONE

Very well, Thomas thought. He would use that dialect. Anyway, it was the most elegant form of the language.

"Lead me to judgment, O, Anubis," he said.

The jackal god grinned at him, his red tongue lolling from his pointed snout like that of a dog's.

"You know where you stand, human?"

"Certainly." Thomas tried to maintain at least a semblance of politeness just in case he was wrong—and there was only the slightest, tiniest chance of that—and he wasn't facing a construct of the Captain's mind, but rather...something else. Something unthinkably other. "This is the Hall of Judgement, where the dead are separated into the two categories—the Prosperous and the Exterminated—by the scale of Maat, before Lord Osiris himself, God of the Dead."

At first he'd spoken hesitantly. But soon the words were tripping off his tongue as easily as if they were English.

Anubis nodded, as if impressed.

"Come then," he said. He held out his hand, a normal, well-kept human hand, clean and with nicely trimmed nails. Thomas took it. It was warm, as if Anubis were real. They stepped into the corridor, going past the row of minor gods who served as witnesses to the holy rite. Thomas was impressed by the strength of the Captain's illusion. The corridor was stuffy and much too warm. He could feel himself start to sweat. It smelled musty. The dust of the ages covered the floor. They left footprints in it as they paced toward the scale of Maat, which was taller than Thomas, and the things that waited next to it.

The scale was a simple balance with two pans descending from the horizontal beam on delicate golden chains. One of the pans already sat low. A single feather, standing impossibly upright on the tip of its quill, weighed down the pan. This was Maat's Feather of Truth. Ibis-headed Thoth, the scribe of the gods, stood next to the balance. An inscrutable look was on his bird face. Ammut, the demon crouching by the scale, was somewhat more scrutable. He slavered in anticipation of an unfavorable judgement. Beyond, Osiris sat on his throne, mummy-wrapped and unknowable. Isis and Nephthys, his sister-wife and sister, respectively, looked on, also impassive.

Thomas silently congratulated the Captain on his imagination. The Egyptian goddesses were breathtakingly beautiful. Dressed in the diaphanous Egyptian manner, their heavy but firm, large-nippled breasts were totally exposed. Their wide hips and shapely thighs were barely concealed by the gauzy skirts wrapped tightly about their seductive forms. Thomas could even smell the cones of incense burning in the thick, wavy hair that descended in black torrents to their waists. They were intoxicating and distracting.

Thomas wrenched his attention back to what was happening before him. Of course they were distracting. That was why they were present. That was why they were so...womanly. The Captain wanted him to be distracted. He wanted him to fail this test. Whatever it was meant to test. Thomas smiled to himself. He would disappoint the Captain again.

He and Anubis stopped before the scale. This ritual,

THE TWILIGHT ZONE

Thomas knew, was called The Weighing of the Heart. The Egyptians believed that the heart was the center of all knowledge. That that organ contained an indelible record of all the good and bad things an individual had done in his life. The individual's heart had to be weighed against Maat's Feather of Truth. If they balanced, then the individual passed judgement. He would be allowed to join the Prospering Dead in paradise. If feather and heart failed to balance, then the individual was doomed to extermination. His heart would be snapped up by Ammut the Devourer and he would be damned forever.

Thomas wasn't sure what the Captain meant to test with this elaborate charade. In a way, he realized, it was somewhat appropriate. Today was the First Intercalary Day of the calendar of ancient Kemet, corresponding to June twenty-first of the modern calendar. It was the first of the five feast days before the beginning of the Egyptian New Year. The Intercalary Days, falling as they did outside the normal calendar of twelve months of thirty days each, were considered wild and chaotic. Anything could happen on them. Reserved for feasting and festivals, no important business could be conducted during these days as expected outcomes could be lost in the chaos that accompanied their uncertain presence.

The First of the Days was dedicated to Osiris, king of the dead. Traditionally it was held to be Osiris's birthday, as, traditionally, December twenty-fifth was held to be Jesus Christ's. Perhaps that was why the Captain had brought him this day before this simulacrum of Osiris. In any event, Thomas thought, he was ready to face anything.

Anubis turned to him. "Are you ready for the judgement, O human?"

"I am," Thomas said steadily.

"Very well."

Anubis reached out and plunged his hand into Thomas's chest. The pain was immediate and excruciating. Thomas screamed as he felt the jackal god's fingers close around his beating heart.

This isn't right, he thought wildly. *Something has gone wrong.*

He looked at the god's face. The dog grin was unreadable, although on the edge of his vision Thomas could see the Devourer leap forward eagerly.

Despite the pain coursing through his system Thomas realized that he'd been set up. This wasn't a test of some kind. It was a trap, meant to kill.

His knees were sagging from the pain. His teeth were clenched together. His chest heaved but no breath came into his tortured lungs. He reached out and gripped Anubis's arm with both of his.

"Get...your...paws...off...me!" Thomas spat the words in English. The pain made him forget to speak in the ancient Kemet tongue.

He felt his heart move in his chest as Anubis tried to tear it from his body. In response he yanked savagely at the thing's arm with all his strength, and surprisingly Anubis's arm broke away from his body, coming off in Thomas hands.

For a moment they stood looking at each other. There was no pain or anger on Anubis's face. Only a stupid dog grin. Then he and everything around him disappeared. It all vanished suddenly, like slumber after a sudden loud sound close by the sleeper's head.

Thomas stared. He was inside the Captain's study, though he didn't remember entering the room. In fact, he stood right before the Captain's desk. The Captain was looking at him with a peculiar expression on his hard old face.

"What the devil's the matter with you?" he asked, and Thomas collapsed.

He fell, catching himself briefly on the edge of the Captain's desk. He must have blacked out for a moment because the next thing he saw was the Captain hunkering over him, shaking him by the shoulders.

"Thomas, wake up, Thomas!"

He was drenched with sweat and his heart was beating wildly, as if he'd just run a long and difficult race at full speed. He grabbed the Captain's coat sleeve and held on as if for his life.

"What happened?" the Captain asked harshly.

Thomas told him, describing the scene, telling him that he'd first assumed it was a test of some sort, then describing his sudden revelation, the knowledge that if he let Anubis take his heart he would really die.

Benjamin Noir listened with no expression on his hard old face. When Thomas finished, he stood easily. Bearing most of Thomas's weight, he helped him over to a comfortable chair. He set him down, his expression softening into thoughtfulness.

"Something is happening," the Captain said. "I'm not sure what. But this is the second assault on our household this very day."

"Who is it?" Thomas asked, clutching his chest where his heart still raced fearfully. "Who can be doing this?"

The Captain looked at him, his face hard again.

"Who else?" he asked, rhetorically.

"The...the Derlichts?" Thomas asked.

The Captain just stared at him, as grim as a hanging judge.

4.

Jon Noir was more than a little giddy by the time Schmidt slumped down face first on the wooden table, his face red as a beet, and began to snore.

The cooper had drunk continuously for the two hours he'd held Jon as an unwilling guest, emptying more mugs of brandy than Jon could count. Jon himself had downed several mugs at Johann's urging, but at a much more sedate pace.

At first the cooper's conversation had been genial, almost subservient, as he'd praised the Noirs' sterling qualities he'd supposedly heard everyone in Geiststadt enumerate since he and his daughter had moved to the village. But as he'd drunk more and more brandy he'd become maudlin and then belligerent, bemoaning his fate and blaming his difficulties on the residents of Flatbush, where he'd lived before coming to Geiststadt.

"They wouldn't give a man a chance," he'd told Jon blearily towards the end of their mostly one-way conversation. "One mistake! One!" He waved a finger drunkenly in Jon's face to emphasis his point, "and, whooosh!, we had to leave. Me and my little daughter." He sniffed in self-pity. "Anyway, she was only a serving girl. Not like she hadn't done anything like that before. And I didn't even hurt her. Not a bit." He sighed and went face down on the table so hard that Jon heard an audible *thunk* when his head hit the tabletop.

Jon was nonplused. He looked at the drunkenly slumbering cooper, uncertain of what to do. Within moments his daughter arrived, as if she'd been watching from their shop and expecting Schmidt's eventually collapse.

She looked at him and sighed.

"Father drinks," she said, by way of explanation.

"Yes," Jon acknowledged. It seemed the only sensible response. "Do you...do you need any help with him?"

She shook her head.

"It's a fine day," she said. "He can...rest...here for a while. The sun and fresh air will do him good." She glanced at Jon then quickly looked away. "He wasn't always like this," she said. "He's a good man. He's just had a hard time of it, lately. Adjusting to the trouble—to our having to move."

It was on the tip of Jon's tongue to question her about "the trouble" both had alluded to, to ask why, exactly, they'd had to pull out of Flatbush and move to Geiststadt, but he hesitated. Schmidt had given him a not-so-subtle clue before passing out. Perhaps details weren't necessary.

"I'm Jon Noir," he said suddenly.

She looked at him squarely for the first time and again he was captivated by her eyes. They seemed to shine with an internal light of innocence and good cheer that even the present circumstances couldn't completely douse.

"Yes, I know. That is—I've heard your name mentioned around the village." She smiled briefly, shyly. "I'm Trudi. Trudi Schmidt."

"Yes," John said. "I know. It's nice to finally meet you. Formally, that is."

"That was a terrible thing that happened to your friend," Trudi said. "Do you have any idea who did it?"

THE TWILIGHT ZONE

"No." Jon shook his head. "Nor why. Erich was a harmless old man. I don't know why anyone would kill him."

She was as easy to talk to as she was to look at. Jon wasn't particularly shy, but he did have a hard time conversing with girls. Struck by a sudden idea, he said, "Um, listen, I was going to go for a walk on HangedMan's Hill this afternoon. Would you like to accompany me?"

He wasn't usually forward, especially with someone he'd just met. Unlike Thomas. No female was safe in his company. But Jon felt he really needed to clear his head after imbibing the brandy. After finding Erich and bringing him home. A hike would be just the thing. And Trudi was so beautiful and so sad when she looked down on her sodden father.

"I know that—" he began a stumbling explanation, but she interrupted him with a bright smile and decisive nod.

"Yes," Trudi said. "Yes, I'd love to. I'd love to get out into the countryside. I'd love to get away—"

She hesitated, glancing purposely away from her father.

"Let's go then!" Jon said.

He felt excited, by more than just the brandy he'd drunk. By a sense of rebellion, a touch of impetuousness bordering on the wild. Trudi seemed to catch his mood. She nodded wordlessly, her eyes bright and expression suddenly cheerful.

They took the path that was Geiststadt's main street, stopping to exchange greetings and receive condolences with various passers by along the way. Word of Erich's death had spread like wildfire through the village. News of any kind did, and the bad usually moved faster than the good.

Among the villagers they ran into was Rolf Derlicht, one of Agatha's grandsons. Rolf was a husky young man a couple of years older than Jon. Jon had never liked him. When they were children Rolf had used his unusual size and strength to bully Jon—though, to be fair, he bullied most of the other youngsters as well. He even took on Thomas once in a shoving match that had quickly escalated into a serious fist fight. Jon actually hadn't known whom to root for in that one, but for the sake of family solidarity decided to cheer on Thomas. And Thomas had needed his brother's encouragement. Although more than a match for Rolf Derlicht in size and strength, Thomas Noir lacked Rolf's animal ferocity and fighting skills.

Thomas was taking a beating and Jon was seriously considering joining in on his side when suddenly their father broke through the ring of shouting children who were goading the fighters on to greater efforts.

Jon had never seen Benjamin Noir in such a towering rage. He snatched Rolf Derlicht away from Thomas with one hand and pummeled him with open-handed slaps with the other that sounded like gunshots as they exploded upon the young Derlicht's cheeks. He might have beaten the youngster insensible if a terrified Rolf hadn't managed to yank himself free, leaving a torn fragment of his shirt in Noir's grasp. He'd run away, crying, and had never teased the Noir brothers again.

Jon always remembered that long-ago incident whenever he saw Rolf, probably because it had ultimately ended, unfortunately for Jon, with a beating at the hands of his father for not coming to Thomas's aid.

"Hello, Jonathan," Rolf said, stiffly formal, as he always was with Jon. "Terrible news about Erich. My condolences." Although his words seemed kind his voice lacked any sense of sympathy as he looked expectantly at Trudi.

"My thanks," Jon said, just as stiffly. He realized that Rolf was expecting him to introduce Trudi. He thought for a moment of ignoring Rolf's obvious expectation, but then decided that he didn't want to appear boorish in Trudi's eyes. Clearly she couldn't know what had gone on between Rolf and him in the past. As he introduced them, Trudi dropped a graceful curtsey and Rolf took her hand in a lingering manner that to Jon, at least, bordered on the offensive.

"I'm looking forward to getting to know you better," Rolf said, unctuously. "Much better." He paused, as if just remembering something. "By the way, Jonathan, *Grandmutte* wants to speak to you."

"To me?" Jon asked, thrown off his course of growing annoyance by the unexpected request. "About what?"

Rolf shrugged broad shoulders. "I should know? She says to come by the house when you can."

"All right." He would, too, just to satisfy his curiosity regarding this unprecedented invitation. "*Danke.*"

Rolf shrugged, as if to say, it's nothing, turned to Trudi and bowed. "*Auf wiedersehen, madchen.* I'm sure we'll see each other soon, and often."

"I'm sure," Trudi said in a voice that implied no such thing.

Rolf made a vague gesture of farewell, which Jon copied even more sketchily. They parted, Jon and Trudi heading for a less-traveled path that would lead them away from the village and onto the lower slopes of HangedMan's Hill.

"What was all that about?" Trudi asked.

Jon shook his head. "I'm not sure. The Noirs and Derlichts aren't exactly close friends. If they were this particular Noir wouldn't be a friend with that particular Derlicht. You've met his Grandmother Agatha." It was a statement rather than a question.

Trudi nodded.

"She's the head of the Derlicht family. They're the most powerful family in the village—and my father's rival for influence and authority. Over the past couple of years it's been clear that she's been grooming Rolf to lead the family when she's gone. The old bat is older than my father. She can't have that many years left." He smiled. "Have you learned anything yet about Geiststadt's history?"

"Not much," Trudi admitted. "Since we've been here we've spent most of our time making the shop livable and readying samples of father's wares. I haven't really had much of a chance to get know anybody. Except for you, now."

She smiled prettily, which made Jon smile in return.

"I'm sure you've heard about the Noirs and Derlichts," he said.

She waved a hand in a dismissive gesture as they passed the last building on the lower slopes of the looming hillside. Above them now was virtually virgin land, untouched but for the graveyard which lay to their left.

"Gossip," she said.

Jon smiled. "Go on. You can tell me. I'm sure it's nothing I haven't heard already."

"Well," Trudi said, "it's clear that the Derlichts don't like your father. Also..." She hesitated. "... he doesn't attend Church. Nor does any Noir, except the daughters who've married into local families."

"That's true," Jon admitted cheerfully. His father had totally neglected instructing him in religion. That was all right with Jon. He could see the hand of God everywhere about the countryside without the need for a church to view it in or a priest to tell him how to worship. "We Noirs are a godless lot. It's one of the reasons the Derlichts have been suspicious of us over the years. They're good Calvinists, you know."

Trudi gave him a sharp look, but didn't seem as shocked by his frank confession as he'd feared she might be. Another item in her favor, Jon thought. They approached the waist-high stone wall encircling the graveyard that held over a hundred years of Geiststadt dead, stopped, and leaned against it. Most of the graves were marked by wooden crosses. Very few—mostly some of the more notable Derlichts—had stone markers. The wooden crosses were almost all scrubbed of name and date by the elements. No one knew exactly who lay in many of the graves, but the cemetery was well tended with loving care by the community. Jon spent his own fair share of time tending the graveyard, for his mother lay somewhere in one of the lost graves, the only Noir so far laid to rest in Geiststadt.

"Why is this called HangedMan's Hill?" Trudi asked, looking around the bucolic landscape. "It seems very pleasant."

"It is," Jon said. "I love hiking the ridge way. The view from the top is tremendous, and there are scores of hollows and delightful hidden meadows. But there—" He pointed. "Do you see that notch where those parallel ridges nearly come together?"

Trudi squinted, shading her eyes as she stared in the direction he pointed.

"Yes, barely."

"That's the site of the old cemetery. The one used by the Dutch when they originally settled here almost two hundred and fifty years ago. The village was called Dunkelstad then. But it was destroyed and abandoned fifty years before the Derlichts and other families returned to the area and founded Geiststadt."

"What happened to it?" Trudi asked.

Jon shrugged. "No one knows for sure. Some say the town was wiped out by Indians. Others say a plague or disease of some sort. Whatever it was must have been pretty disastrous. Most of the buildings were gone by the time the Derlichts arrived. In fact, their house is one of the very few built on a foundation laid by the Dutch."

"What's this all got to do with HangedMan's Hill?" Trudi asked.

"I'm coming to that. During the Revolution, the Battle of Brooklyn was fought some miles from here. But prior to the battle, a contingent of German mercenaries, Hessi-

THE TWILIGHT ZONE

ans, came through Geiststadt. Despite the fact that practically all of the citizens of Geiststadt were fellow Germans—or maybe because they were—the Hessians pillaged the community. Halfway through the rapine, though, they were taken by surprise by a militia raised from other towns in Kings County. Not actual soldiers, you understand, just armed citizens. Some of the Hessians escaped, but more than half a score were surrounded, captured, and taken to that notch in the ridge way I showed you.

"Once that had been the Dutch cemetery, but it had been abandoned for over a hundred years. It's a spooky bit of land, even now. I've spent many an afternoon wandering about it, myself. I'm not terribly superstitious, but I'd hesitate to go there at night. Many believe it's haunted. Many believe they've seen spirits there at night, searching for...something. Some say a White Lady haunts the burial ground. Some say a whole troop of ghostly phantoms. That's how Geiststadt got its name, you know. 'Spirit Town' or 'Ghost Town' in English."

"What about the Hessians?" Trudi prompted.

"Oh, yes." Jon realized that he'd gotten lost in diverging branches of ancient lore while telling his tale. "Well. They were hung. Most of them. Twelve of them, according to the stories. But there was a thirteenth. For some reason the militia didn't hang him. Perhaps he was the ringleader. The one who instigated the rape of the village. Perhaps the militia had to vent their wrath on someone and hanging that last Hessian wasn't enough." Jon shrugged. "Perhaps they'd just run out of rope, or suitable branches."

"What'd they do to him?" Trudi asked, her eyes wide.

"Why, they..." Jon stopped. His gaze went distant. He was silent for so long that Trudi laid a hand on his arm. He started, and looked at her. He couldn't understand why he hadn't made the connection before.

"They cut his heart out," he said. "And dropped his corpse in an unmarked grave far from his comrades."

He and Trudi looked at each other.

"Cut his heart out?" she asked. "Just like Erich's?"

Jon nodded. "Just like Erich's."

Suddenly, though the sun still shone and the breeze still blew warmly upon their faces, the lower slopes of HangedMan's Hill no longer seemed a cheerful place. The gloom that sometimes descended upon Geiststadt was a nearly tangible shimmer of dark energy. In complete accord they turned without a word and headed back to the village, as if both wanted the nearness of other people rather than the solitude of the now eerie hillside.

McCool couldn't get the water hot enough to suit him.

Callie was heating buckets of it in the fireplace, but it cooled considerably by the time McCool had lugged them up three flights of stairs.

"Faster, you damned bog-trotter," Thomas said as he reclined in his bathing vessel and McColl added another pail to the tepid bath water.

McCool leaned back, gritting his teeth.

"You're not paying me enough to fetch water, Your Honor."

Thomas temper flared. He was not in a good mood. Someone was trying to kill him. He would not overlook or rationalize that. Maybe it was the Derlichts. But why now? Why so suddenly upon his arrival?

"Enough of your insolence. I can return you to the slums where I found you and pick any of a hundred out of the gutter to take your place. You understand, McCool?"

"Yes. Your Honor," he said, his impertinence barely controlled.

That was all right. Or at least sufficient.

"Fine," Thomas said, rubbing a sponge absentmindedly on his chest. "Fetch me another pail of hot water. I must think."

McCool went off without a word. Thomas sank lower in his tub, the water almost covering his face, his knees poking up into the air.

A tub big enough to stretch out in would be nice, he thought, and pipes, perhaps, to carry hot water from a central reservoir.

Unfortunately, though, he had more pressing matters than plumbing to occupy his attention.

If it was the Derlichts trying to kill him, he knew who was probably to blame.

Supper was a sober affair in the Noir household. Seth, of course, had not yet returned from Brooklyn. He wasn't expected back until the next day at the earliest. James and Jon were at the table ready to eat, but Thomas and their father were absent. Jon sent Callie to summon them three times. Three times the summons had gone unheeded.

"Damn it all," James said. "The food's getting cold and I'm getting damned hungry. Let's eat!"

They dined alone. For all James's faults Jon usually got along with him better than anyone else in the family. Tonight, though, James was sullen and uncommunicative. Jon put his brother's mood down to the presence of Thomas, whom Jon had actually yet to greet.

Thomas had been closeted in the study with their father for most of the day, thick as thieves. Jon knew better than to interrupt them when they were in closed session. Besides, he had no real desire to see Thomas. It was bad enough when he *had* to deal with him. He felt no need to seek him out just to say hello.

James started to drink brandy with his meal and was at it long after the meal had ended. Jon went to his room. He tried to read, but couldn't interest himself in either the small collection of scientific monographs he'd accumulated, or even the classic literature in Greek or Latin he usually enjoyed.

On restless nights he'd commonly roust Isaac and they'd go for a ramble by moonlight. But tonight there was something depressive about the dark. Something told Jon that danger was loose in the night. While he normally wouldn't seek out peril for no good reason, neither would he shrink from it. But this feeling deep in his gut told him that an unknown hazard was stalking Geiststadt. Jon didn't want to face it unless he had an inkling of what it was about.

He wasn't, as he told Trudi, superstitious. And yet...

Trudi. Her image came upon him as he tossed and turned in his narrow bed. Something pleasant, at last, to fasten his mind upon. Something beautiful. Something untouched by the miasma that sometimes seemed to come out of nowhere to engulf his fair little village.

He finally managed to fall asleep with Trudi's image in his mind. It was a thin, fitful sleep, hardly refreshing, but it got him through the night. He awoke early as usual, and went down for a solitary breakfast that, as usual, Callie prepared for him.

He was sitting in the kitchen lingering over another mug of strong tea when Manfred Jaeger burst into the kitchen without knocking, panting as if he'd been fleeing the devil himself.

"Have you heard the news?" he gasped, then reported it before Jon could even open his mouth. "Rolf Derlicht is dead—murdered—mutilated."

Jon heard himself question Jaeger from a long distance away, thinking at the same time that somehow he already knew the answer.

"Like Erich?"

The messenger only nodded, his expression wild as he tried to gulp enough air to calm his heaving lungs.

"Where?"

"The cooper's yard. Under the oak."

Jon nodded, almost abstractedly.

Jaeger sketched a vague salute of farewell, then hurled himself back outside to further spread the word.

Jon had been right, he knew now, not to go out the night before. Danger *was* stalking Geiststadt. The savage killer had claimed his second victim.

5.
Friday, June 17th, Second Intercalary Day

"What is this world coming to?" *Hausfrau* Gottchen asked Jon as she stopped him on the dirt lane that served Geiststadt as a main street. "Are we all going to be killed? Are we to be murdered in our beds tonight?"

"I don't know," Jon said, trying to keep up with her questions. "I don't think so. I'm sure not."

The Gottchens were one of his father's client families. They looked to the Noirs for protection in times of trouble, but never before had Geiststadt experienced trouble like this. Trouble usually meant a scanty crop or disease striking the cattle. Life and death, yes, but something you had time to contemplate and plan against. Something money from the deep Noir pockets could help you recover from. It was bad enough when Erich was killed. But if a madman was killing Derlichts, then no one was safe. No plan could protect you. No amount of money could shield you from sudden, terminal disaster.

"They say the body was found in the yard of Schmidt the cooper. I don't know. I haven't seen it myself. Who would want to look upon such a thing?" A sudden thought seemed to strike Frau Gottchen. "This Schmidt, he is a strange man, isn't he? And a stranger, as well. What do we know of him, anyway?"

Jon didn't even try to keep up with her flow of words.

"I don't know, Frau Gottchen," he said, which seemed

a suitable reply most of her questions. He bowed and said a hasty goodbye and hurried off before she could launch another stream of unanswerable queries.

Isaac fell in beside him and they both headed towards Schmidt's yard.

"Callie woke up both Captain Noir and your brother Thomas with the news," Isaac said. "The Captain wasn't happy. Seems like he thought that Erich might have been killed by the Derlichts for some reason."

"I don't see why," Jon interrupted.

"I don't see why either," Isaac agreed, "but the Captain thought Erich's killing might be part of some kind of plot against the Noirs."

"Rolf's killing would seem to argue against that theory," Jon muttered.

Isaac nodded. "Anyway—the Captain don't want the body disturbed until he can come and look at it himself. He told me to find you and make sure it stays put until he arrives."

Jon nodded. That was reasonable. Though it was a mystery what his father might see that he himself, for example, couldn't see.

A crowd—by Geiststadt's meager standards—had gathered around the cooper's yard by the time Jon and Isaac arrived. Benjamin Noir's fear that Rolf's body might be moved or otherwise tampered with seemed entirely groundless. No one wanted to touch it. No one wanted to even get near it. Jon could understand why. No one wanted to be contaminated by the terror and sudden, awful violence that it represented.

The crowd parted wordlessly as Jon and Isaac approached. A dozen whispered conversations slipped into silence as they neared the death scene.

Rolf Derlicht's corpse sprawled upon the wooden table where Jon and Johann Schmidt had sat drinking brandy the day before. His bloody torso lay on the top of the table while his legs dangled over the edge. The bench on that side of the table had been knocked over. Rolf's right arm was bent at the elbow. The hand and forearm hooked under the edge of the table, holding the corpse in place. His left arm was pointing straight out at a right angle to his body. His fingers were clenched in a fist, except for his index finger, which was extended, apparently pointing.

Jon leaned down close to the body, sighting along the arm. It wasn't exactly clear what, if anything specific, Rolf seemed to be pointing at. Perhaps the cooper's combination house and workshop. Perhaps Noir Manor, which lay past the cooper's shop, farther out on the edge of Geiststadt. Perhaps anything in between.

Rolf had been brutally slain by a knife. Like Erich, his chest had been opened and the heart removed. Jon made himself examine the wound closely. The technique seemed similar to that used on Erich, though Jon was not an expert on either surgery or butchery. The main difference in the deaths lay in the placement of carved letters spelling out I AM RETURNED. In Erich's case they'd been incised into his cheeks. In Rolf's they'd been cut across his forehead. The childishly executed cupid hearts, this time, were carved on his cheeks.

"What is all this fuss? What? Eh?"

A thick, harassed-sounding voice pulled Jon upright.

THE TWILIGHT ZONE

He turned to see a bleary-eyed Johann Schmidt approaching, Trudi hustling in his wake. The cooper was dressed in rumpled, brandy-stained clothes, probably the same he'd worn the day before. Jon could smell the liquor on him from ten feet away. He looked perplexed and angry at the same time, and centered both emotions on Jon. The crowd had parted silently, precipitously at his approach, allowing him to reach Jon's side undetected.

"This, Herr Schmidt," Jon said simply, and stepped aside.

The cooper caught sight of the body for the first time, as did Trudi. Both stopped dead in their tracks. Trudi gasped. Her hands went up to her cheeks in an expression of horror that would have looked childishly comical if it also hadn't seemed so sincere. Schmidt blundered to a halt. His red face went white in the space of a single breath as all blood drained from it, seemingly puddling, Jon thought, in his doughy gut. The cooper put a hand out in sudden terror or denial, and shook his head swiftly. It took him a couple of moments to find his speech, and even then he stuttered.

"N-n-no," he finally said. "This has n-n-nothing to do with m-m-me. N-n-nothing," he repeated, and turned and like a bull pushed his way though the crowd, which had closed again around the murder scene. He staggered blindly, shoving those he stumbled against with stiff, outstretched arms. Several fell to the ground. Many muttered angrily at Schmidt as he plowed a path back to his home, and, Jon suspected, a bottle of brandy.

* * *

Thomas awakened with Callie standing over him, a concerned look on her ancient, wrinkled face.

"What is it now?" he asked with a sigh, settling down comfortably on his feather bed.

"Another killing," she said economically.

"Indeed?" Thomas sat up, interested. "Who, this time?"

"Rolf Derlicht."

"Rolf, hmmm?" Thomas didn't even try to conceal his smile. "No loss, I say. Though this is rather a fatal blow to the Captain's theory."

Thomas didn't like the way Callie looked at him. There was bitter knowledge in those ageless eyes sunk in an aged face. He could never keep a secret from her. In many ways her powers were as potent as the Captain's, though her's were the rude untutored abilities of the savage hedge wizard while the Captain's were those of a studious, erudite man. Still, over the years he had learned not to be contemptuous of the old woman's talents. She had uncanny sources of knowledge and a strength of will second to none. Thomas knew that he had to be careful around her.

"The Captain wants you to go with him to examine the body."

"All right." That was a chore he wouldn't particularly mind. "Be a dear and tell McCool to fetch me a cup of tea while I dress."

Callie swept out of the room in silence.

What to wear to a body viewing? Thomas thought. On one hand, it wasn't exactly a highly fashionable event. On the other, almost the entire village was sure to be present and he wanted to make a good impression. No sense, however, in wasting his very best for this sort of thing. In fact, Thomas wondered idly, if anything could conceivably happen in Geiststadt that would call for his very best.

Fresh underwear and stockings, of course. Perhaps his Hessian boots with the black silk tassels. The grey trousers tailored to be worn tucked into, not over, the boots that were polished to a mirror-sharp sheen. His lavender waistcoat with high rolled collar. Linen shirt with cravat, of course. To top off the ensemble his double-breasted morning coat that fit him like a second skin. Better do without the white gloves, he thought. That would be gilding the lily just a little bit.

Thomas had finished dressing and was giving his pocket watch its morning wind when the Captain appeared in the doorway, watching him with silent disapproval.

"Ready?" Benjamin Noir asked, sourly.

Thomas put the watch and chain into place in his waistcoat and tugged the garment into its exactly precise and proper place.

"Ready," he said, reaching for hat and cane waiting on top his dresser.

The Captain stepped aside, letting Thomas precede him down the stairs. McCool met them halfway up, carrying an ornate silver tray with tea cup and saucer, sugar bowl, creamer, and cozied teapot.

"Ah," Thomas said. "I guess I'll take my tea in the kitchen after all."

McCool turned without a word and led the procession downstairs.

"Tea?" Thomas offered. "It's a special blend I order from Coronation. In London."

"There's a body out there—"

"Exactly," Thomas said. "A body. Rolf's not going anywhere. Except, perhaps, to Hell. He can wait."

Benjamin Noir stood before the table, glowering at Thomas. Finally, he nodded.

"Perhaps you're right." He sat down suddenly, and transferred his glower to Isaac, who was standing by the fireplace. Benjamin Noir gave him orders to tell Jon to guard the corpse. "I want to examine it myself," he said to Thomas as Isaac ran from the kitchen.

"Examine it for what?" Thomas asked mildly.

"I don't know," Benjamin Noir admitted. "Clues. Indications as to who killed him. And why."

"It sounds to me like the work of a madman," Thomas said, pouring tea for the Captain, who took the cup with a grunt. "Perhaps we'll never know why he died. Or even who did the killing."

"A madman." The Captain paused with a spoonful of sugar halfway to his cup. "I thought you were better trained than that, boy. Everything has a reason behind it. Everything has meaning." He snorted. "Are you being obtuse for a reason, or are you just being lazy?"

"No, not at all," Thomas said mildly. "It's just that Seth will be bringing the magistrate's men from Brooklyn. They're the experts at solving crimes. Ferreting out clues and all that."

"Those dunderheads! They couldn't find their asses if they were looking for their hip pockets. No." Benjamin Noir shook his head. "Besides, they know nothing about

THE TWILIGHT ZONE

Geiststadt. About what has happened here over the years."

"That's all for the best, isn't it?" Thomas asked. "We don't want them to know our business."

The Captain nodded. "Exactly. That's why I'd like to find a solution to this, this insanity, perhaps even before they arrive."

"I don't suppose we have time for some toast then?"

"Toast," Captain Noir muttered. Suddenly he put his teacup down and looked at his son with a questioning expression in his usually hard eyes. "You have a theory about the killings?"

Thomas shrugged. "With Rolf apparently the second victim, it seems unlikely that they're part of some kind of vendetta against the Noirs."

"Then what's behind it all?" the Captain asked.

"Vengeance of a sort. Perhaps blind vengeance against Geiststadt as a community."

"Then you *do* have a theory about these murders?"

"Let me think about it a bit more," Thomas said placidly. In reality, he didn't want to lead the Captain right to it. He wanted him to figure it out for himself. "Ah." His eyes lit up as Callie slipped a plate onto the table before him. "Toast."

The Captain waited with commendable patience as Thomas carefully applied butter and jam to several slices of toast while McCool hovered around in the background trying to appear useful. Thomas ate slowly and neatly, sipping his tea and wiping his lips between bites with a linen napkin that had been on his tray.

"Finished?" the Captain asked as Thomas popped the last bite into his mouth.

"Hmmm," Thomas said, chewing. He stood up, brushing imaginary crumbs from the front of his waistcoat and trousers. "That's better. Never view a body on an empty stomach." He smiled brightly at McCool, as if in great good humor. "Isn't that right, Tully?"

"If you say so, Sorr," McCool replied, marginally more respectful to Thomas in front of Callie and the Captain.

If anything, the crowd had grown by the time the Captain and Thomas, followed by McCool at a respectful two paces, arrived in the cooper's yard. Jon was still examining the body while the crowd continued to speculate uselessly in quiet murmurs. A pretty blonde girl, unfamiliar to Thomas, was isolated in a no-man's land between the table and surrounding mob whose members were more than a little unwilling to approach the corpse. She herself seemed unwilling to face the multitude of eyes cast upon her by the crowd, and unable as well to look upon the corpse, cold and stiff and bloody on her father's table. She looked sad and frightened and worried as her eyes cast around her like those of an animal's in a trap.

Thomas Noir saw her, and was struck by a wave of desire that almost overwhelmed him. Almost. But not quite.

"Jonathan." His brother looked up. Their eyes met and Thomas smiled to himself at the expression that flitted across Jonathan's face. Dislike, distaste, distrust. But all overwhelmed by the over riding realization that he couldn't act on those feelings. Jonathan Noir was in a position of subservience to Thomas and he knew it. "Sorry we haven't had the opportunity to speak 'ere now, dear brother. Fatigue from my journey, don't you know. To meet again under these sad circumstances." Thomas pulled a linen handkerchief from his sleeve and patted his forehead, playing the gentlemen to the yokels all around him. They ate it up, murmuring appreciatively. Now to show his hard, decisive side. He put the handkerchief back up his sleeve and took a long step forward, so that he could peer over Jon's shoulder. He pointed at the body with his walking stick. "Who could have done such a terrible thing?"

Jon looked at him sardonically, as if well aware of Thomas's play acting.

"That's the question, isn't it, brother?"

"Indeed." Thomas whirled suddenly, his gaze for the first time openly falling on the young girl who had the undefined role in the little drama before them. "My name is Thomas Noir, *madchen.* I hope that this—" Thomas paused, glanced at the body "—that is, Rolf Derlicht was neither kin nor close friend."

"I—I barely knew him. My father and I are newly come to Geiststadt."

"Ah." Thomas turned and looked at his brother, trapping him. For the sake of basic politeness, he knew that Jonathan couldn't avoid introducing them. He knew also, for some reason, that Jonathan didn't want to. Of course, he could contrive to meet the girl soon enough later on, but he so enjoyed making his brother perform in public.

He enjoyed it even more when Jonathan knew he was doing it.

"Thomas," he said in as friendly a manner as he could manage, "this is Trudi Schmidt. This yard belongs to her father, Johann Schmidt, a cooper. They moved here from Flatbush only a few weeks ago."

"I see." Thomas stepped toward the girl and took her hand. His gestures were fluid and dramatic and so quick as to not be denied. Now Thomas knew why Jonathan was reluctant to introduce them. She was an exquisite thing. Five years from now she'd be just another dumpy *hausfrau*, coarsened by work and childbirth. But now she was quite gorgeous with a fresh beauty and lively vitality that even this horrible scene could scarcely dim. He bent over her hand and kissed the air above it. It was prettily done, nor overdone.

"Trudi," Jonathan continued in the same tone of forced friendliness, "my brother, Thomas."

"You two can continue to exchange significance glances concerning the girl," Benjamin Noir said in an icy voice, "Or you can try to turn your brains to something more useful. For example, discovering clues about the identity of the killer. Like—what is Derlicht pointing at?"

"I noticed that," Jon said.

Thomas glanced, almost unconcernedly, at the corpse.

"Looks to me like he's pointing at the cooperage."

"But why would he do that?" Trudi asked.

Excellent, Thomas thought. Encourage that question. But he only shrugged, preferring to let the onlookers draw their own conclusions, now that Trudi had invited their speculation.

THE TWILIGHT ZONE

"Or," Jon said dryly, "he could just as well be pointing at Noir Mansion."

"Yes." The Captain pulled at his beard thoughtfully. The stone amulets braided into it shifted silently in its thick coils. "Or at anything between. Still, it's something to keep in mind. Perhaps we'd better question Herr Schmidt."

"My father's not well," Trudi offered immediately. "He went to bed early last night. Both of us slept until the commotion in our yard awoke us a little while ago."

"You know this for a certainty?" the Captain asked, much to Thomas's relief. Thomas didn't want to get on the girl's bad side by questioning her harshly. You could rely on the Captain, Thomas thought, for a thorough interrogation. He had a flair for it. And he certainly seemed to enjoy it.

"Of course," Trudi said.

"How is that, girl?" the Captain asked. His natural acerbity showed through, though he tried to keep his words softer than normal. "Do you generally sleep within sight of each other?"

"No, of course not," Trudi said. There was a general hum of excitement from the on-lookers that Trudi seemed to take for a bad sign. "But, I-I'm a light sleeper. I would have heard my father get up and move around."

"But you heard nothing," the Captain insisted. "You slept soundly all night."

"Yes. Yes, I did."

The Captain spread his hands in a there-it-is gesture. Thomas had to bite his lips to keep the smile off his face. The Captain had managed to turn the girl's words against her, at least in the crowd's mind. So, she had heard nothing. Who wouldn't say that to protect their father? A man newly moved to Geiststadt. A man whom nobody knew. A man to whom the victim seemed to be pointing, perhaps clenching his fist with his very last breath. A man who, clearly, drank more than he should. And why did he drink to such excess? To forget something, perhaps?

It's easy to turn a small, insular community against a newcomer. Especially one who has left his prior home under somewhat mysterious circumstances. Especially one who has an all-too apparent vice.

What, Thomas wondered, *would happen next*? He wanted the pot to bubble, but not boil out of control. Not yet, anyway.

"Let's drag the cooper out and question him," someone shouted from the back of the crowd. The group shifted, seeming to sway back and forth like a multi-legged beast. Voices murmured in agreement with the shouted suggestion.

Benjamin Noir held out a hand.

"No sense in being hasty. He's not going anywhere. I'll make sure of that." He turned to Isaac. "Get some men to watch his workshop," Benjamin Noir said in a quiet voice, and the burly young farmhand nodded and went off to do the Captain's bidding.

"We do not know," Benjamin Noir continued, "nor can we assume, that Herr Schmidt has done anything wrong. But we must make sure that he can give an account of himself."

The crowd murmured agreement and looked about

uncertainly. Because if Schmidt wasn't responsible for the murders, that meant someone else was. Someone who had lived in Geiststadt for a long time. Or, if not someone then, perhaps, something.

And to the villagers both those thoughts were intolerable.

It was a long day, unsatisfactory on all accounts. Jon spent it trying to catch up with the unending chores that were necessary around the farm. He wanted to investigate the murders, to help pacify the fear that seemed to have settled over Geiststadt like a deadly fog, choking everyone with its acrid, bitter stench.

But he couldn't figure out how to do that. There were no concrete clues to investigate. No lines of inquiry that could lead to a possible solution of the terrible mystery. His father had come away from his interrogation of Johann Schmidt grim-faced and close-mouthed, but there was nothing unusual about that. His father was almost always grim-faced and close-mouthed. Schmidt closeted himself in his shop the rest of the day—probably drinking—and so did Trudi.

Jon wanted to see her again, but could think of no excuse for a visit. He hadn't liked the way Thomas had looked at her. Nor did he like the fact that his brother had accompanied their father to question Schmidt. Knowing Thomas, he'd probably spent his time conversing with Trudi rather than working on anything related to the murders.

Though, Jon thought wryly, he could hardly blame him. That's what he wanted to do himself.

As the day passed, Jon also started to worry a bit about

Seth. The trip to Brooklyn shouldn't have taken this long. Seth should have been back with the magistrate's men by midday at the latest. By late afternoon, though, they still hadn't shown up. Perhaps there had been a delay of some sort in Brooklyn, or perhaps they'd had a minor accident on the road, either coming or going. In any case, Seth was late and there was little they could do at their end but dispatch another messenger to Brooklyn with the news of the latest killing.

Jon was scattering corn and old bread for the chickens, thinking about meeting Rolf Derlicht the day before, and how Derlicht had said that his grandmother Agatha had wanted to speak to Jon.

That request was out of character, Jon reflected. The usual attitude of the Derlichts to the Noirs was one of haughty neglect. If they deigned to take notice of a Noir at all, it was with the air of a superior to an inferior. In their view *they* were the family with money and power. The Noirs were upstarts. Actually, this attitude had made it easier for Jon's father to make some inroads on Derlicht authority in Geiststadt, though the entrenched clan still controlled most of the village.

Perhaps that was what Agatha Derlicht wanted to discuss. Though why with him and not Thomas or their father, Jon couldn't say. Perhaps she had some information on the murder. Now murders. But why share it with him, and not his father?

Well, Jon thought, *there was only one way to find out what she wanted.* He was not eager to beard the lioness in her den but that was what had to be.

Jon called over one of the farmhands, who was dili-

THE TWILIGHT ZONE

gently trying to look like he was working, and handed him the sack of chicken feed. For a moment Jon considered going home to wash up and change into clean clothes for this unprecedented visit, but in the end decided not to. Agatha Derlicht would receive him in his working clothes, he thought, or not receive him at all. It would be her choice.

Derlicht Haus was on the north side of the village, the end opposite from Noir Manor. It was situated on a stretch of level land away from the banks of Skumring Kill. The house was surrounded by a number of barns, root cellars, out-houses, chicken runs, icehouses, and various other buildings, some already a century old. Most showed their age. The house itself was a dreary pile of wood and stone built, as he had told Trudi, on the foundations and cellars of one of the old Dutch mansions when the village that occupied the plain before Hanged-Man's Hill had been called Dunkelstad.

Derlicht Haus was only two stories tall, but it covered a lot more ground than Noir Manor. It had been added to over the years with a kitchen, porch, and even another wing of rooms tacked on in a similar but not identical architectural style, giving it an organic, hybrid appearance that Jon found vaguely unsettling.

Farm hands and servants watched his progress warily as he approached the front door and knocked once with the ponderous brass knocker that was some kind of semi-human looking wild animal with a brass ring in its mouth. He waited patiently while the uniformed butler, an old Negro named Pompey, came to the door. Jon was unsure if Pompey was slave or servant, but he projected the rarefied attitude of a duke. Or perhaps a minor prince.

"Yes?" Pompey's hair was cotton white and had all but vanished from the top of his head. He'd looked like that ever since Jon could remember. Callie said that the old Negro had been with the Derlichts long before the Noirs had come to Geiststadt.

"I'm here to see Frau Agatha," Jon said. Pompey continued to look at him like an eagle considering his prey, so Jon felt compelled to add, "Rolf, uh, Rolf mentioned to me yesterday that she wanted to see me. Under the circumstances, I don't know if she's accepting visitors, but I thought her request might be important."

That seemed to satisfy Pompey. He inclined his head like an emperor and gestured to Jon to enter.

"Yes, sir." Despite his age the butler's voice was still a deep, strong baritone. "If you'll come in, I'll see if madame is receiving."

Pompey left Jon in the first floor parlor, closed the door after him, and disappeared soundlessly into the bowels of the house. The room was neat and well-furnished, though in the style of the previous century. It was dark with only small windows that let in a minimal amount of light. It was a gloomy room. As far as Jon could remember from the few times he'd actually been inside Derlicht Haus, that adjective could pretty much apply to the entire domicile. It seemed a place of little light and happiness, though in fairness Jon thought that sometimes you could describe Noir Manor in much the same way.

The door opened suddenly bringing him out of his

THE TWILIGHT ZONE

reverie. Pompey stood aside and Agatha Derlicht swept in to the room. She was wearing one of her fancy gowns, but its fashionableness was muted by the fact that though in impeccable repair it was probably fifty years old. And it was dead, unrelieved black. Jon wondered if she was wearing it to mourn Rolf Derlicht's passing, but then he remembered that Frau Agatha wore black so often that there was speculation around Geiststadt that it was her favorite color.

"Shall I bring tea, madame?" Pompey asked.

She favored him momentarily with her cold gaze.

"No. This is not a s-s-social call."

"Very well, madame," the butler said. He withdrew, closing the door behind her as she swept into the room and took a seat on a venerable sofa set before the unlit fireplace.

She and Jon looked at each other for a long moment. Jon could read nothing from her cold gaze and immobile features. In that way she was a match for his father. In his more whimsical moments Jon often thought that Agatha Derlicht and Benjamin Noir should have wed, thus merging the Noir-Derlicht families under a single roof and solving the problem of ruling Geiststadt. It would have made, though, for some grim family dinners. And considering Frau Agatha's age he never would have been born. Of course, the upside of that was that Thomas wouldn't have been born either.

"You may sit," Agatha Derlicht finally said, nodding to a nearby chair. At least, he thought she was nodding. It could have been the minute tremors which shook her entire frame almost constantly. Nevertheless, he sat where he thought she'd indicated.

'Thank you." Jon perched uneasily upon the seat. The fear to settle back and make himself comfortable was only partially subconscious. He cleared his throat. "Sorry," he said, "about Rolf. He was..."

"He was a *schiesskopf*," Agatha Derlicht said without a smile. "But he was a D-D-Derlicht. When I'm gone he w-w-would have become head of the family. Someone k-k-killed him. I want that someone found, and punished. B-b-before..."

Jon nodded as she paused.

"Before someone else dies," he said.

"Exactly." She paused again, her head bobbing in time to the unseen metronome, which controlled her tremors. Then, unexpectedly, she sighed deeply and fractionally relaxed her rigid posture. She looked, Jon thought, suddenly almost human. Suddenly old and tired and frail. "It was easy before you N-N-Noirs arrived. When our word was law. We would have qu-qu-questioned everyone. Some s-s-severely. We would have discovered the murderer in short or-or-order. But—times have changed. G-G-Geiststadt is bigger. There are more people. Too-too-too many to control like we used to."

"That approach would have worked," Jon said thoughtfully. "If the murderer is a person."

Agatha Derlicht looked at him thoughtfully.

"I am an old woman. I have seen...th-th-things...here in Geiststadt that are not readily explainable. Especially since Be-Be-Benjamin Noir has come—I have no need to tell you the story of the day of your birth. B-B-But even

THE TWILIGHT ZONE

before his arrival there had been...odd...occurrences. So p-p-perhaps you are right. Perhaps we should be aware of the possibility of an...inhuman agency having a hand in the killings." She shook her head. "I don't know."

Jon kept his face carefully expressionless.

"You were always a smart boy," Agatha Derlicht spoke, half to herself, her stutter vanishing as she seemed to concentrate her thoughts. "Trustworthy. Respectful. Hard-working. I never understood why your father favored Thomas over you. Well." She shook her head. "That is not my business. This is." Her gaze sharpened again, her spine stiffened. She became her old formidable self. For a moment she even stopped shaking. "We are rivals, the Noirs and Derlichts. But not in this. We must join forces to destroy whatever it is that threatens the peace of Geiststadt. That is what I wanted to tell you yesterday. Today it is even more true."

Jon nodded.

"Whether, as you said, the killer is human or not."

There was no reason why Jon should trust Agatha Derlicht. Their families were life-long rivals. Even enemies. Still, she was the one proposing an alliance, a pooling of effort to find a solution to a problem they both faced. His father seemed to believe that Schmidt might somehow be involved with the killings, but—as usual—he hadn't confided anything to Jon. Hadn't even discussed the situation with him, though, just the day before he'd apparently thought the Derlichts might be involved. Personally, Jon hesitated to condemn Schmidt just because he was an easy target, a newcomer to the area, even if he obviously had personal demons.

"I have no proof," Jon said cautiously. "None at all. But the nature of the killings. Their savagery. The words carved into the victims faces..."

He fell silent. Agatha Derlicht prompted him impatiently to go on.

"Well," he said, "it may sound...silly...superstitious. But remember the Hessian?"

"Hessian?" Agatha Derlicht asked.

"The old story about the skirmish fought in Geiststadt during the Revolution. The militia captured some of the mercenaries who'd attacked the village. They ended up hanging them all. Except one."

"Yes," Agatha Derlicht said. "All but one. Whose heart they cut out before burying him in an unmarked grave in the old c-c-cemetery."

She and Jon looked at each other a long time.

"What are you thinking?" Jon finally asked.

"I'm thinking that what I said a few moments ago is still true. H-h-human or not, the killer must be stopped before more d-d-die."

"If...if the killer is not human," Jon said hesitantly, still unwilling to put into plain words the terrible thing that he thought, "where would we find him?"

"I-I-I t-t-think you know the answer to t-t-that," Agatha Derlicht said, shaking even more than usual as she forced the words from her mouth.

"And how do we stop him?" Jon asked quietly.

Agatha Derlicht either shook her head in denial, or gave herself over to a fit of shuddering. Jon couldn't tell which.

6.

Again that night, Jon Noir couldn't sleep.
This time he couldn't conjure Trudi's image to comfort himself. Thomas's face intruded on the scene whenever he thought about her. His brother had been insufferable at dinner. All dressed up as if he were attending a fancy ball, Thomas exhibited the manners of a supercilious gentleman who found himself surrounded by amusing bumpkins. Only their father, of course, was free from his barbed wit. Jon thought that James was going to attack him when the fish was served. Somehow his brother managed to control his anger and then drown it in brandy. James was sullenly drunk before desert. After dinner Benjamin Noir and Thomas closeted themselves in the study again.

Seth was still absent, hopefully safe in Brooklyn or somewhere on the road. But despite the fact that his father had men watching Schmidt's place, Jon couldn't help but feel a growing concern for his missing brother who might be wandering somewhere between Brooklyn and Geiststadt with a killer still on the loose.

James had settled in for a night of serious—even by his standards—drinking. Jon couldn't bear to watch. He took himself to his room, but natural history and literary classics both failed to grip his mind. He had paced restlessly for awhile and that too soon began to pale as a means of passing the time.

He threw himself on his bed and stared at the ceiling,

his skin literally seeming to crawl at the touch of blanket or sheet, anger building and growing. He knew he couldn't contain it much longer, but he was utterly unsure where to direct it.

At everything, he thought. Every damn thing. His father. Thomas. Even Trudi, for the way she'd looked at his damn brother that morning. But mostly, of course, he was angry at the killer, the unknown maniac, human or otherwise, who was transforming Thomas's return to Geiststadt—a difficult situation, at best—into an impossible one. Over the years Jon had learned how to deal with Thomas in the course of an ordinary day. Mostly he ignored him, sometimes he lead with a judicious jab to keep his brother unbalanced and uncertain.

But the murders had thrown everything into an uproar. They had to stop, of course, both for the sake of Jon's sanity and for the safety of the villagers. They had to stop, before the killer struck again.

Jon suddenly sat up on the bed. He hadn't been doing a damn thing to stop them. He'd been uncharacteristically passive, waiting for someone else, his father, perhaps, to act.

Why? Jon wondered. Was he afraid? Any sane man would be, he told himself, but any sane man would also realize that it was unlikely that the killings would just stop on their own. Some sinister plan had been put into motion and the murders wouldn't stop until the plan was fulfilled. Whatever it was.

He stood and went to the old clothes press that slouched drunkenly in the corner of his bedroom. It contained his extra clothes, and odds and ends that he'd

THE TWILIGHT ZONE

accumulated over his life. A coat for the winter. The fowling piece that he used for duck hunting in the fall. He took that out, considered it, then put it back. No. Stealth would be the key to this operation and he couldn't drag an ancient blunderbuss around the woods quietly. Especially if he actually had to use it. He didn't want to go totally unarmed, though, as the killer, human or not, had an obviously deadly blade of some sort.

Jon settled on the old bayonet he'd mounted on a wooden handle and then honed to razor sharpness. It was unique, something between a long dagger and a short stabbing spear. He paused, considering, and then decided he'd be a fool not to ask Isaac to come along. Isaac was strong as an ox and fast as a panther, besides having a sharp pair of eyes and ears. Killer-hunting would be dangerous, certainly. But somehow the thought of sharing the danger made enduring it seem more palatable.

He went quietly out of the house, stopping at the kitchen to make up a sack of food in case they'd be out most of the night. Isaac had a powerful appetite and Jon himself wasn't a light eater, either.

Callie was in the kitchen, sitting before the fire, rocking and warming herself, watching the flames dance.

"Where you going, boy?" she asked.

"For a hike," he said lamely, knowing that she would know that this was not one of his usual nighttime jaunts.

"You taking that big boy with you?"

"Yes'm," he said nodding. "If he wants to come along."

"Good. He'd follow you into Hell, boy." She looked

from the fire dancing in the fireplace into his eyes. "You be careful that's not where you end up."

Jon paused. "Do you think the killer is human, Callie?"

"It uses a blade. If it uses a blade to cut, it can probably be cut by one. Probably." She rocked on, her gaze back on the fireplace. "My eyes are cloudy. Maybe I'm getting too old to see clearly anymore."

Jon had a sudden thought. "This isn't...I mean, you don't think this is something my father is involved in, do you?"

"It could be...something...coming for him," she said. "The Captain's led a strange life. He's made enemies." She stopped rocking and looked at him again, and Jon was astonished to see the concern in her eyes. She's actually worried, he thought. She's worried about me. But she wouldn't come right out and say it.

"I'll be careful, then." Jon said.

Callie set the chair in motion and looked back at the fire.

"You always was a smart boy," she said.

He left her there, rocking, and went out into the yard. It was quiet, with an undercurrent of the usual familiar farm sounds on a warm near-summer night. The livestock were all settled in the barn, the chickens were asleep in their coops, muttering in their dreams. Jon loved the night as he loved the day. He regretted the hours lost to sleep that made the nocturnal portion of the daily round less familiar to him.

The night was the time of the quiet creatures, the small hunters, and clever gatherers. The bat, fox, and raccoon. There were still said to be some wildcats in the more in-

THE TWILIGHT ZONE

accessible parts of HangedMan's Hill, but wolf and bear were already creatures of the past. It was too bad, Jon thought. He'd give a lot to hear the howl of a wolf on a warm night with the full moon shining down upon them both like a gentle silver sun.

He went quietly to the bunkhouse where the unmarried hands slept. Eighteen men worked the Noir's farm. Well, seventeen, now that Erich was gone. Eight were family men. They had their own cabins on the fringe of the estate. Some sharecropped, some worked the Noir herds and planted crops for their own use, or to sell with the larger Noir harvests in neighboring communities that were becoming more towns than villages. Brooklyn had grown so large that it was no longer self-sufficient, and the gaping maw of Manhattan was less than two days away by cart. The soil was rich, the land bountiful. The farmers of Geiststadt made a good living selling their wares in the markets in the west, as long a there was no drought, nor locust, nor snow in June.

Jon entered the bunkhouse where the ten—no, nine—farmhands lived. He moved quietly as the Indians who once lived on this land, now vanished like the wolf and bear, but Isaac was awake when Jon reached his bed.

"Going out?" Isaac asked in a low voice.

Jon nodded.

"Hunting the killer?"

Jon nodded again. "It'll be dangerous."

"In that case," Isaac said, rising from the bed fully dressed as if he'd expected Jon to come by at any moment, "I'd better take this."

He held his shiny straight razor up by its wooden

handle. The blade was four inches long and shone bright like a crescent moon in August. Isaac flipped it shut and put it in his right shoe. Jon clapped him silently on the shoulder, and they slipped out of the bunkhouse, leaving the snoring field hands behind.

Thomas was bored, but he dared not show it. He'd learned that the Captain didn't tolerate inattention. Indifference in the face of his studies would lead to a whipping faster than anything else. And, though the Captain was an old man—an old, old man, Thomas thought—he dared not arouse his wrath. He was bigger than Thomas and despite his years still stronger. And meaner, Thomas thought. It would never do to forget that.

The Captain sat at his desk, perusing his manuscripts as if he didn't have a care in the world. As if bloody bodies were an everyday occurrence in Geiststadt. He was a cold-hearted old bastard. Thomas would give him that.

Thomas, sitting in a less comfortable chair behind his own inferior desk set perpendicular to the Captain's, squinted, then opened his eyes wide, bringing the faded papyrus as close as he dared to the glass-enclosed oil lamp. When he was only eleven, he'd held a manuscript he'd been trying to decipher too close to an open flame and it had caught fire. The disaster was only a minor one. Only that one papyrus had gone up in smoke, though for a moment or two a fiery fate for the entire study had been a near thing. He'd carried the marks of *that* beating for a long time.

This manuscript, while ancient, was probably relatively

THE TWILIGHT ZONE

recent compared to some in the Captain's collection, being written only a couple of hundred years before the birth of Christ. They couldn't be any more certain of its age. Relatively late for an Egyptian papyrus, it was written in a rather debased form of demotic script. Recently added to the Captain's collection, it had been obtained from his Egyptian agents since Thomas's last visit home. It had been found, so they'd said, in a cache recently discovered in the vast ruins of the temple of Karnak and smuggled out of the country right under the eyes of the ruin's excavators.

It was unquestionably authentic. Thomas had handled enough ancient papyri to be rather good at sniffing out the forgeries. Besides, the Captain's antiquity agents knew better than to defraud him. It was well known that the Captain had other agents whose only job was to deal with forgers in decisive and decidedly unpleasant ways.

The scroll, formed by separate sheets of papyrus glued together into one long sheet, was in remarkable condition for a paper document nearly two thousand years old. Thomas handled it carefully. It consisted mainly of a long-winded summary of specific rituals that were to be performed on various days of the Egyptian religious calendar. Thomas was already boringly familiar with most of them. The ancient Egyptians were more religious than Protestants. Their temples were kept busy seven days a week.

But here—here was something interesting. Something new. At least something Thomas had never seen before.

The section of the scroll was titled "The Chapter of

Vanquishing Apep." Thomas settled in to read it more closely.

Apep, according to common belief in ancient Kemet, was the great serpent who embodied the destructive forces of Chaos, the primeval state of the universe. He had existed even before Order brought the world out of Chaos, living in the dark watery abyss, which had existed before time. He'd survived the cataclysm of creation, which spawned the world and heavens and eventually humanity. He still attacked the great boat of the Sun God, Ra, every day just before dawn. This part of the scroll contained rituals to help Ra and his minions lest Apep eventually destroy Ra's sun boat. If that ever happened Chaos would overwhelm Order and the world would end.

It was interesting reading, Thomas thought. Not to be taken literally, of course, in this enlightened age. At least Thomas didn't believe in the old stories. He was less sure about the Captain. He'd never had the courage to question Benjamin Noir about his beliefs. To be sure, there was something to the magic that the Captain practiced. It worked. Thomas had seen enough empirical evidence to convince him of that. It didn't work in every instance, of course. But what did? But Thomas had benefited enough by it over the course of his life to believe in it's general efficacy.

But Chaos Serpents? Sun boats? Immortal gods who had the heads of animals and traversed the sky every night bringing the sun back to safety every morning so that it could arise again over the Earth? No. He didn't believe in that at all. Even if he'd almost been killed by

Anubis. An Anubis that was, he was certain, a creation of the Captain's mind.

Thomas glanced at the Captain, hard at work transcribing copious notes into his ponderous personal journal from the scroll he was perusing. Benjamin Noir looked up, frowning, as if he'd felt Thomas's eyes on him. Perhaps he did, Thomas thought. He was almost inhumanly perceptive.

Thomas smiled as best he could and dropped his gaze down to his own papyrus. He didn't want the old man to probe too deeply into his thoughts. He was afraid of what the Captain might possibly see.

Jon and Isaac stopped for a moment at the Glass House. For some reason the stench of the Corpse Flower was far more potent at night. The House's interior smelled like a battlefield on a summer day after a slaughter. The smell drove Isaac out immediately. Jon withstood it to take a few measurements and jot down some more notes about the plant's condition, batting at the night-flying moths surrounding the plant as he did so. He stared at the botanical monstrosity for a long moment, then realized he was only wasting time, holding back because that fear was still there, keeping him from beginning his search for the killer.

Jon sighed. He joined Isaac outside.

"Let's go," he said, and they headed for the graveyard. Not the recent, well-tended cemetery where the dead of Geiststadt lay, but higher up on HangedMan's Hill where the forgotten of Dunkelstad had been planted into the earth.

The land was quiet and dark. The moon was a miniscule sliver hanging high in the sky. The stars glittered over head without illuminating the landscape through which they moved. They were as quiet as the land itself, at one point passing so close to a fear-frozen rabbit that Jon could have reached out and speared it with his bayonet if he'd wanted to. He had no desire to kill, so they passed the creature by, heading upslope to the outskirts of the abandoned cemetery.

"What are we looking for?" Isaac asked. His voice was so quiet that it could have passed for a whisper of the night wind, but Jon heard him clearly. It seemed that all his senses were razor sharp. He could smell the grass underneath his feet and hear the patter of the breeze as it sifted through the leaves above his head. He could see almost as clearly as if it were day. The musty spice of the once-hallowed earth he stood upon was strong on his tongue, as if he could taste it on the air with every breath he drew into his mouth.

"I don't know," Jon replied, just as quietly. He felt strange and powerful at the same time, but he didn't know where the strength came from or what to do with it. He only knew that something was calling him deeper into the graveyard.

He followed his intuition and Isaac followed him. The simple wooden crosses that had once marked the Dutch graves were all long gone. Even their burial mounds had sunk into the earth, smoothed by almost two centuries of wind and rain. Plants grew lushly in the boneyard, as if the ground was abnormally fertile. Flowers were abundant, though almost all their blooms were closed

THE TWILIGHT ZONE

for the night. The once-civilized roses that had marked a few of the graves had gone feral. Their blooms were smaller and stems thornier. They grew in great thickets which Jon, and Isaac behind him, skirted as they made their way into the cemetery's heart.

They stopped and waited. It was as if Jon could feel all the life around him, in the trees and among the bushes and even burrowing in the ground. And the death, as well. The sense of strangeness that had enveloped him was still there. It was almost palpable. He reached his hand out as if to touch it.

"What do you want of me?" he asked in a clear voice.

The answer came suddenly from all around him. He couldn't be sure from exactly where. It seemed like everywhere. He looked at Isaac, but his companion's face was blank. He couldn't hear the words that Jon was hearing so clearly. He shivered, as if someone had brushed a feather across his naked brain.

There was a murmur of many voices. Jon Noir spoke English, German, Latin, and Greek, but he couldn't understand what these said. Partly because so many speaking at once, partly because the words, though naggingly familiar, seemed to slip around the edges of his consciousness. They were like English and German and even something like Latin, but they weren't those languages. Jon concentrated.

They were...

He frowned. Almost, he had it, then it slipped away. He clenched his fists and Isaac, standing concerned at his side, suddenly gasped aloud as he saw Jon's eyes roll up in their sockets until only the whites showed. Instead of trying to understand the river of voices flowing over him, Jon narrowed his focus, trying to understand only a tiny stream, a single current. Partial understanding came. A word here or there, maybe the essence of a sentence.

The voices were speaking Dutch.

The dead resting beneath his feet were speaking to him, Jon realized. Not all of them. There weren't enough voices to account for all the bodies buried in the old cemetery. Maybe twenty. Maybe more. Speaking all together, all at once, in the unfamiliar language. He couldn't understand the specifics of what they were saying, but he knew that they were pleading with him. For what he could not tell.

Jon suddenly turned his head and looked up at the far corner of the cemetery, the far edge where the outlines of a single large pit marked the internment place of the twelve Hessians killed nearly sixty-five years before. Of the burial place of the last Hessian, the thirteenth, there was no sign.

It was as bright as day in that corner of the graveyard. Jon could see men in ragged uniforms, some of them bloody, with broken bones that somehow still held them up. They spoke, and Jon could understand them. They spoke German that was a little different than that he was used to, but he understood them.

"Do not blame us—"

"It is not our deed—"

"We have paid—"

"Already—"

"Too much—"

"Too much—"

"Look to the living—"

They might have said more, but Isaac suddenly gripped his upper arm with a hand as powerful as a vise and even shook him a little with the urgency of his need.

"Jon! Jon, wake up. Look, Jon!"

Jon focused on reality and followed his friend's gaze upslope from the graveyard into the notch in Hanged-Man's Hill where the two ridgelines came together. Something was standing there in the notch. Something white and faintly glowing. He couldn't be certain because of the distance and the bushes obstructing the view, but it looked like a human figure. Jon couldn't tell if it was male or female, young or old. But it seemed to be watching them intently.

Jon couldn't resist his sudden urge to call out.

"Hey!"

He waved. The figure continued to look down upon them, then turned suddenly and fled. It disappeared among the trees in moments.

"Do we go after it?" Isaac asked gamely.

Jon shook his head. "There's no chance to catch it in the dark. Tomorrow, we'll follow its trail."

"All right." Isaac looked at his friend in intent silence. Finally, he asked, "What was you listening to?"

Jon closed his eyes, suddenly very tired.

"Dead men speak, Isaac," he said. "Dead men."

A light was shining inside the Glass House when Jon and Isaac returned to the manor. It was late. Jon was tired, but he knew that he couldn't sleep. He said good-night to Isaac at the bunk house door and his friend went inside to get a few hours sleep before the start of the next day. But Jon knew that his night wasn't over yet.

As he suspected, his father, lantern in hand, was standing before the Corpse Flower, staring at it as if it could reveal to him the secrets of the universe. And maybe, Jon thought, it could, and would, before its bloom died back. He was only happy that his strange acuity of senses seemed to have disappeared. He didn't think he could stand the aroma of rotting flesh that was the Corpse Flower's perfume if his senses were still as strong as they'd been in the graveyard.

His father glanced at him as he came into the Glass House.

"You've been out wandering in the night again," his father said in his deep, sepulchral voice.

Jon nodded.

"What did you find?"

"Dead voices," Jon said. "Dead people."

His father nodded, as if he'd said "Rabbits and squirrels" instead.

"The *heka* is strong there," he said.

"*Heka?*"

Jon felt his father's eyes on him, peering as if he wanted to pierce through to his son's soul. Benjamin Noir shook his head suddenly, an expression of almost human doubt on his face. Jon was shocked. He had never seen that look on his father's face before.

"Sometimes," he said, in musing tones, "I wonder if I didn't make a mistake with you."

THE TWILIGHT ZONE

Jon would have said something in the sudden silence, but he was too stunned.

"You look like your mother, boy, but my blood runs strongly through you, as well. Maybe as strongly as it runs through your brother. Perhaps I should have educated you both—but, no. I had to concentrate on the one, the thirteenth, and so neglect the other." Benjamin Noir's gaze turned inward, and he spoke again as if to himself. "But perhaps there's still time."

He looked at Jon, the old fire back in his eyes. "Yes, *heka*. That is why I moved to Geiststadt." He gestured, encompassing, it seemed, all of Noir Manor and the surrounding land. "For whatever reason, the land here is drenched with *heka*."

"But what is it?" Jon asked.

"The ancient Egyptians knew it by that name, boy. It's power. Energy the Creator used to make the world. It holds the universe together. It brought life to this world. The modern Arabs call it *barraka*. Many living beings, human and otherwise, possess it. Even some places and objects do. Anything strange, abnormal, exotic, or ancient. Deities possess it in great quantities. Kings do. The dead have it. Especially the walking dead." His father looked him in the eye and suddenly Jon feared him, feared him as never before in his life. He suddenly looked unhuman. More than human, or perhaps less. His face was the mask of a terrifying ancient god. Not cruel but merciless. Unconcerned with human trivialities. "I am the thirteenth son of my father, boy, and I have it!" His voice was like that of a lion, or a fire roaring out of control. For an instant he seemed invincible and immortal, but then suddenly he was just a man again, strong and vibrant beyond his years, but just a man. When he spoke it was in a quiet, almost introspective voice.

"But not enough," he said, and his broad shoulders slumped almost imperceptibly. "No. Not enough."

He turned without a word and, taking his lantern with him, left Jon alone in the dark in the Glass House, the stench of the Corpse Flower all around him.

7.
Saturday, June 18th, Third Intercalary Day

Jon thought that it would be difficult to sleep, but he was wrong. His mind was in turmoil, but his body was exhausted and for once it won its battle with his brain. He sank into a deep sleep and awoke with the sun already risen. He slept, he thought, like the dead. Though that metaphor was no longer as apt as it once seemed to be, as apparently the deads' sleep was more restless then he'd ever realized.

Jon had always been a rationalist. If he believed in a God at all, it was in some far off, largely beneficent but mostly preoccupied figure who, once he'd set the world in motion had gotten distracted by other affairs and let it pretty much roll along on its own. He had no specific theological beliefs. The Roman—or Egyptian, for that matter—cosmology seemed as likely as the Christian. Or as unlikely.

But now. Now he had positive proof of the soul, of survival of the spirit after death. He had seen the revenants with his eyes, heard them with his ears. It was solid evidence that he had to believe. He knew that his father had spent all those years in the study of esoteric knowledge of some sort or another. It had seemed that Benjamin Noir had spent his days chasing will-o-the-wisps and imaginary wisdom. Now, it seemed that perhaps his father had been right. This business of *heka*...

Jon hesitated at the entrance to the kitchen. Callie was

in her normal spot, cooking breakfast, but he was surprised to see Thomas already at table. His servant, McCool, was standing behind him, shoveling food down his gullet when not waiting on his master.

"You're up early," he said to his brother.

"Good morning to you, too," Thomas said after chewing a mouthful of eggs and sausage. "It happens that I have a lot to do this day."

Jon didn't even try to suppress his smile.

"Really? You're actually going to do some work around the farm?"

Thomas carefully spread some marmalade on a lightly toasted chunk of bread.

"Heavens, no. Why should I get my hands dirty when we have you for that?"

Jon grunted. He went to the fireplace where Callie had made him a plate of eggs, potatoes, and sausage. He took the food and a steaming mug of tea from her with thanks, and went to the rough-hewn table where he sat across from his brother. He pitched into the food. After a couple of forkfuls he looked up to see Thomas watching him closely.

"I understand you had quite the adventure last night," Thomas said.

"Who told you that?"

"The Captain, late last night as we worked in the study." Thomas paused. "He seemed...not quite himself. Pensive. One might almost say doubtful."

"Did he?"

"Yes." Thomas's gaze narrowed and his expression

hardened as he continued to stare at Jon. "Don't forget your place around here, brother."

"My place?" Jon put his fork down and returned his brother's level stare. "What would that be?"

"*I* am the thirteenth son," Thomas said with some emphasis. "*You* came after."

"I know that," Jon said in a low voice, his hand going unconsciously to the birthmark that arced across the base of his throat. He touched it lightly, not-quite memories of almost twenty-one years ago flitting across his mind too quickly for him to catch and examine.

"I am the rightful heir to the Captain's knowledge," Thomas said.

Jon shrugged casually and returned to his food.

"Maybe. Our father mentioned that to me last night, though." He chewed thoughtfully on a slice of fried potato. "He told me he was re-thinking that idea."

He knew that he'd hit home when he saw the anger on Thomas's face.

"You lie!" Thomas exclaimed.

No, Jon thought, *I exaggerate*. But he wouldn't say that to his brother. He took a slurp of tea from his mug as Thomas rearranged his features into a bland mask.

"We shall see, brother," Thomas said in a casual tone that Jon knew concealed seething anger. "Perhaps you'll take to the studies. Perhaps you won't."

"Perhaps." Jon knew that Thomas was angry, even worried. Thomas didn't like to share anything—material items, attention from others, or even something as hard to quantify as the prestige of being Benjamin Noir's thirteenth son, but still his reaction to Jon's subtle taunting seemed too intense. Unless, Jon thought, there was more significance to all this than he'd realized. His intuition told him that everything was building towards a climax that would decide much of his future. Perhaps even much of the future of Geiststadt and of the entire Noir family.

"Anyway," Thomas said with his elaborate casualness, "I'm sure it'll all work out in the end. Other things concern me today."

"Oh?" Jon asked, amused at his brother's attempts to conceal his real feelings, "like what?"

Thomas toyed with his silverware.

"Oh, like that delightful girl I met yesterday. What was her name? Trudi? Too bad her father is such a drunken sot. I thought I'd go over to their place and get to know her better. Perhaps console her by letting her get to know me."

Jon suddenly sat upright and immediately cursed himself for his lack of control. Not only had he let Thomas know he'd scored in their interminable little game, but more importantly he knew that he'd just set Thomas on Trudi's trail. Thomas would pursue her now just because he knew it would bother him. Jon didn't want Trudi to be some kind of trophy in a game between him and Thomas. For one thing, he doubted he could defeat Thomas in this competition. His brother had an uncanny way with women. For another, there was something about Trudi that attracted him more than any woman ever had. He barely knew her, but he knew that he badly wanted to know her better. He wanted her to

THE TWILIGHT ZONE

know and care for him. Suddenly it seemed the most important thing in the world to him.

Thomas, watching him, rose with a smile that was more of a smirk, and pushed away from the table.

"McCool," he said, "go up to my room and fetch that perfume I picked up the other day. I fancy that it would be a good gift for the young lady."

"Yes, Your Honor." McCool sketched a casual salute and went off on the errand as Thomas smiled down on Jonathan.

"It's all the rage in Manhattan. All the fashionable young ladies use it. I'm sure it'll make a favorable impression on this country girl."

"I'm sure," Jon muttered as he stood and stalked out of the kitchen, his breakfast only half finished. His brother's low laughter followed him.

Thomas wore his finest waistcoat and shirt and newly shined Wellington boots. He was as splendid a picture of young manhood, he was sure, as could be found east of Manhattan, including all of Brooklyn and Flatbush, let alone Geiststadt. Just to be doubly sure, however, he stopped off in the study to examine a certain papyrus that just might pertain to the occasion. He would work the spell, if needed, that evening. With Callie's help, of course. For now, Thomas decided, he'd try his native charm on the girl. Often, that was all that was necessary.

He and McCool made their way to Schmidt's shop. McCool carried the gift nicely done up in tissue paper and ribbon. Thomas always had a few bottles of the cheap perfume on hand, just in case.

It was, Thomas thought, a pleasant morning, if one

liked country scenery. He saw Trudi in the yard, scattering feed to a small flock of chickens, and felt the day's prospects suddenly brighten. Jonathan was right about the girl. There was something almost irresistibly attractive about her. Thomas had known more beautiful girls. Certainly more sophisticated girls.

But Trudi had an innocent, almost naive air about her that Thomas found refreshing. Her youthful good looks were also more than adequate. The pleasure of having her for herself, alone, might be even greater than the pleasure he'd get from taking her away from Jonathan.

She saw him approach, and smiled. The chickens cavorted at her feet for more feed, but she stopped to drop a pretty curtsey in response to his elaborate bow.

"Good morning Miss Schmidt," Thomas said. "A delightful day made even more delightful by your presence."

"Thank you, Mr. Noir."

A slight blush stole upon her cheeks at Thomas's words. That's a good sign, he thought, a very good sign. He put his hand out without taking his eyes off Trudi and McCool slouched forwards with his usual insouciant grin, placed the tissue-wrapped package in Thomas's hand, then quickly stepped backward.

"A small token of welcome to Geiststadt," Thomas said, handing her the package. "Forgive its lateness, but please accept its sincerity."

"Why, Mr. Noir—"

"Please," Thomas said, flashing his most engaging grin. "There are so many Mr. Noir's around here that that form of address is much too confusing. One might think

THE TWILIGHT ZONE

you were addressing the Captain. Or even my brother Jonathan." His laughter showed the absurdity of that notion. "Call me Thomas, for the sake of clarity, if nothing else."

"Very well...Thomas," she said. She put the feed basket on the ground for the chickens to fight over and unwrapped the tissue paper, exposing the delicate hand-blown glass bottle. "It's beautiful," she breathed.

Thomas smiled. "Here." He stepped forward among the squalling chickens, who, he felt, were detracting from the scene. "Try some here."

He lifted the glass stopper from the bottle and took Trudi's forearm in his other hand, rotating it to expose that the underside of her wrist. Delicately he trailed the stopper along her wrist and was happy to note a tiny shiver along her arm, almost suppressed. If he hadn't still been holding her, he would have missed it.

He released her hand and she brought it close to her face and sniffed. She smiled.

"All the fashionable young women in Manhattan are wearing this scent," he said, smiling back. It was somewhat of an exaggeration, of course, as this was a nice enough but relatively cheap perfume he bought by the pint. But she couldn't know that. "You, of course, would fit right in with them."

Trudi's smile turned to gentle laughter.

"You flatter me."

"I only speak the truth!" Thomas protested, again flashing his engaging grin.

"Manhattan." He frowned momentarily as her attention

turned away from him to some internal desire of her own. "It must be wonderful."

"Oh, it's fairly nice," Thomas said. "I'll tell you all about it."

He smiled to himself again as he succeeded in dragging her attention back to him.

"Oh, yes, please. But first let me put the feed away. Then I must make sure my father has had his breakfast. I won't be a moment," she said, and turned and ran back to the shop.

"Fairly nice," McCool said in a dead-on imitation of Thomas's voice.

Thomas glanced at him. "Well, I'm sure it's no Tipperary. That's where you came from in the *Auld Sod*, eh?"

McCool spit on the ground. "Fuck Tipperary. And the *Auld Sod*. I was starving there."

Thomas nodded. "Don't you forget that."

They waited together. When the first scream came they looked at each other. Thomas's face was blank of emotion, McCool's blandly innocent. They ran together to the shop. The screams hadn't stopped. They were coming louder and closer together. When they entered the shop they saw Trudi standing at the entrance to the room where Schmidt slept, which was partitioned off from the work area by cloth hangings too ragged and disreputable to be called curtains.

Trudi was staring at her father's bloody corpse. It sprawled across the bed, throat slashed, blade still embedded at the end point of the cut. Screams welled from her throat one after the other although her face was curiously blank, as if she didn't even realize she was screaming.

THE TWILIGHT ZONE

Thomas grabbed her arm and turned her into his body, sheltering her from the gruesome sight of her father's corpse. She went to him willingly, putting her face against his broad chest, resting in the refuge of his arms.

"Shhh, shhh," he said, patting her hair with the gentleness of a mother cat calming a frightened kitten.

Her screams subsided into sobs. Thomas looked at McCool over her head, and nodded. McCool darted out of the room for help as Thomas continued to hold the grieving girl.

The love spell, he thought, might not be necessary after all.

Jon felt almost foolish carrying his homemade bayonet spear. The old graveyard was utterly without menace in the bright daylight. The fear-filled atmosphere the night before had vanished with the darkness. It was now just another lovely late spring day, with the official beginning of summer—and Jon and Thomas's birthday—only three days away. Thomas. He forced the image of his brother and Trudi from his mind.

It was still before noon. Jon had stopped briefly in the Glass House for a quick look at the Corpse Flower before picking up Isaac at the cow barn and heading for HangedMan's Hill. He didn't want to make this little jaunt on his own. Besides, Isaac was almost as good a tracker as he was himself.

But first they had to discover if the strange glowing figure from the night before had even left tracks. Jon had the disturbing notion that the thing they'd seen was probably a ghost, or specter of some kind. In that case it could hardly leave a material trace of its passing. He supposed, anyway, not being an expert on the physical manifestations of psychic presences. On the other hand—they had undoubtedly *both* seen it, and Isaac had seemed both deaf and blind to the evening's other, assuredly spiritual manifestations.

All of his doubts were laid to rest when Isaac called Jon over to where the forest margin blended into the grassland. Isaac pointed wordlessly, as if he didn't want Jon to be influenced by anything he might say about his discovery. Jon sank down to his knees next to his friend, his sharp eyes picking up the clues left on the ground and among low-lying branches of the surrounding trees. He nodded.

"Looks like this is it," Jon said. He reached out and gently swept his hands over a patch of moss whose delicate stems were crushed and bent as if someone had stood in place for awhile, watching something in the graveyard below. To confirm this, Jon stepped gingerly in the same spot, turned, and looked down upon the cemetery. He fingered a broken branch at the level of his throat. "Whomever stood here had a fine view of the graveyard—they snapped off this branch to make it even clearer."

"Way shorter than me," Isaac said. "Shorter than you, even. A child?"

"Or a small woman," Jon said. He fell back to his knees and closely examined the nearby ground. There—a small dislodged stone. Further on a broken stem from a leafy shrub, snapped when whoever—or whatever—passed by and brushed against it.

THE TWILIGHT ZONE

"It's a trail, all right," Jon said.

"Left by a human being," Isaac said. "Thank the Lord."

Jon grinned, but he couldn't tease his companion too much. He'd been just as worried as Isaac that they were after a ghost.

It was slow going. It took over an hour to follow the infrequent visual clues—crushed or broken plants, disturbed sticks or stones, scatterings of fallen leaves that had once been piles—a quarter mile before it led to a somewhat more traveled trail.

This more clearly defined path probably had started out as a game trail, used by the deer, raccoon, rabbits, and other wild denizens of HangedMan's Hill to travel to favorite eating or drinking spots, but it had been definitely been used by at least one person. Occasionally the two hunters could discern human footprints. All seemed to have been made by the same set of small, badly worn shoes.

The trail snaked up HangedMan's Hill, taking them deep into a forest largely untouched by the villagers who lived in the flatland below. Certainly some hunters may have passed through occasionally, and Jon and Isaac may have come close sometimes during their rambles across the countryside, but the center of Geiststadt life was the plains below the ridge way, not the hills themselves. After only a short time on the game trail they both realized that they were in an unfamiliar part of the heavily forested hillside.

It was dark inside the forest, cool, and quiet. They could smell the rich loam at their feet, piled thick with decades, probably centuries, of dark humus compounded of fallen leaves and rotted branches and moss encrusted logs.

Jon was enjoying the various rustic sensations that so fully enveloped his senses that he almost passed another faint path that forked off the game trail, leading up the mouth of a small, knife-edged gorge. He caught Isaac by the arm and pointed. Isaac nodded. Their silence was unintentional—an unconscious desire to fit in with the magnificent forest which surrounded them.

They paused at the gorge's threshold, listening to a soft murmuring babble that seemed to accentuate the silence rather than break it. They followed the sound and discovered a wandering forest stream. Jon stooped and drank a handful of water. It was sweet and cool. Isaac joined him and they drank until their thirst was slaked, then they continued on their way on up the gorge. The path was now was almost as obvious as a city street.

The canyon dead-ended thirty yards before them, apparently untouched by human hands. They looked at each other uncertainly. Jon shrugged. He put a hand to his mouth, cupping it.

"Hello," Jon called out. "Anyone here?"

The silence, but for water running over stone, continued, and for a moment Jon thought that their trip had been in vain. Then he felt, somehow, the irresistible pressure of eyes gazing at him, and he turned to see a small, raggedly dressed old woman who had come upon them from the rear, silent as creeping death.

"Agatha Derlicht!"

As soon as he blurted the name, Jon knew he was wrong.

THE TWILIGHT ZONE

She was too short for one thing, and her hair, though clean and snow white, was wild and unbound. Her clothes were much patched and needed patching where they weren't. But he knew why he'd thought she was the eldest Derlicht when he first glimpsed her. Her resemblance to the old woman was unmistakable. She had the same thin face—though even more weathered by sun and wind than Agatha's—the same blade of a nose and hawk-like eyes.

Her eyes were wild when they first focused on the boys, but she seemed to recognize them and relax at least a little.

"No," she croaked in a voice that seemed rusty from disuse. "No. Not 'Agatha,'" she said. "I am Katja Derlicht."

"But—but," Jon stuttered. "You've been dead for fifteen years!"

She laughed wildly, like one insane.

"Only to my oh-so-loving family," she said when she finally regained a semblance of control.

"I don't understand," Jon said.

Katja's bitter gaze turned inward, as if her sharp old eyes were fixed on a scene occurring in some other place, at some other time.

"She kept me locked up in that dark old house for years. For years. She knew I loved the sun and flowers and wind on my face. She knew I hated small, enclosed places. But she kept me chained in a little room with a little window so I couldn't feel the rain or dance in the moonlight or talk to the birds and the foxes. But I escaped from my rotten prison. Fifteen years ago I broke my bonds. I escaped to the sun and moon and stars and have never looked back!"

"Why?" Jon asked. "Why did your sister keep you locked up all those years?"

Katja looked at him and he could feel the power of her eyes. It was like the *heka* that his father had told him about. There was no denying that the old woman was animated by some kind of supernatural energy.

"She knew I was different," Katja Derlicht said. She smiled and for a moment her face was transformed. The madness was gone. Her features were transfused by a gentle light, as if shining from within. "If I'd been fifty...even forty years younger when your father had arrived in Geiststadt...Well, no use sighing about what might have been. I was the age I was. Your father wanted a young wife. Still, it seems to me that if Fate had only been kinder, Noir and Derlicht would have become one twenty years ago." Katja Derlicht's expression became troubled, but the sadness that touched it was a human sadness, not insanity. "Fate being what it is, I see trouble ahead. Years. Decades. Centuries, even." She sighed and turned her worried face to Jon's again. "But you, you of all Noirs who could have been my child, be careful. The next days are critical. Danger abounds."

"The killer?" Jon asked eagerly.

Katja Derlicht nodded.

"Is he of Geiststadt?" he asked.

"It is hard to say," she said. "But I think not."

"Is he...human?"

"I think that has already been answered for you."

THE TWILIGHT ZONE

"By the ghosts, you mean? The spirits who spoke to me last night."

She only nodded.

"I really did hear the voices of the dead, then?" Jon asked, wonderingly.

"You are your father's son. It's not surprising that you have some of his abilities."

Jon suppressed a shiver. "Even if I don't want them?"

Katja Derlicht frowned sternly.

"Don't turn your back on your talents," she said. "They may mean the difference between life and death some day. Some day very soon now."

Jon nodded abstractedly. It was all rather difficult to take in. He had known that his father had been exploring strange paths all these years. But he had never pried into his father's business. It seemed, though, that perhaps he was involved more deeply in the doings of his father than he realized. Probably all the Noirs were. Maybe even all of Geiststadt.

Jon looked at Katja Derlicht and nodded solemnly.

"You're right," he said. "I'll be careful. But what about you? You're all alone out here."

She laughed, and this time she sounded almost human.

"Alone? Hardly. I have the sun and stars and moon for companionship. The birds and rabbits, foxes and possums, are all my friends. This is where I had longed to be all my life. I am in no danger now."

"All right." Jon nodded dubiously. "Can we come see you again?"

"I'd like that," Katja Derlicht said. "I do miss the sound of human voices sometimes. Living human voices."

Jon and Isaac exchanged glances.

"Do you want us to bring you anything?" Isaac asked.

"My needs are few," she said, "and taken care of by all that is around me."

She gestured at the forest and hillside and stream, and Jon knew that, odd as it seemed, the old woman was indeed content with her strange life, and now at peace with the world.

"Been out tramping in the woods again?" Thomas was perched comfortably on a chair on the porch. It was mid-afternoon and sunny, with the *uraeus* figure beaming like a beacon above the doorway to Noir Manor.

Jonathan put one foot on the staircase leading to the porch and stopped to look at his brother.

"Yes," he said, "I have. How have you been wasting your day?"

Thomas smiled like a hungry cat that spies an unlucky mouse well within reach.

"Hardly wasting it, my dear brother," he said. "Fortunately I was at the proper place in the proper time to console Trudi."

"Console Trudi?"

Thomas's smile widened as he saw the sudden look of concern on Jon's face.

"What for? What happened?"

"Her father is dead," Thomas said carelessly. "Killed himself, it seems, in remorse over the murders."

"Dead?" Jon asked, stunned. "Killed himself?"

"Do try to keep up, dear boy." Thomas stretched languidly and made a production out of consulting his pocket watch. "The Captain should be down any time now. We're going to examine the body. Care to come along?"

"Not really," Jon said. "But I will."

"Too late," Thomas murmured, "and a penny short. As usual."

This killing, Jon thought, was not like the others. Not at all.

Five of them were in the room with the corpse. Jon. His father. Thomas and his man McCool. And Agatha Derlicht.

The reconstruction of events was simple. Perhaps deceptively so. Johann Schmidt had apparently sat on his bed fully dressed and taken a sharp edged woodworking tool to his own throat, cutting it through in a single motion. He had fallen back among his bedclothes and quickly bled to death. Both the body and blanket were stiff with clotted, dried blood that was attracting hordes of flies. A scrap of paper next to Schmidt's pillow had been touched by the spray of blood that had burst from the cooper's throat, but the brief message scrawled upon it by a shaky hand was untouched.

"Forgive me," it said, in German. It was unsigned.

Thomas was the first to speak after everyone had looked over the scene. Naturally, Jon thought, he would be.

"It seems we have our murderer," he said.

"You think so?" Agatha Derlicht asked in a voice glacially cold and pure.

"I do," Thomas said with a nod. "You see, the murders

began soon after his arrival. As has been established," and here he nodded at their father, "Schmidt was running from something. Perhaps some violent act. Maybe even other killings. We know for sure he drank to excess. We know he had high emotions."

"James drinks too much," Jon said quietly, "and we know that your emotions can be...excessive. Yet no one has accused you of murder."

Spots of red on Thomas's cheeks showed Jon that he'd struck home with his thrust, but his brother controlled himself.

"That's foolish," he said. "Why, I wasn't even in Geiststadt when the first murder was committed, and as to a possible motive—"

"The boy wasn't accusing you," Benjamin Noir said without emotion. "He was merely making a point."

He was hovering over the body. Suddenly he reached out and removed the blade from Schmidt's neck. It wasn't a knife. It was an odd tool with a pointless curved blade set at a right angle to a wooden handle. Only the top edge of the blade was sharp.

"What is this thing?" Benjamin Noir asked.

"It's called a froe," a strange voice said.

They all turned to look to see three men crowded at the entrance to the room, Seth slightly in the lead. Jon was relieved to see brother finally returned to Geiststadt with the magistrate's men. Seth looked harried and puzzled, as usual.

The man on his right was older, perhaps in his sixties. He was fleshy in the face and body. He was bald on top and the hair on the sides of his head was white. His clothes were well-made and expensive-looking. Jon thought that Thomas could only dream of such finery. There was something naggingly familiar about his appearance Jon knew he had never seen him before, but still—

The man on Seth's left was middle-aged, soft-looking, and dressed cheaply and unremarkably. There was nothing familiar about him at all. In fact, he looked like one of those colorless men whom you'd forget the instant they were out of your sight, whom you'd have to know for years and years before you'd remember his name. He was the one who had spoken.

"It's used for cutting barrel staves out of wooden planks," he said in a mild, unassuming voice.

"Or throats," Thomas added wryly.

The three newcomers advanced into the room. Shock blossomed on Seth's face as he realized that there was a corpse on the bed.

"Is it—he—dead?" Seth asked.

"Yes," Jon said quietly. "It's Johann Schmidt, the cooper."

"Schmidt? But he just moved to Geiststadt. Who'd want to kill *him*?"

Jon didn't offer an explanation. He stared more closely at the older man, who had followed Seth into the room, the nondescript fellow at his side. For the first time, Jon got a good look at the older man's face and he realized who he was.

"Why—why," Jon stuttered, completely at a loss. He had seen the man's engraved picture both in newspapers and as the frontispiece of several books about old New York. "You're Washington Irving!"

The older man turned to Jon and bowed slightly.

"Yes," he said. "At your service, sir."

Jon was too stunned to reply.

"Washington Irving, the author?" Thomas inquired in the sudden silence.

"Yes." The old man smiled at Thomas. "You've read my books?"

Thomas shrugged with a semi-apologetic smile.

"Not really. I don't read much in the way of popular fiction."

"Oh," said Irving, his smile suddenly gone frosty.

"I have," Jon volunteered. "I love your tales of old Dutch New York."

And he did. He wasn't just saying that to make Irving feel better after his brother's jibe. Irving was probably the finest author that a young America had so far produced, though lately he'd been devoting much of his time to writing tales and travelogs set in Europe, abandoning his native New York for more far-away, and more literarily-accepted locales.

"Thank you," Irving said,

"If I may ask, sir," Benjamin Noir asked in a tone that implied he would, whether or not he may, "to what do we owe the honor of your visit?"

"As those who have read me may know—" Irving glanced tellingly at Thomas, who was suddenly looking elsewhere "—from 'The Legend of Sleepy Hollow,' perhaps, or 'The Student of Salamanca,' maybe, I have something of an interest in the gothic. The...supernatural, some may say. I was visiting my good friend Franklin Brooks, the Brooklyn magistrate, when this young man—"

here he paused to nod at Seth "—brought the story of the most extraordinary, uh, situation to our attention. It sounds like a perfectly thrilling story. Esquire Brooks kindly allowed me to indulge my interest by letting me accompany Constable William Pierce—" here he paused to nod at the third man "—to investigate the circumstances surrounding this murder."

"I see," Benjamin Noir said, glancing at Agatha Derlicht. She looked back at him blandly, but Jon caught the meaning of their exchange. Neither one of them wanted a famous author poking about Geiststadt, looking for quaint stories regarding its inhabitants to tell to the world. "Well, welcome to Geiststadt, then, Mr. Irving. Constable Pierce. I am Benjamin Noir."

"Thank you," Irving said. After his initial comments identifying the woodworking tool, Pierce seemed content to let Irving speak for him. "Is this the murdered man?"

"It's *a* murdered man," Thomas murmured, "probably self-murdered. But you're two corpses too late if you're looking for the original."

"Eh?" Irving looked at him with some irritation, as did Jon.

"What my brother is trying to say," Jon said, stepping between them, "is that there's been more...killings." He hesitated a moment over the last word, unwilling to commit himself to one side or the other of the suicide issue. "There's been three...deaths...now in Geiststadt."

Washington Irving and Will Pierce exchanged startled glances.

"By gosh," Pierce said, his voice as mild as his looks. "We'd better get to the bottom of this."

"Yes," Benjamin Noir said dryly. "We'd better." He looked thoughtfully at his sons. "Gentlemen, these are my sons, Jonathan and Thomas. Jonathan can take you to view the bodies of the previous victims, if you so desire. They've been kept on ice, awaiting your arrival."

"Splendid," Irving said. He glanced at Pierce. "Wouldn't you say so, Constable."

"Hmmm?" Pierce had been peering closely at Schmidt's corpse. He turned his mild gaze to Irving. "Yes. Yes, I suppose so."

"Fine," Benjamin Noir said with a frown. "Jonathan can explain matters—the circumstances of their death—as you inspect the bodies. Thomas, come along with me. There's some things that we have to look into."

Benjamin Noir nodded to Agatha Derlicht, whom the men had seen fit to ignore during the course of their discussion. Agatha nodded back a mere millimeter, and Thomas followed Noir out of the room without a word.

"By gosh," Constable Pierce said as the Noirs strode out of the room, "he seems an authoritative fellow."

"He was a sea captain," Jon said by way of explanation. "Now, if you gentlemen will follow me, I'll see if I can enumerate the curious events of the past several days."

"That's why we're here," said Irving.

8.

Thomas excused himself as soon as he could from the Captain's study. The old man was again looking for answers to the events unfolding about them in his manuscripts, scrolls, and horoscopes. Thomas saw an opportunity, and knew that he should take advantage of it as soon as possible. But, as always, he wanted reserves in place in case the unthinkable happened and his own personal charm somehow failed.

He found Callie where he thought he would, warming herself by the roaring fireplace in the kitchen, though the afternoon temperature was already at least eighty degrees. The old woman seemed to have shrunk over the years, becoming a tinier and even more wrinkled version of herself with each passing season. Soon, he thought, she'd be no bigger than the collection of shrunken human heads with lips and eyelids sewn shut that she kept in her sleeping quarters just off the kitchen. Those heads had given him frequent nightmares as a child. He'd dreamed that they'd whispered words barely understandable through their sewn-shut lips. Telling him stories of Callie's people. Of headhunting and lavish banquets of long-pig on white Caribbean beaches during nights of the full moon.

She looked up at him, still rocking as he approached her place by the fire. Her dark eyes gleamed like beetle's wings shimmering in the moonlight.

"What do you want now, young master?"

Thomas smiled his charming smile.

"Maybe just to say hello, Callie," he said, slipping effortlessly into Callie's native language, almost forgotten now by the rest of the world. *"To see how you're doing."*

Callie's response was a sharp cackle that had little of humanity in it, and even less humor.

"Do not lie to me, young master. You don't care how Callie does. You want something. You need something from me. That is the way you are. You are your father's son."

Thomas's smile became fixed, but he kept it in place and nodded. Callie had been the closest thing to a mother that he'd had when he'd been growing up. But she'd really been more of a stern taskmistress than a loving parental figure. Whereas Jonathan had been given over largely to the care of his various sisters after their mother had died giving them birth, Callie had cared for him as a baby. She'd washed him. Dressed him. He suspected that she would have fed him from her own body if her milk hadn't dried up years before. But it had never been out of love. Rather, it seemed, out of duty to the Captain.

She'd taught him her own tongue. It was almost a private language that in all of Geiststadt only Thomas and Callie and the Captain understood, that very few people in all of the rest of the world knew.

The Captain had said, whenever anyone cared enough to ask, that he'd found her in Cuba. That she was the only daughter of a noble Spanish house that had been slaughtered in a native uprising. The truth of the matter, which again only Thomas, Callie, and the Captain knew,

THE TWILIGHT ZONE

was close, but ironically twisted from the fiction the Captain perpetuated. Callie was from Cuba. She was from a noble house. One that went a lot further back in Caribbean history than the Spanish did. She was a Karibe Indian, descended from a line of chieftains, shamans, and witches. Once a powerful and populous tribe that dominated many islands in the far-flung Caribbean, the Karibes had been in decline long before Callie's birth. Decimated by savage, interminable internecine wars, Callie's people were finally finished off by centuries of slavery under the Spanish. She was one of only a handful of pureblood Karibes left in the world. There were warriors, headhunters, priestesses, slavers and slaves, cannibals and kings in her ancient lineage. And she was the sole repository of all their ancient and powerful knowledge. She had more *heka* than anyone Thomas had ever met. Except the Captain.

"*There is no escaping your wisdom, old one,*" Thomas said in the ancient language. "*You are right. I come for your help.*"

"*About what?*" Callie asked.

"There is a girl—"

"*A girl?*" the old witch asked scornfully. "*At this dangerous time! Murder and death all around you. And you occupy yourself with a girl? There will always be girls, young master. Always.*"

"But this one is special," Thomas pleaded. "*And now is the time to strike.*"

Callie started rocking again, her head nodded in time to the rhythmic rolling of the chair.

"*It's the cooper's daughter, isn't it?*"

"*Yes, wise and ancient one.*"

"*Don't patronize me, boy.*" She continued to look into the fire as she spoke. "*You know that Jonathan loves her already. And she could very easily come to love him in return.*"

Thomas only smiled.

"*I see.*" Her sigh was like a soft breeze on a summer night, unseen and barely heard. "*All right. You are the thirteenth son of the thirteenth son. Your destiny is great. Your desires must all be met.*"

Thomas had heard that before many times.

"*You'll help then. Like you did with that girl, what was it? Almost eight years ago?*"

Callie stood, slowly and with effort.

"*Yes. She was your first, wasn't she?*"

Thomas nodded. He'd been thirteen and he was in love. Well, he'd thought he was. She was eighteen, buxom and beautiful, but cold to his youthful wooing until Callie took a hand. It lasted most of a summer, until the girl got pregnant. The Captain paid the family off and she disappeared. Thomas had never seen her again.

"*Very well. I will make the dough and bake the image. First, though, you know what we need.*"

It was a statement, not a question. Thomas nodded. He was willing to trade a little pain now to ensure a lot of pleasure in the near future. Hopefully, the very near future.

Callie took a pewter mug from its hook near the fireplace. She got the needle from where she kept it, stuck in a knot of her hair. It was a splinter of bone from a human femur honed sharp as, well, a needle. Thomas rolled up his sleeve.

Constable Pierce didn't say much. Washington Irving did most of the talking, in the form of an endless stream of questions that nearly made Jon Noir hoarse as he tried to answer them all. By the time they'd looked over old Erich's body Irving had been briefed on the history of Geiststadt and the relationship between the Derlichts and the Noirs. As they viewed Rolf Derlicht's body Irving's questions elicited the recitation of supernatural occurrences connected with Geiststadt, though Jon edited these so that his own experiences were glossed over. He wasn't comfortable enough to entirely accept them himself, let alone discuss them with strangers. Particularly strangers who were connected with the magistrate's office or who were widely read popular authors.

"This Corpse Flower that you mentioned earlier," Irving said as they left the Derlicht's icehouse where Rolf's body was stored against the heat of the late spring day, "sounds fascinating. I'd love to see it. How about you, Constable Pierce?"

"Good gosh, yes," said the mild-looking man, which were about two more words than he had spoken during their lengthy inspection of the bodies. "I don't think we have any of those in Brooklyn."

"No," Jon said. "I wouldn't think so. I haven't had a chance to look in on it myself today. I'll be happy to take you to the Glass House for a tour. We also have some very interesting carnivorous plants that I believe would also be scarce in Brooklyn. Not to mention our Egyptian lotuses and lilies."

"Sounds fascinating," Pierce said without too much enthusiasm.

As they went down the main street of the village, ignoring—or at least pretending to—all the whispers and stares that followed them, they passed Thomas Noir. He was dressed, Jon thought, like a city fop. And he was headed right for Schmidt's shop.

Trudi, Jon thought with a sinking feeling.

Thomas bowed deeply and smiled. Pierce and Irving nodded back to him pleasantly. Jon grit his teeth, and took their visitors on to the Glass House and its collection of exotic flora.

What a nice day this was turning out to be, Thomas thought, as he bowed in the direction of the investigator, writer, and brother.

The Third Intercalary Day in the calendar of ancient Kemet. Only two days till the first day of the year. In the contemporary calendar, the first day of summer. And, of course, his birthday. How time flies. As the first of the days between years was dedicated to Osiris, the second to his son Horus, the third belonged to their implacable enemy, Set, or as he was also sometimes called, Seth.

Knowing his own colorless lapdog of a brother, Seth, Thomas thought this mildly amusing. Set could have almost been Thomas's own patron saint. Or god. The Egyptians considered him the god of evil, the personification of drought, darkness, and perversity. He was the enemy of all that was good. Impatient to be born, he'd

THE TWILIGHT ZONE

torn himself from his mother's womb. He murdered his own brother, Osiris, mutilated the corpse, and scattered parts of it up and down the length of the Nile. He persecuted both his sister, Isis, who was Osiris's wife, as well as Horus, their son. The enemy of light, his head was the head of a beast unknown to man. His weapon was the primeval knife that was the symbol of dismemberment and death, and the fact that he had red hair made all redheads in Egypt feared and scorned for three thousand years. But yet, when Horus the Avenger finally defeated him after a cycle of battles that had lasted eighty years, the gods spared his life.

Why? Thomas asked himself. Because they knew they needed him. They needed his strength and cunning to face the Apophis serpent in the final battle between Order and Chaos. In the end, they could not do without him, and that, he thought, was the perfect metaphor for his own life.

Thomas didn't believe these old myths literally. No sane man did, although he wasn't sure about the Captain. But they were an instructive guide to the depths lurking underneath the apparent ordinariness of life. For example, the Captain needed Thomas's strength and cunning, even though he also feared him for those very qualities. Thomas wasn't sure why the Captain needed him. Perhaps because of something the old man had done in the past, as Benjamin Noir now seemed to believe that these unsolved murders were a sign that something in his checkered history might be catching up to him. On the other hand, Schmidt's death seemed to have given the old man pause. Maybe Benjamin Noir didn't know *what* to believe.

Good, Thomas thought. Let him worry. In the meantime, Thomas had his own needs to consider. His own desires.

He entered Johann Schmidt's workshop. It was virtually deserted and quiet as the proverbial grave. Only Trudi was present. Red-eyed and white-faced, she sat listlessly at Johann's work bench, staring silently off into space. She looked as morose as a mother cat whose litter had just been drowned. She was so immersed in her grief that she didn't even notice Thomas enter the room.

"My dear Miss Schmidt," he said, glad that he'd finally found a reason to wear his best outfit. He'd had McCool polish his Wellingtons till they shone. He wore over them his tightest- fitting trousers, revealing his length and strength of leg. His best waistcoat, of amethyst colored ribbed silk and wool, with a stand-up collar and square cut-away front, was resplendent. As was the morning coat he wore over it with faultlessly articulated m-notch lapels and a roll collar cut high in the back. He'd spent almost twenty minutes on his cravat, discarding a pile of ill-tied ones at his feet as McCool looked on—uselessly—in amusement, until he finally achieved the drape and flow he was reaching for. He was, he knew, a charmingly handsome devil.

She jumped as the sound of his voice transported from her inner world of grief back to the bleak reality of the real world.

"Mr.—Mr. Noir, I didn't hear you come in."

THE TWILIGHT ZONE

Thomas put a look of concern on his face as he approached her forlorn figure.

"I'm sorry to have startled you. But please. Remember that you promised to call me Thomas."

She nodded. Thomas smiled. She was vulnerable, devastated by the death of her father and the realization that she no longer had a means of making a living. She was alone in the world with no man to protect or provide for her.

Thomas knew that he had captured her attention. Between his charm and the ensorcelled doll Callie had made in her image and fortified with Thomas's own blood, it would be easy to capture her heart.

Dinner at Noir Manor that night was unusual. Everyone, even Thomas, was on their best behavior. James stayed away from the brandy. Thomas and Benjamin Noir were punctual. And there were guests.

Much to Jon's surprise, his father had offered to put up Pierce and Irving, who had initially intended to stay at The Hanged Hessian. Benjamin Noir wanted them close where he could keep on eye on them. As unlikely as it seemed, he obviously didn't want the constable sneaking around and looking at things he shouldn't be, nor did he want the famous writer penning revelatory commentaries exposing all the Noir secrets to the reading public. His father told him as much in a brief, whispered meeting before dinner where he gave Jon the job of being their guide during their stay in the village.

Or, as Benjamin Noir put more truthfully and succinctly, "their watch dog."

Constable Pierce was, as seemed his wont, quiet during dinner, uttering his favorite phrase, "Oh gosh, yes," several times, and little else. Irving was much more voluble. Suspiciously, to Jon at least, Thomas was at his most charming. He drew Irving out and got him to tell tales of his literary adventures in publishing as well as stories of his journeys across Europe. Thomas seemed entirely sincere about his interest in the latter. The Noirs and their guests sat at table until well into the evening as Irving spun stories of his travels through England, France, Italy, Greece, and Spain.

"Wonderfully interesting," Thomas commented as he, surprisingly enough, poured the last of the brandy for James who, even more surprisingly, had remained sober as the evening wound down.

"Yes," Benjamin Noir agreed. "I'm sure we'd all like to hear more, but it's getting late and tomorrow will be a busy day. The pastor is in from Brooklyn. He's staying with the Derlichts. If you'll agree to release the bodies, Constable Pierce, we should hold the funerals tomorrow. The bodies aren't..." Benjamin Noir hesitated, and rephrased his final sentence. "They won't last much longer."

"We don't want the ice to get contaminated," Seth said primly. "We've got a whole summer's worth of ice that could be ruined if the, uh, process is dragged out much longer."

"Good gosh, yes," Constable Pierce said. Then he made his longest speech since arriving in Geiststadt. "We can learn nothing more from the bodies. It's time for their decent Christian burial."

"What about Johann Schmidt," Benjamin Noir said thoughtfully. "What can we do about his body?"

"Eh?" Constable Pierce asked.

"I don't think they'll want to bury him in consecrated ground. Him being a suicide."

Constable Pierce pursed his lips, stopping Jon from voicing his opposition to the suicide theory.

"I can't agree with that conclusion as yet," the Constable said.

"Trudi will be glad to hear that," Jon said with some relief.

Thomas cleared his throat, magically, it seemed, bringing all eyes around the table to him.

"Yes, she will. But don't worry about her, dear brother," he said with a cryptic smile.

Jon frowned. "What do you mean?"

"I mean that her future is assured. This afternoon Miss Schmidt consented to be my wife."

A hubbub of surprised congratulations broke out around the table as Jon stared at his smiling brother in stunned silence, and his father regarded his thirteenth son with open speculation on his usually inscrutable face.

9.

Sunday, June 19th, The Fourth Intercalary Day

Jon woke in the morning more tired, it seemed, then when he went to bed. Much to the astonishment of most of the on-lookers he'd refused the night before to join the congratulatory toast to Thomas as James broke out a fresh bottle of brandy. Instead he'd left the dining room in silence, a stony expression on his face. He went directly to his room, threw off his clothes and collapsed into bed. But sleep would not come. When he finally dozed after hours of fruitless tossing and turning his sleep was light and broken by a series of fleeting, barely remembered, but horrific dreams.

As usual, he was the first one up that morning. But he had no enthusiasm for the coming day. He dressed mechanically and went down the stairs to the kitchen where Callie was already making tea and readying breakfast for the still-sleeping members of the household and their guests.

She looked at him critically.

"Didn't sleep well, did you, boy?"

"No."

She put the mug of strong tea on the table before him. His hands automatically cupped it, but he seemed to lack the will to lift it to his mouth and drink.

"Your brother has taken the girl from you." It was a statement, not a question.

THE TWILIGHT ZONE

Jon looked at the old woman, who returned his gaze with her usual impenetrably stoic expression.

"How could he?" Jon asked bitterly.

"How?" she laughed. "Your brother is a charmer. With help from the other world."

"You mean a spell or something?" Jon asked, only half-believingly.

Callie shrugged. "What does it matter? It is done. He wanted her. He takes what he wants." She paused, and looked at him for a moment as if in pity of the obvious misery on his face. "Though—"

Whatever Callie was going to say was silenced as another voice chimed in, "Good gracious, that tea smells marvelous."

They turned to see Constable Pierce standing in the kitchen entrance, looking even more mild and sleepy-eyed first thing in the morning than he did during the rest of the day, if that were possible.

"I will get you a cup," Callie said flatly.

The small man seated himself at the table across from Jon. They looked at each other silently for a few moments.

"I was going to drop by Miss Schmidt's," the constable finally said, "to tell her that I've released her father's body for burial. Would you care to accompany me?"

"Yes," Jon said. Perhaps if he could see her. Talk to her. Perhaps he could find out if things had really gone as far as his brother had claimed. Thomas was known to exaggerate. Or make grossly inflated claims. Perhaps this was just another of his wild notions, devoid of actual truth.

"Thank you, yes," Pierce said politely as Callie put a mug in front of him on the kitchen table. She acknowledged his thanks with a silent nod and returned to her chair in front of the fire, rocking and soaking up the heat and staring at the dancing flames as if they were a true oracle of the future.

Thomas slept soundly. He always did. He awoke each day refreshed and with no regrets, no matter what had happened the day before. He was not one to dwell on the past. He preferred to anticipate the future.

He was also a vivid dreamer, but he never had nightmares. He always maintained perfect control of his dreams, as he did his life in the waking world. This dream started pleasantly enough. He was walking down the church aisle after the wedding, accompanied by his new bride. Trudi looked beautiful. That was good. If he was going to have a wife, she had to be beautiful. Thomas didn't really need a wife, but it would give a gloss of stability and respectability to the Noir family. Children would probably prove useful, as Seth and Jon and he, himself, were to the Captain. There was always the possibility of a child like James, though...

The church was crowded with familiar faces. He supposed that it was the tiny Geiststadt church where a pastor came once a week from Brooklyn. But Thomas didn't know for sure because he'd never been inside the church. The Captain was missing. That was good, too. It meant that he was dead. That was why all the peasants were bowing and scraping. He, Thomas, was now the Lord of Noir Manor.

THE TWILIGHT ZONE

The only unhappy face in the crowd was Jonathan's. No surprise there. He was angry that Thomas had taken Trudi from him. Which was part of the reason—maybe the main reason—why he'd decided to marry her. He liked to take things from his brother. He'd done it all his life. This was just the latest, though maybe the best, thing he'd ever stolen from him.

Still, he should try to keep his brother happy. In some way. He was useful after all. He ran the farm. Thomas wouldn't have to worry about getting cow shit on his boots, yet could still be Lord of the Manor. Well, he'd devote some thought to it. There must be some bone he could throw Jonathan.

As can happen in dreams, the scene changed instantaneously without a sense of transition. Thomas was suddenly in his bedchamber in Noir Mansion, but it was a transfigured room. It was three times the size of his actual room, and furnished in a rich, luxurious manner that bordered on the decadent. The bed was an enormous four-poster with silken sheets and velvet curtains, drawn back now as Thomas lay on it in anticipation. Full-sized floor mirrors glittered around the bed, throwing back Thomas's reflection from all angles.

He watched Trudi avidly as she stood at the foot of the bed, smiling languorously at him. Her smile was knowing and experienced, not at all like that of the innocent girl she'd seemed to be. She stepped out of her dress and slowly, seductively, removed all her undergarments until her naked glory was revealed to Thomas's appreciative eyes. Her breasts were full and heavy, her arms round, her hips wide, her thighs sleek and strong.

Thomas approved. He'd made a good choice. It'd be some time before he tired of her quite apparent charms.

She leaned forwards, putting her hands on the bed's thick, soft, luxurious mattress. Her heavy breasts swayed with her movement, their reflection caught from all angles in the mirrors that surrounded the bed. Thomas patted the mattress by his side.

"Come, my dear," he said. "Time for you to be instructed in your wifely duties."

"Time for you, my dear," she said in a sweet, husky voice full of promise, "to receive your just desserts."

Thomas liked the sound of that.

Her smile widened, widened, and widened, her mouth melting and changing to that of a beast's muzzle. Her teeth grew into fangs. Her sweet voice turned to a terrible roar as she sprang onto the bed on all fours.

Suddenly terrified, Thomas could feel her hot breath all the way from the head of the bed. Her body was that of a voluptuous woman, but her head was the head of a lioness. Thomas recognized her. Somehow his Trudi had become Sekhmet, the fierce lioness-headed goddess of destruction and revenge. The punisher. The terrible Fury who when angered had to be restrained by all the rest of the gods combined lest she destroy all of humanity.

Thomas cringed as she crawled on all four towards him. This is another test, he thought, it has to be. A test. Just a test. Then he remembered that the last strange ordeal he'd thought a test had really been meant to kill him.

He screamed and scrabbled away from her. She rose up on her knees and threw her head back, her breasts jutting forward, and roared in fury. Then she exploded into a hundred little black shapes that hurtled toward Thomas, flapping their wings and screeching.

Birds. A flock of small black birds. Jonathan, Thomas thought giddily, would know what kind of birds they were. They collided against him and the bed's headboard. He threw his arms over his face just in time to protect his features. He could feel their tiny bodies striking him. Most bounced away harmlessly. Some stuck by claw or beak. They picked at him, screeching insanely in tiny, twittering voices. He wanted to strike at them but was afraid to take his arms away from his face. Afraid of what their beaks and sharp little claws would do to his face. To his eyes.

Realization came out of the dream fog, out of his bewilderment, that this was a chaos sign. A flock of birds, random and unpredictable, was a mark of the Apophis serpent. Someone was again trying to kill him with magic. Perhaps an enemy of the Captain was trying to remove him from the chessboard. Was trying to neutralize his presence in whatever game it was playing with the Captain. But Thomas could waste no time worrying about that. He had to protect himself. He had to think of something. He had to summon some sort of aid, or he could very well die in this dream.

Set was the answer. He was the most puissant of the gods. He had been spared by the gods, specifically, as insurance against the might of the Chaos Serpent. Thomas called out aloud, crying Set's name, praising him, promising him a lifetime of prayers, worship, and sacrifice for his help.

As suddenly as it had appeared, the Chaos Flock was gone. After a moment of silence Thomas took his arms from his face. They were nicked and scratched. Blood ran from them in a score of places, but there were no serious wounds. Set had saved him. Thomas smiled, his heart beat starting to return to normal.

Then he felt the tiny, almost weightless feet scurrying upon the sheet under which he lay.

Thomas looked down to see a horde of scorpions swarming up his bedclothes. There were scores of them. They were malignantly black. None were more than an inch or so long, but their minute size did not comfort Thomas. He knew from his reading of magical texts that generally speaking the smaller the scorpion the deadlier their poison.

He was petrified with fear as they swarmed over him. They got under the sheet. They got under his silken robe and the garments he wore below He could feel their dozens of little clawed feet prickling his skin as they scuttled over every portion of his body, from his feet to his legs to his groin, abdomen and chest. Under his arms and over his throat. On his ears and in his hair.

His only hope, Thomas thought, was to lie perfectly still. Lie perfectly still and not move an inch. Not a fraction of an inch. Give them no reason to strike.

One crawled over his mouth, its tiny clawed feet probing his lips. Another scampered from his forehead over his left eyebrow and climbed over his eye lid and the eye itself. Thomas clenched his teeth in agony not to blink. A pair scuttled about his genitals, but he did not flinch. His heart was beating so rapidly that he could feel it vibrate in his chest. But that, surely that, wouldn't entice the creatures to sting.

The moment endured, it seemed, for an eternity. Thomas prayed silently to Set for relief, but the god would not answer. To Hell with him, Thomas thought. He was just a figment of some sun-crazed Egyptian's mind. Or maybe Set did help, for the creatures did not sting. Thomas started to think that maybe this *was* just a test, or maybe his prayers were efficacious. Maybe, like Sekhmet, like the Chaos Flock, the scorpions too would just go away.

And then an agonizing pain struck him in the left armpit.

A scorpion had planted its stinger in Thomas's flesh. It was like a needle driven to the bone, a white-hot burning needle that was razor-barbed and coated with poison that slowly spread to the meat all around the insertion point.

Worse, as if that were a signal, others struck almost simultaneously. On his neck and legs and abdomen and hands and back and too, too many places to count, scorpions plunged their stingers into his flesh. His body exploded in a universe of pain.

Thomas gave a strangled cry and convulsively flung himself up out of bed. He was falling. He was falling, he knew, to his death. When he struck the floor he would be dead. His life would be over before it had even been lived. He would be cheated of his rights, his inheritance, of all the years he should have had as the head of Noir.

And he heard a voice roar in disbelief in his head, "No!

No, he is NOT the one!" and the pain suddenly all left his body and he crashed to the floor beside his bed.

"Owwwww."

Tangled in his sheets, Thomas automatically rubbed his elbow where it had struck the floor. He was soaked with sweat and his heart was hammering like a steam engine gone mad. But there was no blood on his arms. There were no scorpions on him or anywhere in the room. He was alive and intact but for a sore elbow.

And despite all the pain, all the terror which had gripped him in his awful dream, he had recognized the voice in his head. He knew, now, who was trying to kill him.

It was the Captain's voice, Thomas thought. Benjamin Noir's.

Geiststadt's joiner, Karl Hellig, and his teen-aged apprentice were delivering the coffin, one of three they'd stayed up all night making, just as Jon and Constable Pierce arrived at Schmidt's shop.

"Gonna bury 'im today?" Karl asked.

"Gracious, yes," Constable Pierce said. "He hasn't been kept on ice, has he?"

"Nope. Just laid out on one of the tables in his shop." Hellig paused. "Girl's been in there all night. No one wants to sit with her."

"Can't say I blame them much," Pierce said.

"Not going to want him buried in the cemetery either, I reckon."

"That's outrageous," Jon said.

Hellig was a Derlicht man, but he'd help put up Noir

Manor over twenty years ago and he'd been paid in gold, not chickens. Benjamin Noir had sent a lot of other business his way over the years, as well. He scuffed the ground, spat.

"I'm just saying, is all. The people are upset. They think he's the killer."

"Well, now," Constable Pierce said thoughtfully. "There's no real evidence of that. Indications, maybe. Nothing conclusive."

"You don't think he did it, then killed himself in remorse?" Jon asked him.

"Good gracious," the constable said mildly, "most killers lack remorse, my boy. That's why they're killers. The good cooper seemed to have demons, all right. Maybe they eventually drove him to kill himself. But did they drive him to kill others?" Pierce shook his head. "That's the question. Yes, it is."

"People here think he did it because he's a stranger," Jon said.

Pierce looked at him. "You're all strangers to me, son."

Jon nodded thoughtfully. Possibly the constable had depths to him that weren't readily apparent.

"Can you give me a few moments with Trudi alone?" he asked.

Pierce looked at the joiner and his apprentice. "Well...he's got to be put in the coffin. Lid has to be nailed down. She might not want to see that. Maybe you should take her somewhere while that's being done."

"All right."

He rapped softly on the door. They all waited, long

enough for Jon to consider knocking again, but Trudi finally opened the door.

"Hello," Jon said.

She looked at him silently. It was clear that she hadn't slept. It was clear also that she was being dragged down by a grief that was almost too great for her to bear. Jon's heart near broke when he saw the sadness on her face, in her red, tear-swollen eyes.

"Pardon us, miss," Heller said, touching his forehead. "We have to, to..."

"Yes," she said listlessly. "Go on in."

Heller nodded. He and his apprentice carried the coffin inside the shop. Pierce looked at Jon mildly for a moment, nodded, and joined them inside, leaving Jon and Trudi alone in the doorway.

"Trudi...I..." Jon wanted to put his arms around her and hold her, but he remembered Thomas's words from the night before and they stopped him cold. "I know you're not feeling well—"

"My father is dead," she said in a low voice. "He was my only family. With him gone I have no one. I have no way of making a living..."

"Is that why," Jon asked, "you're going to marry Thomas?"

Trudi's expression changed. Her eyes went distant, her voice hollow, almost as if she were talking to herself.

"Thomas will take care of me," she said. There was no passion, hardly any expression of emotion at all in her voice.

"And you," Jon asked, "and you love him?"

"I love him," she repeated.

THE TWILIGHT ZONE

"You don't even know him," Jon said, aware of the sudden anguish in his voice. "You just met him yesterday. You don't know what he can be like."

"I love him," she said again, in a tone as remote and distant as if she were commenting on a dream she'd once had, but mostly forgotten.

Jon looked at her. There was something wrong—something *very* wrong in Geiststadt. And it had all started with his brother's return to the village. It was all, somehow, centered around Thomas Noir.

Thomas was still in bed when Callie came up to his room to announce breakfast.

"Time to rise, young master," she told him. "Everyone else has already breakfasted."

"Everyone?" he asked from the sanctuary of his bed. "Even the Captain?"

"The Captain? Of course."

"And how was he this fine morning?"

She looked at him, a deep frown throwing the wrinkled geography of her ancient face into high relief.

"As always," she said.

Thomas nodded. *Not for long*, he thought.

"There is much to be done today," Callie said. "Mr. Irving wishes to see you. He is in the waiting room. The Captain wishes to see you in his study."

"Then I'd best get going, hadn't I?" Thomas asked with a try at his usual grin. From the expression on Callie's face, it wasn't a complete success. "Tell Irving I'll be with him presently. And send McCool to me."

"That redheaded devil," Callie muttered. "He does

nothing but slink around the house all day, drinking our tea and eating our food."

"He has his uses," Thomas said. "Now go."

Callie looked at him, her expression unreadable.

"You're not the master yet," she said. Though she dared not say it aloud her tone implied that perhaps he never would be.

"Lucky for you, old woman," Thomas said with more confidence than he felt.

"Why is that Master Thomas?" she asked, unafraid. "You'd throw me out of the household, who's looked after you since that cursed night you were born?"

"I need no one to look after me now, old woman," Thomas said. "So what use are you?"

She nodded at him grimly. "You are your father's son. You have little of your mother in you, boy. Not like your brother."

"Thank God for that," Thomas said heartily. "Jonathan's a fool, a soft fool. He'd allow useless old women to sit rocking before the fire all day while he played with the cattle and corn. But not me." Thomas allowed his anger to show through. "Not me. I have ambition. I have plans."

"I'm sure you do, young master," Callie said, backing out of the room, her ancient face again an unreadable mask of uncountable wrinkles and hard, staring eyes. There was a flintiness about her, Thomas thought, a toughness, that was almost inhuman.

He threw himself out of bed the moment she shut the door, poured tepid water out of the pitcher sitting on the night stand next to his bed, and splashed his face. No

THE TWILIGHT ZONE

time to wash more thoroughly. No time to take care with his dress. He had to see what that infernal busybody, Irving, wanted. First, though, McCool.

Thomas's man entered his bedroom when he was only half-dressed. He wore his usual mock-subservient expression.

"Yes, sorr?" he asked laconically.

"Today," Thomas said, "as soon as it's feasible."

"Why the rush?" McCool asked.

Thomas looked troubled. "I think he's trying to kill me."

McCool laughed. "What a lovely family you have, Your Honor."

"Shut up," Thomas said. "You forget your place."

"No, sorr. Not me, sorr. Never, sorr."

Thomas looked at him. Here was another who had to go, once he had the power. But the smile on McCool's face was more genuine than mocking. He was a man, Thomas thought, who loved his job.

"We must kill the Captain."

"You mean," McCool said silkily, "*I* must."

"Yes." Though he had always known that it would come to this, though all his plans had been laid to bring this much-desired outcome to fruition, for the first time Thomas felt as if he were taking an irrevocable step down the road to Hell. But, Thomas thought, it wasn't his fault. He had to do it. The Captain was forcing his hand. Besides, there were no Gods, Christian or Egyptian ruling the universe. There was no right or wrong. There was only survival.

"You have to kill the Captain, before he kills me."

It was the first time Jon had been in church since his sister Sara had wed four years ago.

It hadn't changed. It was still darkly claustrophobic, still too crowded with densely packed bodies. The fact that it was a triple funeral instead of a wedding had curiously little effect on the minister who'd come from Brooklyn. He was remarkably phlegmatic in expression, dour in tone. Apparently, it was all one to him whether he was marrying or burying.

Jon and Seth were the only Noirs in attendance, besides Sara and Emily, who, since their marriages, were no longer Noirs in name. Isaac and the other Noir field hands were there with their families, as well as nearly the entire non-Noir population of Geiststadt. There'd been some ugly whispers when Johann Schmidt's casket, accompanied only by Trudi, had been carried by Hellig and his apprentice down the aisle and placed with the other coffins near the altar, but the whispers had been silenced when the pastor abruptly began the service as if—as was probably true—he had other places than Geiststadt that he wished to be.

The service itself seemed interminable, as was the hellfire sermon preached in German to a mostly approving townsfolk. It was not to Jon's taste. He soon found his attention wandering, but there was nothing in the church for it to fasten upon.

The pastor seemed to take forever to finish, but finally he thundered his last damnation and the congregation sang their last gloomy hymn and began to file out of the

THE TWILIGHT ZONE

small church. The funeral procession formed immediately as pallbearers brought the coffins out one by one. Jon served as one of Erich's bearers, along with Isaac and four other Noir workmen. Rolf Derlicht was borne to the horse-drawn funeral carriage by a quartet of stalwart Derlicht retainers. Agatha Derlicht, shaking with her usual incessant tremors, led the way. Rolf's coffin was put in the carriage first, then Erich's was placed next to it. Jon paused, looking around.

"Where's Schmidt's coffin?" he asked.

Isaac shrugged. "I didn't see anyone near it when we were taking up Erich, excepting Miss Trudi."

Of course. Trudi had no one to act as pallbearers for her father's coffin.

"Come on," Jon said. Isaac followed him back into the church, along with a couple other Noir field hands Jon gathered. Trudi was standing alone and forlorn by her father's coffin. Hellig had been scared off by the reception Schmidt had gotten when they'd brought his coffin into the church.

"Let us take him," Jon said quietly, and she nodded in silent gratitude. They lifted the coffin and carried it outside, placing it in the wagon atop Erich's and Rolf Derlicht's. The black-garbed wagon driver clicked his tongue and flicked the reins, geeing up the two horses who sedately plodded towards the cemetery. Most of the village followed in procession, led by the pastor.

Jon was near the front rank, near but not next to Trudi, Isaac trudging along at his side. He was desperate to talk to her, to again plead with her about her disastrous decision to marry Thomas, but he knew that this was not the place, nor the time, to bring up such a delicate subject. His only hope, he realized, was to be patient. To wait for some time to pass so that the wounds opened by the tragic and violent loss of her father could heal at least a little.

"Jon—"

He heard Isaac say his name in a low, uncertain voice. Felt him tug at his shirtsleeve. He glanced at his friend, who had a worried expression on his face. He was looking around uneasily as the procession trudged slowly up to the graveyard. They were outside of Geiststadt's loosely defined village limits, not far from the enclosed cemetery grounds. He looked at Isaac inquiringly, wondering what was bothering him.

"The birds, Jon."

Jon Noir frowned. He glanced around and then saw what Isaac was indicating with a slight gesture of his head. The birds.

Crows. They were a common species around Geiststadt, around any rural agricultural village where they made their living off the fields and garbage dumps of men. But they never acted like this. Hundreds of them were perched, silent and unmoving, on the stone wall that surrounded the burial ground. They were absolutely silent and seemed unnaturally fixated on the approaching procession. They could have been dead and stuffed but for the intent stares of their unblinking eyes and the occasional silent ruffle of feathers as the funeral cortege ground to an uncertain halt before the cemetery gate.

"What does this mean?" the pastor from Brooklyn wondered out loud.

THE TWILIGHT ZONE

Damned if I know, Jon thought to himself, but he contented himself with a shake of his head and a noncommittal shrug. No one else had any answers either. The pastor stood for a long moment, as if in total uncertainty himself, and then finally turned his gaze to Trudi.

"I'm sorry," he said. "I don't know what this, this gathering of crows means. Perhaps nothing. But perhaps it is a sign from God that we cannot allow Johann Schmidt's body to be buried within the cemetery."

"Why not?" Trudi asked, astonished.

"I understand it's probable that he's a suicide," the pastor said stiffly. "If so, he cannot be buried in hallowed ground. I don't know what else this, this extraordinary omen can mean. It must be a sign from God."

"It hasn't been proven that Johann Schmidt killed himself," Jon said hotly.

"He was a suicide and a murderer," someone said from the mass of townsfolk behind them, and many repeated the ugly words in angry murmurs.

"It hasn't been proven," Jon repeated.

"This sign is good enough for me," someone said.

"Because of some inexplicable behavior by a bunch of birds—" Jon began angrily, and Isaac laid a hand warningly on his arm.

"You can say nothing to change their minds," Isaac said quietly, so only Jon could hear. "And who knows what will happen if you whip up their anger."

Jon nodded. He could see the wisdom in his friend's words. There was a sudden stirring in the crowd. As Trudi protested willing hands came forward and dragged her father's coffin from the wagon, setting it none too gently upon the ground. Jon went to her side and put his hand on her arm, but she only stared wordlessly, stiffly, at her father's coffin as the procession started up again.

As they crossed the boundary into the graveyard, the flock of crows exploded into the sky as if whatever bonds holding them to the stone wall had simultaneously burst. But unlike all crows Jon had ever observed, these were quiet, their raucous caws unnaturally stilled. They winged in patternless chaos in the sky over the burial ground, then flew off and disappeared among the trees on the higher slopes of HangedMan's Hill.

For a moment, standing there in the warmth of a late June afternoon, Jon shivered. He felt the cold touch of death pass by ever so close, then vanish.

Trudi cried, and there was nothing he could do to comfort her.

"What will we do?" she asked, disconsolate. "What we will do with my father?"

Jon and Isaac looked at each other for a long moment, then Isaac looked up towards the old burial ground of Dunkelstad. Jon nodded.

"There's always the old cemetery," he said as gently as he could. "We could bury him there. Isaac and I. If you want."

Trudi looked at him. There was nothing but misery and sadness in her eyes.

"It's still sacred land, Miss Trudi," Isaac said. "Once was and always will be."

Finally she nodded. Jon and Isaac shouldered the burden of coffin and body. They never could have done it just by themselves, Jon knew, without Isaac's ex-

THE TWILIGHT ZONE

traordinary strength. They made their way slowly and carefully up slope, further up the hillside to the abandoned cemetery.

It was, Jon knew, going to be a long, hot afternoon.

10.

Noir Manor was virtually deserted inside and out. Callie was in her usual place rocking before the fireplace, thinking whatever thoughts occupied her mind nowadays. James was already drunk in his room, thinking whatever thoughts occupied *his* mind. Everyone else was at the funeral, except, Thomas was sure, the Captain. The Captain didn't attend rites of passage concerning others, especially if they were held in churches. Thomas wondered if he'd even attended his own wedding.

Thomas hunted him throughout the house. The first place he checked was, of course, the study. But for a change that room was empty. The Captain had been spending almost all his time there since Thomas had come home from the city, seeking clues to the identity of the murderer. It wasn't that he was expecting to find something specifically related to the killer in his old manuscripts. Rather, he was looking for a spell or a procedure that might help him uncover a clue. Something that might enable him to open a window into the past to witness the crime. Something that might help him check the psychic residue left at the murder scene. Something that might help him build a picture of the slayer somehow, someway.

He might, Thomas thought, eventually succeed. The Captain had a brilliant mind, was terrifically knowledge-

THE TWILIGHT ZONE

able about using *heka,* and had the endurance of a bloodhound once he found a trail.

Thomas wasn't going to give him that chance to succeed—but maybe, in a way, he had already. Maybe the old man had somehow uncovered Thomas's secret plan, which was why he was trying to kill him. That was why the Captain had to die. Now.

But not in the study. Though that would have been a fine and private place for the killing. Thomas flopped into the Captain's chair and thought for a moment about where else he might be.

The cellar work room, possibly. Maybe he was down there mixing a potion or intoning a spell. Thomas's throat was suddenly dry. He swallowed, carefully inventorying the messages carried from his various senses to his brain. He was relieved to detect nothing out of the ordinary. Everything seemed normal. No one, at the moment, was invading his brain with false images of an unreal reality.

He rose from the chair and went through the near-deserted house quickly but quietly. He was nearly overcome by a sudden sense of urgency. He wanted to get this done. Done now.

He went down the back stairs to the cellar below with McCool flitting silently at his heels. He stopped to light a lantern in the cellar below, then went down the stairs to the crypt without making a sound. The door to the sub-cellar was closed and locked. It was possible the Captain was inside. He would often lock himself in so he wouldn't be bothered in the middle of long or difficult experiments.

Thomas turned and motioned to the darkness at the

head of the stairs. McCool was at his side in a moment, moving noiselessly as a ghost. Thomas gestured at the lock. McCool nodded. He had some talent in this area, as well.

The somewhat cumbrous lock yielded within moments to McCool's pick. The two men looked at each other. The tension ratcheted up another notch in Thomas's gut. Though they couldn't actually surprise the Captain if he was in his one-room laboratory, in a way this was the ideal place to confront him. There would be no chance of witnesses. No possibility of anyone observing them as they met him over his alchemical workbench.

Move fast, Thomas told himself. *Move fast, move fast, move fast.*

He nodded at McCool, flung the door to the workshop wide open and leaped in, holding his lantern high.

The room was dark—the Captain wasn't there. The door to the workshop hit hard against the wall with a hollow *thooom* that sounded like distant thunder. Thomas caught it as it rebounded towards him, the nervous energy surging through his system damped by a wave of disgruntlement tinged with a tiny bit of relief.

"Where is the old sod?" McCool asked, disappointment savage in his voice.

Thomas shook his head. He aimed the lantern around the room just to be absurdly sure. But there was nothing in the chamber other than the usual workbench, alchemical accoutrements, bookshelf stuffed with the familiar array of volumes, manuscripts, and papyri, and the large, immovable safe that contained the Captain's rarest, most dangerous, and costliest items and potions. Thomas also suspected that it protected a bag or two of gold coins, but he couldn't be sure because he'd never seen the inside of it.

They backed out of the workshop.

"The Glass House," Thomas said suddenly. Suddenly, he was sure. He knew that the Captain was there as sure as he knew McCool was a cold-blooded killer hired from the Five Points gang of Irish thugs called the Dead Rabbits. There was no doubt. They were heading for the final confrontation. "I'll go in the front way," he said. "You take the back."

"You daft?" McCool asked, most disrespectfully. "I ain't killing no one in a house with glass walls."

"Everyone's at the funeral. There's no one around to see us," Thomas said with more than a trace of impatience. "Besides, it's almost impossible to see inside because of the thick vegetation. This is our best chance to strike."

"You're sure he's there?" McCool asked.

Thomas nodded. "Oh, yes," he said. "Sure as certain."

"How?" McCool asked with narrowed eyes.

Thomas just looked at him. Finally the Irishman turned, muttering, and made his way back up the stairs. Thomas followed. He had never been so sure about anything in his life.

They saw no one as they left the manor and split up, McCool looping around to the rear entrance of the Glass House. Thomas calmly strode through the empty manor yard to the front. He spied the Captain right away as he entered the building.

Benjamin Noir was standing before the Corpse Flower.

He glanced around briefly as he heard Thomas enter, then returned his attention to his botanical monstrosity. Thomas had all he could to not put his handkerchief in front of his nose. The thing stank horribly. He waved in an irritated fashion at the buzzing flies the stench attracted. The Captain continued to stare at his hideous flower for several moments as they stood side by side.

Finally, Benjamin Noir sighed. It was, Thomas thought, most unlike him.

"Have you ever felt," he said to Thomas, "that you've wasted a good portion of twenty years of your life?"

Thomas shook his head.

"No. Of course not. Though you have." Benjamin Noir finally looked at him. "I don't know where it could have gone wrong. You were the thirteenth. The thirteenth son of a thirteenth son—"

"Did that matter so much?" Thomas interrupted.

"Did that matter?" the Captain exploded. "Did that matter? By the great Hermes Trismegistus, it meant everything!"

Thomas felt vaguely disappointed even as he saw, over the Captain's shoulder, Tully McCool approaching. Flitting silently from bush to planter, from cover to cover, the long-bladed dagger gleaming in his hand.

"Did *I* never matter to you, then?" Thomas asked. "Or just the fact that I happened to be your thirteenth son?"

The Captain laughed. "I needed a thirteenth son," he snapped. "What did it matter what he looked like or what his name was. I needed that son!"

"Why?"

"Haven't you learned *anything*, boy?" the Captain

THE TWILIGHT ZONE

asked with angry exasperation. "Don't you realize how rare a thirteenth son of a thirteenth son is? Your *heka* is overwhelming—should be overwhelming." He shook his head and looked thoughtful for a moment. "But it isn't. It just isn't."

"You sired me for the value of my *heka*?" Thomas asked.

"Fool," the Captain said without much rancor. "I sired you as a repository for *my heka*. For my will. My consciousness. My personality."

The revelation struck Thomas like a physical blow.

"I'm getting old," Benjamin Noir said, as if to himself. "This body won't last much longer. But—" he looked at his son, the fires blazing in his dark eyes again *"—I will not die*. I will not rot like a dead dog in the ground. I spent years siring children so I could have the thirteenth son whose body would be strong enough to withstand the transference spell. Whose body would serve as my vessel until I could sire another thirteen sons and move forward another generation, and then another, through eternity. But *you're weak!"* The Captain lifted his clenched fist as if to strike Thomas, who flinched backwards at the rage in the old man's eyes. *"Weak!* You almost died, twice, when I attempted the transference. I cannot be trapped in a dying body. It would mean my own death—"

Thomas suddenly snarled like a beaten dog that raises its head to defend itself at last.

"Your death is closer than you think, old man."

"What do you mean?" the Captain ground out through clenched teeth.

Thomas laughed. It was suddenly funny. All the Captain's plotting. All his plans. All gone for nought.

"Turn around and see."

The Captain whirled suddenly, as if warned at the last second by more than Thomas's sardonic comment. Tully McCool stood within striking distance, blade in hand. The Captain started to roar out a protective spell, or perhaps a curse, but McCool, whose skills had been honed in many a street fight and clandestine assassination in the tough neighborhood called Five Points, struck a sudden and sure under-handed blow.

The blade sliced up like summer lightning. It slid in between the Captain's ribs and struck home to his heart. McCool's hand thumped against the Captain's chest. Words wriggled on the Captain's writhing lips, but either anger or death kept him from articulating them.

He half turned, his long arms flung wide. McCool released the blade, letting him go. He stared at Thomas for a long moment. Thomas stared back, unable to keep the relieved and mocking half-smile from his lips.

I showed you, old man, he thought. *I showed you who was the better. Smarter. Tougher. I showed you.*

Thomas Noir caught his father's body as the old man fell limply into his arms.

It was a long afternoon.

Isaac went down to the manor and fetched some shovels, as well as rope that they'd need to lower the coffin, while Jon waited in the abandoned graveyard with Trudi. Now that he had the opportunity to talk to her, he discovered that he couldn't find the words. He couldn't tell her what Thomas was really like. If she really loved him, she wouldn't believe him. If she didn't love him and was intent on marrying him for money and security, the truth wouldn't matter. He didn't think Trudi was like that, but how well did he know her? How long had he known her? Not very well and not very long. He could be wrong about her, but he didn't think he was.

That left only one improbable conclusion. She did love Thomas, even though she'd known him for less time than she'd known Jon. Thomas sometimes had that effect on women. It wasn't quite...natural.

Isaac arrived with the shovels. Jon took one and glanced around the cemetery.

"This looks like a nice spot," he said to Trudi.

She looked up at him, her eyes dull, almost uninterested. She had been quiet the whole time Isaac had been gone, sitting silently by her father's coffin. It was almost as if she were a different woman than the one he'd met just a few days ago. Of course, she was now alone in a strange community. Her entire world had come crashing down around her. It was natural that she'd be somewhat numb, that she would retreat to some inner place where she'd feel safe and protected.

"Yes," she said. The stretch of ground that Jon indicated was an isolated patch away from any trees whose roots they'd have to dig through, or thick patches of brush that they'd have to clear away. "Thank you both for doing this."

"Our pleasure, Miss Trudi," Isaac said, and began to dig.

Jon joined him. Trudi fell silent. She looked down at

the ground at nothing as Jon and Isaac dug her father's grave.

The sun rose overhead. It was a hot day, almost unnaturally so, and still. There was no breeze to stir the leaden air. Sweat dripped from their faces and ran freely down their backs and sides. They worked steadily, stopping only for infrequent breaks. Fortunately the dirt was soft loam rather than hard clay. It came up easily on their shovels. Before they had gotten three feet down they stopped for a moment to watch the funeral in the Geiststadt graveyard break up. A long line of people was already making its way back down to Geiststadt where Agatha Derlicht was hosting a wake for her grandson and for the memory of old Erich as well.

"Guess they're done," Isaac said. It was the first words they'd spoken since they started to dig.

"Guess so," Jon replied. Like Trudi, he didn't feel much like talking.

Isaac obviously realized this. He took up his shovel and began to dig again. After a few moments he stopped when his shovel scraped something hard.

"Something down here, Jon," he said.

A round white dome had been exposed by a stroke of his shovel. Jon looked at him. They both knew what it was.

Jon kneeled in the dirt and brushed away the soft loam with his bare hand, exposing a greater expanse of naked bone. It was a whole skull, rather well preserved. Jon thrust his hand into the dirt around the skull, soon exposing more remains as Isaac watched. Even Trudi watched, though her eyes betrayed no more interest than if they were digging up potatoes rather than bones from an unmarked, unknown grave.

"I wonder who it is?" Isaac asked.

"You know," a voice said from behind them.

Isaac was so startled that he dropped his shovel. Jon sat back suddenly on his heels and even Trudi showed expression on her face as she turned to look at the speaker.

It was Katja Derlicht. She was standing underneath a thick-branched oak, twenty yards from the three young people, looking curiously ephemeral in the deep shade. No one had heard her approach.

"Ah," Jon said. "You, uh..."

"Startled you all?" Katja asked when Jon seemed unable to finish his sentence.

"Yes. Startled us."

The old woman smiled. "I'm sorry. I didn't mean to. I've been so long in the forest that I've taken its silence. I move like a tree branch. Like a flower tossed by the wind. Silent and unseen."

"That's all right," Jon said. There wasn't much else he could say. He rose, brushing the loam off the knees of his pants. He gestured towards Trudi. "Katja Derlicht, this is Trudi—"

"I know who she is," the old woman said with a gentle smile that she turned upon Trudi Schmidt. "I grieve for your loss, dear," she said, "but it must be some comfort to know that your father has gone on to his just reward."

That's probably, Jon thought, *exactly what she's afraid of*, but he smiled as Trudi thanked the aged woman with a trace of her old smile back on her too-wooden, too somber face.

"You said," Isaac said tentatively, "that we know who this skeleton is. Was. I mean."

Katja Derlicht turned her smile to him.

"Of course."

Jon and Isaac looked at each other. Suddenly Jon had the feeling that if there was enough of the skeletal remains they'd see that its rib cage had been crudely hacked apart so that the heart beating beneath it could be removed.

"The Hessian," Jon said. "The Hessian who was not hanged."

She nodded.

"What are the odds," Isaac said "that we would find his body now?"

"There are no coincidences," Katja told him. "Only undiscovered connections."

Jon squatted down over the body. Almost of his own accord his hands went out to smooth the dirt away from the remains of the lost and forgotten corpse. When he was done, he'd exposed all of the skeleton. It was very well preserved. Fragments of uniform still enshrouded the corpse. A row of buttons lay among the bones of the hacked ribcage. Bits of leather also lay in pieces among the bones and, amazingly, leather boots, still mostly whole, covered the remains of the feet and lower leg bones.

Wordlessly, Isaac and Jon climbed out of the grave. From the deep shade that enveloped Katja Derlicht like a shawl hundreds of little lights suddenly shone. They

THE TWILIGHT ZONE

danced around her like tiny sparks tossed on an unseen wind, swarming like silent, glowing bees. After a moment they darted out from the shade of the trees, tumbling in a shifting spiral into the hard daylight where their glow was dimmed, but still visible.

"Fireflies," Jon breathed.

He had never seen them out in daylight before. He had never seen them swarming like this, either. They came towards Jon and Isaac, but suddenly dipped down when they reached the open grave and landed on the Hessian's skeletal remains. They stayed a moment. Their light dimmed and died. Then they took off again, their flight choreographed, it seemed, in a complex, undecipherable pattern. They swept past Katja Derlicht and vanished into the upper slopes of HangedMan's Hill.

"What do we do now?" Jon asked in a quiet voice.

"Gather up his remains," Katja Derlicht advised them in quietly, "for reburial. Make sure you get them all. Then put Johann Schmidt to rest in the grave. It seems like an appropriate place."

The three young people looked at each other. Trudi seemed more alert, more alive, than she had all day.

"I think she's right," Trudi said. "I think this would be a good place for my father to begin his search for rest."

"All right," Jon said. He turned to look at Katja Derlicht. He wanted to ask her many more questions. But she was gone.

The worst part was the blood, though to be honest, there was less than Thomas had expected. McCool, when queried, said sardonically, "Well, I stuck him through the heart, didn't I? Stopped pumping almost at once." He paused, looking at Thomas as they stood over Benjamin Noir's body. Thomas had caught the Captain as he fell, then eased the body to the floor. "I expect you want me to finish it?"

"Finish it?" Thomas asked, distracted. He could hardly believe that his scheme had worked. That the Captain was dead and he was heir to the Noir estate. After planning it for so long, somehow it all seemed somewhat anticlimactic. But, he reminded himself, it wasn't over yet. Not by a long shot. "Yes. Yes, I suppose so."

They had to keep up the pretense. That had been part of the plan, to sow confusion by pretending a supernatural killer was stalking Geiststadt for spectral revenge. Schmidt's killing was just an attempt to induce more confusion, to break the established pattern. Also, parenthetically, it served to make Trudi vulnerable and dependent on Thomas's sudden offer.

"But quickly!" Thomas said. He glanced around the Glass House. They were still quite alone, but also quite vulnerable to someone stumbling upon their little drama.

"Quick as a pig to the slaughter!" McCool said, gleefully. He did seem to enjoy his work. He straddled the Captain's body and with a single stroke of his razor-sharp blade sheered through the old man's coat and shirt from neck to waist. He plunged the knife into the Captain's chest and began to saw through the ribs.

Surprisingly, Thomas found that he couldn't watch. He turned his head, looking up and away as if he were checking for lurkers among the verdant foliage that made

THE TWILIGHT ZONE

the Glass House a riot of color. McCool glanced at him, grinned, and went back to his butchery.

"Jaysus, these flies," was his only comment as the horde of creatures attracted by the odors dispersed by the Corpse Flower were already finding their way to the Captain's fresh and bloody corpse.

"All right," McCool said after a moment. "What do we do with it?"

He stood, holding a small oiled cloth sack in his bloody hands. He handed it to Thomas, who accepted it distractedly. He was, he suddenly realized, holding the Captain's heart in his hands.

"You'd better go rinse your hands in the lotus pool," he told his co-conspirator.

"Good idea."

"Hurry up." Suddenly Thomas was impatient. He wanted to get out of the Glass House. It was warm inside. Too warm. And it smelled of death.

McCool plunged his hands into the lily pool and rubbed vigorously. The bag Thomas held in his hands suddenly seemed unbearably heavy. Unfortunately, Thomas thought, there was no feather to weigh it against. The Captain's soul was undoubtedly demon-fodder this very moment. Thomas, glancing around the Glass House, was struck by a sudden idea. The Corpse Flower. The Captain had loved it so, let his heart nourish it.

Thomas dug a hole in the back of the tub behind the great bell of the immense flower, and buried the bag as McCool rinsed the Captain's blood off his hands. He rejoined Thomas after a moment, but hesitated as they started to leave.

"Half a mo'," he said. "Almost forgot."

He took his knife out and leaned over the Captain's body and carved the usual letters and symbols upon it. Since Benjamin Noir was so heavily bearded there was no room for them on his face. He chose the Captain's upper chest above the gaping hole through which he'd removed the man's heart.

"Jaysus," McCool complained. "His damn chest hair is almost as thick as his beard. Maybe I should shave it first—"

"That's good enough," Thomas said. Suddenly he was wild to depart. It was as if warning bells were going off in his mind.

Finally McCool was done. They stopped at the outer door and glanced about the yard, making sure no one was in sight. Thomas nodded. The coast was clear.

They walked nonchalantly out of the Glass House, immediately separating. McCool went around to the manor's rear. Thomas went up the stairs to the front entrance.

"Hello," a voice suddenly said and it was only the total exertion of his iron will kept Thomas from jumping into the air. "Nice day, eh?"

Thomas turned, forcing his features into a politely neutral mask. Washington Irving was reclining on the settee at the end of the porch, a glass of brandy to hand.

"Yes," Thomas said as heartily as he could. "Very."

"Missed you at the funeral," Irving said.

"Yes. Sorry I couldn't make it."

"Sad business. Even sadder, the villagers wouldn't let

Fraulein Schmidt bury her father in the cemetery. She was quite disturbed. Couldn't blame her, really."

"No," Thomas said. "No, you couldn't." About the last thing in the world he wanted to do was hold polite chitchat with this old man. On the other hand, he had to seem natural. He couldn't dash away without seeming to be concerned about his betrothed's well being. "What happened?"

"Well, your brother Jon and that large Negro boy took him up to bury him in the old cemetery and the most extraordinary thing happened. This flock of crows—"

"Sorry," Thomas said suddenly. "Must run."

He left Irving on the porch with his glass of brandy. Jon, he thought. That figured. He was still trying to hold onto her. He barked sudden hard laughter as he went up the stairs to his room. He'd take care of that, now that he was the head of the family.

Still, he reminded himself, he had to be patient. He had seen his father's will. It left him everything, but he couldn't be the one to bring that up. Be patient, he told himself. Be patient just a little longer.

It wasn't until he gained the sanctuary of his room and sat down in his comfortable chair with a contented sigh that he noticed the large, blotchy blood stain on the right thigh of his burgundy-colored trousers.

The question running through his mind as he sat motionless in his chair was, did Irving notice it, as well?

11.

Trudi had gone back to her father's shop to find something to hold the Hessian's remains, while Jon and Isaac continued digging the unmarked grave deeper so that it could decently contain the encoffined body of Trudi's father.

"I don't even know what we're supposed to do with these bones," Jon said.

Isaac glanced at the remnants piled neatly by the side of their former grave.

"Don't ask me," he said. "I don't want nothing to do with dead bones. Especially the dead bones of someone cut up and killed. Especially someone cut up and killed who was pretty mean himself."

"Katja Derlicht seemed to think it was important that they be disinterred. The way she spoke indicated that fate guided us to dig in this spot." Jon paused. "I suppose they have a lot of *heka*."

"What's that?" Isaac asked.

"*Heka*? It's...I'm not sure. It's magic, that's for sure. Maybe—it's more like fuel you use to do magic. Like oil you burn in a lamp. My father knows all about it. He's just started to teach me about it recently. Very recently."

Isaac stopped digging himself and leaned on his shovel. He looked seriously at his friend.

"Jon—" He started, stopped for a moment, then started again. "Your father took me in five years ago. He didn't have to. He could have sold me. Could have turned me over to the slave catchers. But he let me build a life here. He made me work hard, but he paid fair. Some day, because of him, I'll be able to buy my own place, maybe."

"So?" Jon interrupted.

"So—what I'm sayin' is I got reason to be grateful to the man. And I am. But...he's a hard man to warm to. He never treated you right, nor any of your brothers and sisters 'cept Thomas."

"You think I don't know that?"

"I think you try to forget it," Isaac said. "People talk, Jon. They respect him, maybe, but they're also afraid of him. He's a witch man, Jon." Isaac shook his head. "It'll all come to no good in the end. I know it. You were free from that part of him. It didn't touch you. Sure, maybe you don't go to church regular, but your soul is good, Jon. Your soul is bright. You won't burn in Hell."

"But my father will?"

Isaac just nodded.

"Maybe he will," Jon said softly.

"This talk of...*heka*...of whatever...Maybe's he's trying to draw you in, like Thomas. Thomas will follow him to Hell. Mark my words. But I don't want you going down, too."

Jon smiled, touched by the worried look on his friend's face.

"Don't worry about me, Isaac. I've got a lot of years left before the fires of Hell singe my hindquarters—"

"Don't none of us know how many years we got, Jon," Isaac said soberly. "Look at Mister Derlicht."

Jon was saved from continued contemplation of his

mortality as Trudi approached, bearing a small elongated wooden cask that had been made by her father.

"This should do to contain the...remains," she said after a moment of silent groping for the proper word.

Jon nodded. He vaulted easily out of the pit and took the wooden cask from Trudi. It was about the size of a coffin made for a child. He knelt down on the grass beside the remains of the unnamed Hessian and carefully transferred them to the cask. They fit perfectly, almost as if the container had been made for them.

There are no coincidences, Katja Derlicht had said before she'd mysteriously disappeared. Jon was beginning to think that she was right. Only, Jon thought, he had to be smart enough to understand the unseen connections, and he doubted that he was.

They'd almost dug deep enough. After a few more shovelfuls of dirt Jon and Isaac looked at each other and nodded. It was finished. It took some doing to properly lower the coffin. Isaac finally had to scramble into the grave and support the narrow end as Jon at one end of the rope and Trudi at the other, slowly lowered the casket into the hole. Isaac had barely enough room to lower the end he was supporting, then squeeze aside and clamber out with Jon's help.

Jon wanted to go home, put his feet up and have a long, cool glass of cider, but they weren't finished yet. Together, he and Isaac filled in the hole, finally tamping the leftover dirt into a two-foot-high mound.

"I'll make a cross as soon as I can, Miss Trudi," Isaac said, when they were done.

"And we can plant some flowers," Jon offered.

THE TWILIGHT ZONE

"You've both been so kind," she said, blinking back tears.

Jon felt acutely uncomfortable. He wanted nothing more than to take her in his arms and comfort her, but he couldn't. Circumstances wouldn't allow it. They bound him tighter than unseen chains.

"It's nothing," he finally said. "The least we can do."

Finally, as if she could hold back no longer, the tears came. They streamed down Trudi's face as, helplessly, she went to Jon and Isaac both, hugging them and sobbing aloud. Isaac and Jon looked at each other helplessly, then back down to Trudi. They each held her awkwardly until she cried herself out and finally released them.

"I—" she started to say, but shook her head as if the words couldn't get past her lips. "Thank you," she finally said.

"Whatever you need," Jon told her, "whenever you need it, you can call on me."

It looked like she wanted to speak again, but settled for a single quick nod of her head. If she couldn't say anything more, Jon thought, certainly he couldn't. Together, the three of them went down the slope of HangedMan's Hill to Geiststadt. They parted at Trudi's home.

"Remember what I said," Jon murmured.

She nodded, and as if not trusting herself to speak, turned and ran into the shop.

"Your brother," Isaac said, "should be taking care of her, if they're really to be married."

"You don't believe he wants to marry her?" Jon asked. He didn't ask Isaac how he knew of the supposed upcoming nuptials. He knew all too well how fast news traveled in Geiststadt.

Isaac shook his head. "Not for me to say, Jon." He fell silent, a speculative look in his eye. "I wonder, though, at the quickness of it. Suppose he put a spell on her?"

Jon was about to reply sharply, but he caught his tongue. Suppose, he wondered, Thomas did? It would explain the unreasonable speed at which their courtship—though you could hardly call it that—had moved. He doubted that Thomas intended to actually go through with the wedding. He knew that in the past Thomas had made easy promises to other women, and broken them just as easily when it suited him.

"Maybe I should look into it," he finally said.

"Maybe you should," Isaac agreed.

The two friends headed toward Noir Manor in companionable silence. Jon was too tired to make conversation, almost too tired to think. It wasn't a physical weariness. A strange mental malaise was pressing down on him, as if he were moving through water instead of air and the effort cost almost more energy than his mind could expend. He was too tired to discover a solution to his problems and then find the will to implement it.

But he would. He would, after a bit of rest. After a short period of quiet contemplation in one of his favorite places.

"Take the shovels," he said, handing the implement he was carrying to Isaac. "Meet me in the kitchen in half an hour. I'll have Callie rustle up some food and we'll talk. We'll make some plans."

Isaac nodded. "I'm feeling more than a little empty.

THE TWILIGHT ZONE

Maybe we can come up with something after we fill our bellies."

"Maybe," Jon said. *I hope so*, he thought.

He waved at his friend as they split up, Isaac taking the shovels back to their place in the barn, Jon heading for the Glass House. He hadn't had a chance to observe the Corpse Flower for awhile now. He'd been too occupied with other things. A few minutes spent pondering the enigma that was the Corpse Flower would be more refreshing than eight hours of dreamless sleep.

He entered the Glass House wondering how much longer the flower would remain in bloom before its stalk collapsed, when he saw the strange bundle stretched out before its basin. He stared at it for several long seconds, realizing almost immediately what it was but refusing to believe the evidence of his eyes.

He walked up to it on stiff, unwilling legs, his mind just mumbling *no, no, no, no, no*, over and over again. He stood over it, sinking down to his knees without realizing it, his hand reaching out and touching the face, cool and dead, dead with bulging eyes unseeing, open mouth unspeaking, missing heart no longer pumping the blood pooled on the floor around it attracting buzzing flies by the score. His father, his great, powerful, commanding, mighty figure of a father was dead. Murdered. Slaughtered viciously like an animal, but with less thought and even less purpose because you killed an animal when you had to eat.

Kneeling over his father's body, hand outstretched and gently resting among the forest of beard that covered his cheek, Jon Noir swore vengeance upon the murderer of his father, human or inhuman, vengeance as awful and bloody as the death that had called it out.

By the time Thomas decided he'd better respond to the commotion a thick crowd had gathered around the Glass House. Everyone in Geiststadt, from Agatha Derlicht on down to the boys who shoveled the horse shit out of the barn stalls was milling around the structure, trying to get a look at the dead man who had once figured so high and mighty in their lives. They crowded around the entrance like children drawn to a puppet show, whispering the news like gossips meeting over a backyard fence.

"He's dead, ain't he?"

"It's too much, too much—"

"I'm scared, I am. Who's to be next?"

"Let me through," Thomas said in his most commanding voice, to little avail. The bumpkins trampled the shrubbery planted around the Glass House, pressing their eager, dirty faces against the structure's transparent sides like urchins peering through the front windows of a candy store.

McCool suddenly appeared from nowhere and cleared a path for Thomas using his strident voice and sharp elbows.

"Coming through! Look out! Let us through!"

They met James at the entrance. He was coming out the door, his clubfoot dragging on the ground, his pale face empty.

"Is it true?" Thomas demanded, trying hard to keep his expression stern and concerned at the same time. "Is it the Captain?"

THE TWILIGHT ZONE

"It is," was all James could say, and he dragged himself to Noir Manor as fast as his crippled leg could take him.

Enjoy the brandy, Thomas thought. *It'll be your last.*

It was stifling inside the House. The Corpse Flower reeked. The press of bodies in the enclosed room didn't help, nor did the smell emanating from the Captain's corpse.

Jon was standing to one side, leaning against the great tub that held the Corpse Flower. Isaac was at his side. Seth looked pale and uncomfortable, but then he usually did. Callie had come from her accustomed spot in the kitchen. Somehow she'd had no trouble making her way through the crowd. Maybe it was because she was so small. Maybe it was because somehow the crowd unconsciously parted for her. She took one look at the Captain's corpse, said some words in her native language too quietly for Thomas to understand, then left.

Constable Pierce was standing over the body. He was murmuring his customary, "Good gracious." Irving, next to him, managed to look excited and nauseated at the same time. Thomas was worried about him. Worried about whether or not the writer had noticed the bloodstain on his trousers earlier that afternoon. But when Irving looked up and caught Thomas's eye, his reaction, his outpourings meant to be a consolation to a shocked and grieving son—a role Thomas knew that he had to play simply, without extravagance because he realized that he couldn't afford to break nearly twenty-one-year's worth of character—made it almost certain that he'd failed to notice the evidence. There were methods, though, that Thomas could use to make sure. He would, later.

That, basically, had been it. Much sound and fury, signifying nothing. No one had a single clue. Not even a single thought as to what had actually happened. It was time, Thomas thought, to broadcast the seeds of his purported theory far and wide.

"Nothing human could have done this to the Captain," he declaimed in his strong, husky voice, so much like that of Benjamin Noir's that Thomas startled more than a few of the onlookers.

"I beg your pardon?" Constable Pierce asked.

"Nothing human could have done this to the Captain," Thomas willingly repeated. "Physically, he was too strong. Too alert. Emotionally—he was too much loved. He had no enemies in Geiststadt." Thomas smiled at Agatha Derlicht, who had just made her way through the crowd. She looked at him stonily. "Besides—those words carved into his chest: I AM RETURNED."

Thomas fell silent.

"Yes?" Constable Pierce prompted.

"Those words. Those terrible wounds." Unexpectedly Thomas turned to Jon, who was still staring off sightless at some far distant vista playing in his own mind. "What do they suggest to you, Jonathan?"

"To me?" his brother parroted like a dullard.

"Yes. You remember the stories?"

Jon nodded slowly. Every eye in the Glass House was on him. He was looking away, off to one side of the structure. Meeting no one's gaze but seemingly staring at a small wooden barrel-shaped box that Thomas didn't remember seeing there before.

"Yes. They've been going through my head lately, as

THE TWILIGHT ZONE

well. The stories of the Hessian killed and mutilated on HangedMan's Hill all those years ago."

"Tell us," Washington Irving said eagerly.

"Yes," Thomas urged. This was going better than he had planned. Let Jon tell the story. He'd be remembered as the one who placed the blame for the unsolved killings on the ghostly shoulders of the long-dead Hessian. That was fine with Thomas.

Jon started to recount the story of the horrific events of 1776. The audience was enthralled. They hung on his every word, even Constable Pierce. Especially, Thomas thought, Washington Irving.

Thomas left before Jon had finished the tale. He'd heard it all before from Callie's lips. His work done, his seeds planted, Thomas withdrew to Noir Manor to grieve.

Besides, unless he missed his guess, it was time for supper.

12.

Monday, June 20th, the Fifth Intercalary Day

Thomas thought it best to grieve in solitude. He had McCool bring a tray of food to his room and opened up a bottle of a nice hock he'd been saving for a special occasion. Even McCool was in a jolly mood. He'd "sorred" Thomas with only a hint of condescension—though, of course, Thomas was not one to discount past slights. Thomas ate his fill and drank perhaps a little to excess, but still, if you can't celebrate when your ambitions have all been fulfilled, when can you?

Thomas was now master of Noir Manor, and all the properties and monies accrued. It was all in the Captain's will. He'd seen it himself. It was just a matter of being patient until it was brought forth and the terms announced. It wouldn't do, he realized, to discover it himself. Perhaps Seth should. He would, too. It would be just like him to go snooping for it at the first opportunity.

Thomas drowsed in his comfortable chair. The remnants of his meal were on the tray before him. The last of the hock was in his glass.

Perhaps it was the wine. Perhaps it was too much beef for dinner. Perhaps it was too much ambition fulfilled too easily. But Thomas dreamed. Surprisingly, it was a disturbing dream.

Thomas was in his room, sitting in his chair, relaxing now that the day's work was done and his dreams were all fulfilled. Thoughts of Manhattan danced in his head, of fine clothes and even finer women. He would, he suddenly realized have to be very careful indeed in that regard. He was the thirteenth son of a thirteenth son. If the Captain had been right, he, Thomas, would only have to sire thirteen sons himself and he'd gain an entire other life to live. He'd even escape the messy, tedious aspects of infancy and childhood.

Of course, for all the Captain's sureness, something had gone wrong in the process of transmigration. But it was in the books somewhere. He'd find and correct the Captain's error.

As far as he knew, so far he'd sired no sons. There had been two children, but both had been girls. Two others had been aborted. Probably they didn't count, but he'd have to make sure. Perhaps some other children had resulted from some of his very casual liaisons, but he didn't think so. Women of that sort usually knew how to take care of themselves. Besides, if issue had come from any of his informal affairs, almost certainly the women involved would have come sucking around for money. It was in their nature. But that had never happened.

He was grateful to the Captain for his hints to immortality. He knew where he'd probably find the relevant manuscripts. The Captain had a shelf of forbidden volumes he'd kept locked in a special compartment in his crypt. The applicable tome was probably among them. It wouldn't take long to unravel the mystery of the thirteenth son of the thirteenth son.

He'd best get busy, though, and start siring those thirteen sons. It was likely to be a long process interrupted by the birthing of useless girl children. Trudi Schmidt would be good to start on. He doubted that she'd last through the entire process—after all, the Captain had had four wives himself. But he had to make a start somewhere. She was an excellent choice. The village would be sympathetic if they got married soon. Perhaps within the month. After all, they'd both lost their fathers suddenly and violently. They deserved to find some measure of happiness with each other.

On that note the dream shifted again—if he was in fact dreaming—to the scene he'd dreamed before, the scene of their wedding night. It made Thomas slightly uncomfortable. After all, it hadn't gone well the last time he'd had it. But now there was nothing to be afraid of. The first time it hadn't been a real dream. The Captain, who had orchestrated that version of the vision, was no longer around to lead Thomas's psyche down dark and dangerous paths.

Thomas was free to dream his own dreams. Maybe, he thought, as he reclined in his bed and watched his wife's ripe charms emerge as she slowly undressed, that was why his dreaming brain was repeating this scenario. After all, left to its natural conclusion, it would end quite pleasantly.

But, again, something went quite suddenly, desperately, wrong.

Trudi stood smiling and naked before Thomas's bed. But suddenly, without a sense of transition, it wasn't Trudi at all standing there. Nor was it some sort of inscrutable symbol. It was a man. He was shorter than Thomas, but as muscular. Perhaps more so. Worse, there

THE TWILIGHT ZONE

was a hardness to his expression, a look in his dark eyes that said he was used to violence. That he was unafraid of it. Worse yet, though, were the marks of violence on his body.

His face had been battered. It had been beaten by something harder than human fists. One eye was swollen shut by knots and bruises. His lips were bloodied. The teeth behind them were ragged. Some had been knocked cleanly out. Others had been shattered, broken off not far from the root but still set in his puffy and discolored jaw.

He was wearing some sort of military uniform. Thomas had no idea what kind. But it had seen hard use. It was dirty and bloody. His coat still hung over his shoulders, but his shirt had been ripped away. Thomas could see the damage that had been done to his chest. To the ribs hacked and cracked, to the torn flesh that had once covered a beating heart. Thomas couldn't see within the man's chest, but he was suddenly certain that no heart beat there.

He stood before Thomas's chair, a vision of doom and destruction, looking upon him with steady, unblinking eyes.

"Who are you?" Thomas asked. "What do you want?"

The man smiled. It was ghastly.

"You know who I am." The phantom replied in German, though Thomas's questions had been put in English. It was a wonder that his voice could flow intelligibly from his mangled mouth.

Thomas thought of denying any such knowledge, but what did it matter? He shrugged.

"And if I do?"

"If you do," the specter said, almost reasonably, "then I want you to stop."

"Stop?" Thomas asked. Some of him wondered at the utter banality of their conversation. Most of him didn't want to think about it all.

"Stop blaming me for things I haven't done. Stop using my behavior as a guide. As an example for your own conduct."

Thomas couldn't believe it. Here he had finally rid himself of the Captain. And now some other being had arrived from some Godforsaken netherworld to dictate to him. He felt a flash of anger that was more than mere bravado. It was like the squalls that erupted from his lungs at his birth, a raging hatred towards a universe that should have been his own personal domain, yet frustrated his desires at every single turn.

"Be gone spirit!" Thomas roared. "I plotted the death of my own father because he stood in my way. And you're a complete stranger. I care even less for your reputation, let alone your feelings. Get your ugly, filthy carcass out of my sight, or you will know my anger!"

The dead Hessian laughed aloud, and Thomas felt as if the thing's cold hand had touched the base of his spine. He shivered in a sudden spasm of fear.

"Your anger!" the specter repeated, as if those words were a punch line to a very funny joke. He leaned suddenly forward. Thomas could see into the cavity of his chest and confirm what was not there. "Your anger is nothing compared to *mine*, boy. I was a mercenary all my life. I lived in anger for decades. I killed men, women, and children without compunction or thought, let alone regret, and then I myself was taken, tortured, and slain. Anger! I lay for over sixty years in an unmarked grave constantly feeling the pain of my death. It never left me for a moment for all those years. Blades hacking through my pulsing flesh. Snapping my living bones. A cruel hand closing about my beating heart and yanking it from the hole cut into my chest. But that wasn't the worst of it. No.

"I felt for over sixty years the choking earth in my open, screaming mouth. I felt it press down upon me, frigid in the winter, scorching in the summer. I felt the worms eat my tongue, boy. I felt them crawl through my guts. You think to compare your anger to mine?"

Thomas cowered back into the depths of his chair.

"I've done my penance and have achieved my peace. I'll not let you destroy it for me."

The Hessian began to fade, as if he no longer had enough strength to maintain his appearance, even in a dream. Thomas watched him dissolve like a cloud on a windy day, until the specter was nothing but a transparent smear of white across the landscape of his room.

Thomas blinked, suddenly panicked by the realization that he actually wasn't sleeping. That all the while the Hessian had been in his room, he'd been wide awake.

Jon had never realized that life could change so fast.

Four days ago, he'd planned to spend the summer studying butterflies. Now he had to redeem his vow to find a killer. The only problem was, he had no idea how to go about it. He wasn't a constable. He didn't know how to put clues together to solve a crime. If his suspicions were correct—and Thomas, it seemed, was in agreement with his own suspicions—was the crime even solvable? How can you bring to justice a man dead nearly seventy years?

The Hessian's bones were safely ensconced in the wooden casket in the Glass House. Could they be the key to the whole affair?

One person might know. One person seemed to have some faint idea about what was going on. Katja Derlicht. As odd as that seemed. Where did the old woman's knowledge come from? Had she spent her years studying occult knowledge and ancient wisdom like his father? He should go to her. Question her. She must know more about the strange happenings around the village than she'd divulged so far.

What if, though, she was just playing with him? What if she was releasing information in drips and drabs, perhaps wrong information, or information designed to make him draw the wrong conclusions? She was a Derlicht. Could he trust her at all? She had said that she'd harbored feelings for Benjamin Noir. What if those feelings had turned sour over the years, eventually leading her to plot his destruction? What if she had called up the shade of the Hessian to carry out her black desires?

One person might know. Might have the key to understanding Katja's motivations. It was late. Most of Geiststadt was asleep, but it's said that the old sleep little. Jon knew that it had been true of his father. Perhaps it was true of his father's greatest rival as well.

Derlicht Haus was a huge jumble of stone and dark

wood bulking menacingly in the night. Jon stood before it alone. He couldn't ask Isaac to accompany him on this quest. He'd already exposed his friend to much danger. Besides, it wasn't as if he were going through the marsh or the old cemetery on HangedMan's Hill. He was in the village. How dangerous could it really be?

Pompey answered the door as Jon rapped on it with the ponderous bronze knocker. The old butler didn't look surprised, merely supercilious.

"Yes?"

"I have to see Frau Derlicht."

"At this time of night?" Pompey asked. He was dressed in a robe, stockings, and slippers. His puff of white hair was haloed by the ring of light cast by the full candelabra he held high in his right hand.

"It's important—"

"Let him in, P-P-Pompey."

Agatha Derlicht stood behind the old butler, a single candle wavering in her palsied grip. She, too, wore a dressing gown. Her hair had been let down for the night so that it spilled in thick white coils around her shoulders. She looked as old as a saint in the candlelight, but her eyes were as hard as a sinner's.

"Pompey, bring some t-t-tea to the sitting room. Come along," she said over her shoulder to Jon.

Inside the silent parlor it was dark and surprisingly chilly, as if the air in the room had been left over from early spring.

"I'll do that," Jon offered as Agatha Derlicht started to light the multi-armed candelabrum sitting on the mantle, holding her single candle with both hands which were shaking more than usual. She relinquished it to Jon with something of a sigh and tottered over to the sofa, sinking down into it creakily. Jon finished lighting the candelabrum, then sat down in a stiff, uncomfortable chair across from her. Her had never seen her look so old.

"I'm sorry to wake you—" Jon began, but she waved off his apology with a shake of her trembling hand.

"I wasn't sleeping. I've slept little since...since the d-d-deaths began." Uncharacteristically, she looked down upon her hands laced together in her lap, and not at Jon. "The fortunes of both our families have fallen. Rolf was to take over the family when I passed on. He wasn't much—but this is not a good time for the Derlichts. There is no one else. Roderick, perhaps. Perhaps one of the other boys. But I'll need five, maybe six years to get him ready." She shook her head. "I don't know if I have it in me."

Jon looked at her, shocked. When she finally looked up into her eyes, she read his expression easily enough.

"Surprised? No need to be. I'm an old w-w-woman. I'm tired. I'm ready to go to my rest. But I can't possibly, now. Not with Thomas set to take over the Noir fortune. Once he does there'll be no D-D-Derlichts left in Geiststadt within twenty years."

"You can't believe that," Jon said. "I know he can be vicious—"

Agatha Derlicht laughed. For the first time that night she sounded like the formidable old woman Jon had known all his life.

"*Can be* v-vicious? You know your brother. He's vicious as a starving dog denied meat. He wants what he wants when he wants it. He'll let nothing stand in his way. I'm telling you this because you're our only hope. Our only chance for protection against your brother's vaunting desires."

"Me?" Jon asked.

"Of course," Agatha Derlicht said. As she spoke her posture straightened. Her gaze sharpened. She even lost the stutter that plagued her most in moments of weariness and doubt. "Who else could curb his ambition now that your father is gone? Seth? James? Ludicrous, both of them. Unchecked, Thomas will devour all of Geiststadt, and far beyond, to feed his desire for wealth and dominion." She fell silent for a moment. "Your father was powerful in many ways. He had an uncommon strength. He was ungodly and no doubt his soul now wr-wr-writhes in Hell. But he followed an oddly personal road. He had strange interests. He was not adverse to making money, but only to support himself in a comfortable manner and finance his profane researches. He didn't accumulate wealth for the sake of wealth or material things for the sake of showing his wealth to the world. Thomas is different. Surely you realize that."

Jon nodded. His father's greatest desire had been to be left alone. He'd been happy—at least as happy as he ever seemed to be—as long as things were going smoothly and he didn't have to be bothered with mundane matters. Thomas, on the other hand, wouldn't be satisfied unless he could watch the power flow directly from his hands. His father hadn't cared how or when the barn was mucked out as long as the animals were healthy and producing. Thomas wouldn't get involved in the actual mucking, either, but it would have to be done to his precise and exacting order. And he would watch over everything with a magnifying glass to make sure that it was. In the end, he wouldn't be happy until all the barns in sight were under his command. All the barns, as Agatha Derlicht said, in Geiststadt. And eventually, beyond.

"Surely," Jon said, "you can stand up to him."

"For a while," she acknowledged. "And if God grants me enough time I'll raise up a younger Derlicht, my grandson Roderick, or one of his brothers, who will be capable of taking my place."

"What about your sister?" Jon asked, finally seeing an opportunity to turn this disturbing discussion to the path that had brought him there.

"My s-s-sister?" Agatha Derlicht frowned.

"Yes, Katja. I know that..." Jon's voice ran down at the sudden peculiar expression that over took Agatha Derlicht's face. It was something he had never seen on it before. It was fear. Actual undisguised fear.

"My sister Katja is dead," she said in a voice barely above a whisper.

A sudden knock on the door made them both jump. It opened and Pompey entered, bearing a silver tea tray with pot, cups, saucers, and all the accouterments. Jon and Agatha Derlicht looked at each other guiltily as if they were lovers caught at a secret tryst.

"Tea, madame," Pompey announced. He set the tray down on the table in front of her. "Shall I pour?"

THE TWILIGHT ZONE

"No," Agatha Derlicht said. "Th-th-thank you. That will be all."

"As you say." He shot Jon a suspicious, supercilious look and glided from the room, pulling the door shut after him.

They resumed their conversation, the teapot sitting before them untouched and cooling

"That's impossible," Jon said.

"S-s-she's dead," Agatha Derlicht insisted. "S-s-she's been dead for almost f-f-fifteen years."

"That's impossible," Jon repeated flatly. "I've seen her myself, twice, in the last week. I've spoken to her—"

He fell silent at the expression that crawled over Agatha Derlicht's face. It went beyond surprise, beyond fear, well into terror. Mind-numbing, soul-killing terror. He suddenly felt that he'd better explain himself, but was uncertain what words would comfort the old woman trembling before him.

"She told me that you'd kept her in the house. That she escaped some years ago, and has been living as a hermit in a sheltered spot in a small side canyon up on HangedMan's Hill. I—I sort of figured you'd been slipping her food and supplies on the side. She seemed quite well and happy. Somehow in tune with the strangeness that has always been a part of Geiststadt."

"She was t-t-that," Agatha Derlicht said, almost dreamily. "My sister was always odd. Perhaps she should have been born a Noir rather than a Derlicht, though of course there were no Noirs in Geiststadt when she was born. As a child she was always running about the w-w-woods. She refused to dress...appropriately. She liked to go to the old Dutch cemetery. She said she had friends there. When she matured she was quite a beauty. There was trouble with m-m-men. Sev-ev-everal men. She...we finally had to...restrict her...to the house."

"She had a free spirit," Jon interpreted, "so you locked her up."

A flash of anger lit Agatha Derlicht for a moment, then it vanished, as if she'd recognized that there was justice in Jon's words.

"For her own s-s-safety. There was a child. It was stillborn. After that, she was never really healthy again, and her ideas got...odder. She would go out at night. In the winter during storms wearing nothing but her d-d-dress and a shawl. She almost d-d-died several times before we decided to keep her in the house. In a spacious room in the attic."

"For how long?" Jon asked. He couldn't stop himself from asking the question.

"F-f-forty years," Agatha Derlicht whispered. She was silent for almost a moment. "She d-d-died, as I said, f-f-fifteen y-y-years ago. She left a note s-s-saying she wanted her body to be p-p-put in her favorite spot. A s-s-small cave, as you said, on t-t-the Hill overlooking the cemetery. We granted her w-w-wish."

"I'm not lying to you," Jon said in a dogged voice. "I did see her. Isaac, too. And Trudi Schmidt."

For a moment his voice caught on Trudi's name, and he told himself, go on. Go on and try to forget.

"I believe you. But it was not my sister you saw. It wa-wa-was her ghost."

THE TWILIGHT ZONE

Jon swallowed hard. This was not the truth he'd come to find.

"She spoke to me," Jon said wonderingly. "She told me...things..."

"Yes?" Agatha Derlicht said, encouraging him to go on as his voice faltered.

"About the Dutch ghosts of the cemetery. About the Hessian."

"Yes," the old woman confirmed. "Her c-c-childhood f-f-friend."

"The butcher of Geiststadt?" Jon asked. "He was her childhood friend?"

"She was so-so-so sensitive!" Agatha Derlicht said. "We thought she was only responding imaginatively to those strange, gruesome old stories. She told me he was sorry. He was repentant of his crime. She told me he b-b-begged for forgiveness and she was t-t-trying to help him find it. I thought she was only being dr-dr-dramatic."

"If she wasn't," Jon said quietly, "I know where the answers must be found."

If, he thought to himself, I have the courage to seek them out.

They looked at each other for a long moment. Jon remembered Agatha Derlicht's earlier words and sighed. *If not him then who*? It would have to be him. But not tonight. Not in the dark. He couldn't bring himself to go up HangedMan's Hill alone at night.

His visit to Katja Derlicht's resting place would have to wait for the morning, and the light it would bring.

Thomas woke suddenly. It wasn't a sound that woke him.

It was a warning from deep in his consciousness. He blinked rapidly, uncertain and still dazed by sleep. His room was still dark, but he could sense a vague shape looming close by his bed.

The Hessian! Thomas thought. He cowered back uncertainly among his bedclothes, but recognition came suddenly and relieved his fear.

"Bastard!" a familiar, slurred voice said. He could smell the liquor on it.

"Ah, James." Thomas sat up as his brother wove drunkenly on his feet. "How nice of you to visit. What's on your mind, dear brother?"

Thomas struck a match and lit the candle on the nightstand adjacent to his bed. He looked at his brother and winced. It didn't take special familiarity with James's habits to realize that he was drunk. Drunker than a lord. Drunker than it seemed possible to be and still stand on his feet, especially since one of them, Thomas thought, was crippled.

He smelled, too. A sodden alcoholic stench wafted off his wrinkled, stained clothing in almost tangible waves. His hair was in disarray. His eyes were wild and bloodshot. He teetered back and forth as if defying a hurricane, but the only storm he faced was caused by the alcohol raging in his system.

"Bastard!" he said again.

Thomas sighed. Thankfully, he wouldn't have to put up with scenes like this for much longer.

"Don't be tiresome, James. If you've got nothing better to say then drag yourself to bed and sleep it off. I'm sure it'll still be pretty blurry in the morning, but you can always drink more and fall back into a stupor."

"Seth found the will."

"Really." Thomas smiled. That was interesting. Things were progressing faster than he'd expected they would. "Read it, did he?"

"Yesh." James wove in a larger than usual circle and almost went down. "Bastard!"

"Are you now discussing Seth?" Thomas asked with an amused smile, "or still referring to me?"

"Father!" James ground out. "He left everything to you. Everything!"

Thomas smiled widely. It was all coming out, just as he'd planned. Of course, Thomas had had no idea when he'd riffled the Captain's desk and found the will why Benjamin Noir had left everything to him. At the time he'd taken it as just another sign of the Captain's apparent favoritism. Having discovered the old man's despicable plan to take over his body, the legacy was now obvious. Of course, he couldn't let anyone else know what the Captain had intended to do. Not that anyone would believe his story, anyway.

"Well," Thomas said smugly, "the Captain always did like me best."

James screamed like an animal in torment and fell upon Thomas, swinging his fists wildly while sobbing like a sentimental drunk.

Thomas was surprised by his brother's sudden attack. He barely had time to throw his arms up in an attempt to ward him off, then they were wrestling on the bed. James had good size and a certain amount of strength, but he was so drunk that his reactions were slow and his coordination that of a near corpse.

But he stank. He stank and he slobbered great gusts of alcohol-reeking breath. Thomas was nauseated as he fended off James's fumbling punches. He pushed him down to the foot of the bed where he lay crying like a baby.

"But that's all right," James murmured to himself. "That's all right. Seth's going to burn it. He's going to burn the damn will before anyone else sees it. Then it'll be fair."

Thomas leaped up in horror. "Damn him! He wouldn't dare!"

James fixed his bloodshot eyes on him, smiled blearily, and spewed a stream of purple-stained vomit in an arc a good three feet long upon Thomas's mattress and silken sheets.

Thomas's jaw dropped. He was frozen in inarticulate fury, sputtering in anger that had reached the killing point.

"You—you—damned—!"

He whirled suddenly. Every second, he knew, counted. He was moments away from total disaster.

He screamed as he ran from his bedroom, down the stairs, and all the way to the study. He wasn't sure exactly what he screamed. He just made as much noise as he could. He didn't stop screaming until he slammed open the study door and skidded into the dimly lit room and saw Seth sitting at the Captain's desk without lit match or candle in his hands.

His brother's face was sour. His features were clenched

THE TWILIGHT ZONE

as if in inexpressible anger, perhaps at the sheaf of papers spread out before him. He looked up at Thomas and there was actual hate in his usually placid, emotionless eyes.

Thomas's screams turned to laughter. His racing heart slowed and seemed to slip back down to its proper place in his chest.

"You couldn't do it," Thomas said. It was a statement, not a question.

"Did that drunken fool tell you I was going to burn the will?" Seth asked bitterly.

Thomas nodded. "But, of course, you couldn't."

Seth ground his teeth in inarticulate anger.

"Poor Seth," Thomas laughed. "All those years obeying the Captain. Scurrying about at his beck and call. You thought you'd be able to break the spell he had over you once he died. But you couldn't, could you?"

Seth just looked at him, shaking his head in wordless rage as Constable Pierce ran into the room, followed quickly by Jon Noir, Tully McCool, and, lastly, a puffing Washington Irving.

"What is it?" Irving cried. "What's all the commotion about?"

Thomas smiled at him.

"Nothing much," he said to the gathered assembly. "Just a bad dream." But, he thought, there was no sense in taking chances. "Since we're here, though, my brother has found a document he'd like to share with you all. Seth?"

Seth glared at him, his jaws grinding silently. But after a moment, he began to read.

JOHN J. MILLER

"'I, Benjamin Noir, being of sound mind and body, do hereby declare...'"

13.

It was, Jon Noir thought, much too beautiful a day.

It should have been dark and stormy with huge black clouds crying like lost children and wind wailing like animals in pain. Instead it was prosaically sunny, disappointingly mild with gentle breezes sweet with the promise of summer now only a day away.

Still, Jon had a feeling in his gut that things were about to change. Everyone, it seemed, in Geiststadt was walking softly as if afraid to draw attention to themselves. They were conversing in whispers as if aware that someone or something was watching, was waiting, and could strike them down at any moment. Jon could feel it himself. It made him want to cower in his bed with the covers pulled up over his head.

It was not a pleasant sensation.

He ignored it as best as he could as he went through the eerily quiet village. He passed the bunkhouse quickly, almost furtively. He didn't want to bring Isaac along with him. His quest had become totally personal. It was, he felt, up to him to solve the mystery of the awful murders. He didn't even want to contemplate the price of failure.

Jon went up onto HangedMan's Hill, through the old cemetery, and up the game trail that led eventually to the small side canyon where he and Isaac had found Katja Derlicht. The terrain was becoming increasingly familiar, though he knew he'd never feel comfortable there. There was a strangeness to it that made the back of his eyes itch, as if he knew he was being observed by unseen watchers.

The canyon was quiet. Empty of human or ghost. But that odd annoyance, that unscratchable itch, worried at his flesh. He stood it as best he could, and advanced slowly.

The canyon's back wall seemed to be naked rock, but it was covered by a cascade of flowering vines that flowed down the top of the outcrop nearly to the ground. The vines were thick enough to conceal whatever lay behind them.

The prickling sensation in his flesh got worse with every step. Setting his teeth against the bothersome phenomenon, he swept aside the curtain of vines to expose the hollow of a small cave set into the rock wall. There wasn't much to it. It didn't lead very far back though he couldn't be sure because light didn't penetrate inside the hollow.

He could be sure, though, that no one inhabited the cave. It bore no signs of human activity. No furniture, no bed, no hearth. No food stored against hunger. There was only a plain wooden box, and Jon had no desire to check it to make sure what lay within.

"So," a voice said from behind him, "you've finally tracked me to my lair."

The fact that Jon didn't even jump the slightest bit showed how far he'd sunk into stolid acceptance of the strangeness that had ensnared him. He released the vines so that they flowed back to cover Katja Derlicht's final resting place. Or, more accurately, the resting place of her body. He turned to face her spirit.

She stood behind him, a tender smile on her old, pleasantly lined face. As she spoke the irritation that had crawled over Jon's flesh suddenly vanished, as if it were a defense no longer needed. He nodded at her, accepting a marvel he would have scoffed at only days earlier. So much, he thought, can change so fast.

"What are you?" Jon asked, "and what do you want from me?"

"I'm Katja Derlicht," she said. "As simple as that. And I want your help. Not for me, but for all of Geiststadt."

Jon shook his head. "It's not that simple. Not from my viewpoint. You're Katja Derlicht—but you're dead."

"That's right." Her smile widened. "It is as simple as that, for me. Life does not end with death. Many move on. But some feel tight bonds to the land, or perhaps to living people they love and they feel they can't abandon. They might have a great wrong to avenge or a great wrong to pay for. They don't want to, or perhaps can't, move on. Not right away, anyway.

"I spent most of my life imprisoned. I couldn't leave Geiststadt. I hadn't had enough of it. I couldn't move on while I was filled with so much longing for my home."

"But—that night we saw you, the next we followed your trail. A physical trail."

"Of course," Katja Derlicht said. "Do you think ghosts can't affect the physical plane?"

Jon shook his head. "I don't know much about what ghosts can or can't do."

"Yet," she said slyly, "you have no trouble believing

that a ghost is responsible for these terrible killings? Erich. Rolf Derlicht. Johann Schmidt. Now even your own father."

"I-I don't know what to believe. I guess I just didn't want to think that someone I knew—someone I grew up with, would be capable of such vicious savagery. And the clues left on the bodies themselves. The way the hearts were taken. The messages left behind carved into their very flesh."

"A clever human could have done all that," Katja Derlicht said. "To throw suspicion upon someone already dead."

"So, you're saying a ghost *couldn't* have done the slayings?"

She shook her head. The action of head swiveling on neck, of tendons pulling and muscles swelling, looked real. Like she was still alive in a functioning body. It was almost easier to regard her that way. To set the question of her death and spiritual resurrection aside, and concentrate solely on what she was saying.

"Not at all. We can touch the physical world, if we want to."

She approached. Jon steeled herself as her frail, ancient-looking hand reached out and softly lay against his cheek. Its touch was pleasant. Cool. As if a soothing breeze had wafted out from a beautiful forest glade and kissed his skin. Katja Derlicht smiled at the look on his face and drew her hand back and slapped him lightly like a coquettish girl might teasingly treat a wayward but still adored admirer. It stung for a moment, then

THE TWILIGHT ZONE

faded to a pleasing glow that seemed to warm his entire face.

"We can move stones, too, and bend branches. Even leave tracks in the earth, if we desire."

"You laid the trail that led here on purpose, so that Isaac and I could find you?"

"It was a test. One of several you've taken over the past several days. But I didn't, at the time, want you to know of my true nature. I didn't want to take the risk of frightening you away."

"You almost did, anyway," Jon muttered.

"But you persevered as I'd hoped you would."

"How'd I do on those tests you mentioned?" Jon asked. He wasn't entirely comfortable with the notion that he'd been manipulated by unseen forces.

"I wouldn't be here now if you had failed," Katja Derlicht said, smiling. As much as she physically resembled her older sister, she seemed different emotionally. Warmer and much more pleasant. Loving, even.

"I wish I'd known you when you were alive," Jon said. Then he smiled himself. He couldn't have ever imagined that he'd ever say something like that.

"I do, too," she replied. "It would have meant that I'd have probably had a much more pleasant life. But—I didn't arrange all this so that we could moon over what-might-have-beens."

"The killer," Jon said, jerking back to unpleasant reality.

She nodded. "The killer must be stopped. Your fate rests on it." She gestured all around them. "Geiststadt's fate—the fate of all that I love—rests upon it."

"The voices that night—the spirits of the Dunkelstad dead—they told me to seek a human suspect."

"They were right," Katja Derlicht said. "The Hessian is not guilty of these crimes."

"How do you know this?" Jon demanded.

"I've known him since I was a little girl," Katja Derlicht said. "I was ten when he came to Geiststadt and committed his terrible crimes. And then paid horribly for them." She shook her head. "The rest of the village tried to forget him. Maybe they did, but I couldn't. I could hear his agony. I could see a blackness, a tremendous cloud of darkness, hovering over the spot where they buried his mutilated body after they'd taken their anger out on him. For years I was afraid to approach the old cemetery. It took many attempts, but finally I overcame my fear. Even then, it was not easy to achieve rapport with the Hessian's spirit, bound to his grave by a great wrong that he had to redress. Gradually through the years, through fits and starts, I was able to start his spirit on the road to redemption. Even when I was locked in the prison of Derlicht Haus, all those long, lonely, empty years, his rage would reach out for me and, with the sparrows and mice, were my only company. My only solace. It was in those years he discovered the meaning of forgiveness and he started on his way to absolution.

"He had almost reached the end of his long road. And then the killings started. The killings done under his name, without his license."

She spoke softly, sincerely, with ghostly tears shining in her eyes. Jon wondered if he'd reached out and touched them if they'd be wet. If he put his fingers to his mouth, they'd be salty. But he hadn't earned that intimacy.

Katja Derlicht's words, though, had earned her his trust. He believed her. It might be madness, but, good God, he believed that she was a ghost. Was her story of redemption and false accusation any harder to accept?

"If I believe you and the Hessian is innocent of these killings, who committed them?"

She shook her head. "That's not for me to say. A ghost is an insubstantial being, but we cannot be everywhere at once. The killer was been sly and stealthy. He's struck suddenly, unexpectedly. I have no direct knowledge of who he might be. Certainly, I have no proof.

"Despite the ravages the killer has committed on the body of his victims, he's not a madman. No madman would so cunningly lay the blame on another. Another who couldn't argue for his own innocence—or so most would think. No madman could strike four times in five days and not be apprehended. At some point, if he were doing this out of simple lust, he would totally give in to that lust and so reveal himself. No. This killer is cool and calculating."

"He's acting according to a set plan, then."

"Exactly," Katja Derlicht said. "The question is, who profits from these killings? Who gains from the deaths of these four men?"

It didn't take long for the realization to come to Jon. It wasn't totally set yet. There were still points of doubt. Areas of uncertainty. But it was clear as day who profited from the death of Benjamin Noir. Who was the only person who could gain anything from the death of Johan

Schmidt. Who would have achieved emotional satisfaction, at least, from the death of Rolf Derlicht. And even how poor old Erich's death would have served as a smokescreen. Apparently he was even the one who had planted the theory of the Hessian's supernatural guilt in the minds of the villagers. Jon himself had come up with the same theory independently, of course, but he'd kept it to himself and Agatha Derlicht.

Why hadn't Jon seen it before? Was it because he simply refused to believe that such savage treachery couldn't reside in the heart of his own family? How could he have not seen that all the fingers of guilt pointed directly at Thomas?

And—more importantly—now that he realized it, what in the world could he do about it?

Thomas was up all night. He couldn't sleep. He didn't want to eat or drink. He felt giddy as a child anticipating all holidays rolled into one, with his birthday on top. As, in actuality, it was. He couldn't ask for a better present than the one he'd given himself: control of Noir Manor, and all lands, buildings, funds, and other objects accrued to it. He couldn't wait to try it all on for size. He was sure that the title would fit him even better than it had fit the Captain, God—of some sort or another—rest his soul.

In the meantime, there was much to do. He had to get that snoop Irving alone and question him. Make sure he hadn't noticed that incriminating bloodstain. He'd need Callie's help for that. She was good at finding out things. The trousers themselves were safely hidden away. He'd

THE TWILIGHT ZONE

hate to loose such a finely cut pair. After things had died down he'd get Callie to remove the bloodstain. She was also quite good at that.

He supposed he'd also better call on his betrothed. It wouldn't do to neglect her. Then there was the Captain's funeral to arrange. Seth could handle that. Thomas intended to keep him on to handle paperwork and such. With Jon milking the cows and planting the corn, that would take care of most of the work, leaving plenty of leisure, most of which could be spent away from Geiststadt. Speaking of brothers, there was also the worthless James. He'd get the boot as soon as it was appropriate. Perhaps right after the Captain's funeral.

What to do? A hundred thoughts swirled dizzily through his head. He knew now how the Captain felt. How it was to grasp the reins of power in your very own hands. How to wield Life—for Seth and Jon—and Death—for James—like a veritable god.

Thomas made his decision. He reached out and tugged the bell pull that would summon McCool. He waited patiently until the Irishman arrived.

"Yes, Your Honor?"

Even McCool seemed to sense the difference in him. At least, he was more respectful in his address.

"Fetch hot water," Thomas Noir said. "I'm going to take a bath."

Jon peered out from behind his barely opened bedroom door, watching across the stairwell as Tully McCool dragged two buckets of hot water all the way from the kitchen on the first floor. He was huffing and puffing and grumbling to himself under his breath. Jon couldn't understand the words he was saying, but he comprehended their tenor by the expression on McCool's face as he went down the hall, put the buckets down in front of the bathing room's door, opened the door, picked the buckets up, and went into the small chamber.

There came the sound of splashing water as McCool emptied the buckets into the occupied tub, and then Thomas's complaining tones.

"The water's tepid. I don't pay you to fetch tepid water, my good man."

An outraged grumble came from the Gael.

"You don't pay me 'alf enough to fetch any fucking water."

"Watch yourself," Thomas said bluntly. "You can always go back to Five Points if you don't like my money."

McCool's mumbled reply was unintelligible to Jon's straining ears, except for the "yes, Your Honor," which was attached at the end with seemingly less than total sincerity.

McCool left the room, buckets swinging.

"And come back and close the door you damned bog-trotter," Thomas cried. "I'm catching a draft in here."

Jon was close enough to see the rage that suddenly surged over the Irishman's features. His pale skin flushed with anger until his face was nearly as dark as his hair. His teeth clenched in a savage grimace, his eyes wide open and wild, like those of a maddened horse. The change in McCool's normally laconic, mildly mocking posture was amazing.

But it lasted for only a moment. The Irishman mastered

THE TWILIGHT ZONE

his emotions with a facility that suggested long practice, returned to the door, and shut it carefully and quietly. Jon had half expected him to bang it shut as a symbol of his rage, but apparently McCool was subtler than that. As he went down the hall to the landing and back down to the kitchen his face was studiously blank of emotion.

For the first time, Jon realized that there was something in Tully McCool that should be feared.

He didn't know much about Manhattan, but everyone knew Five Points. It wasn't exactly the neighborhood where one would go to find a valet or a manservant. Killers, though, were as common there as dead cats.

A bit of the puzzle locked in, Jon thought. But no proof. He swallowed heavily. He knew where he might find some, though. Thomas was absorbed in his bath. He'd be awhile. McCool was busy fetching water. He'd be occupied as long as Thomas. Longer, in fact. Someone had to empty the basin, and that someone wasn't going to be Thomas.

Now was as good a time as ever.

Jon took a deep breath and slipped out of his room, silently pulling the door closed behind him. He crept down the hallway. Thomas, now singing to himself as he soaked and scrubbed in his overblown wash tub seemed utterly unaware of his passage.

Jon made it to his brother's bedroom and slipped inside, quietly shutting the door. The only noise he heard was the thudding of his own heart as he prepared to violate the privacy of his brother's room, something he'd never before even conceived of doing. He had no idea of what to look for or what he might find, but surely there must be something that, however tenuously, would connect his brother to the killings—if, indeed, he were guilty of them.

A quick glance around the room told him little that he didn't already know. His brother had expensive tastes and he indulged them as fully as he could. His furniture—bed, chairs, nightstand, wardrobe—were all much nicer than Jon's. Jon sat down on the bed and felt as if he were sinking into a pit full of feathers.

More comfortable, too, he thought. *No time to waste*, he quickly added. *No time.*

He pulled open the nightstand's upper drawer. Inside were some papers. Old manuscripts, scrolls similar to those his father had owned. Also a small flask. He shook it. It sloshed. Open, it smelled of fine brandy. Jon was tempted to try a sample, but knew better than to drink of an unknown potion in his brother's room. He put it back and rummaged around. His hand closed around a slim, round object and he pulled out Thomas's watch, given to him by their father just last year.

It was weighty in Jon's hand. It had a good, solid heft to it. It felt warm, as if it'd been sitting in sunlight for a while rather than a dark drawer. Jon looked at it closely. He was drawn to it. He'd admired it in the past as a finely wrought artifact. He'd never felt covetous about it. But this time he had to stiffen his resolve to put it back in the nightstand drawer. It was almost as if the watch itself was whispering to him, offering itself, urging him to take it, no one would miss it, it would feel so good in his waistcoat's pocket.

Nonsense, of course, Jon said to himself, shutting the

drawer. Thomas would miss it in an instant. And what could he do with it? Put it in his desk and take it out under the cover of darkness to stroke it like a miser gloating over a pile of gold coins? He wasn't here to rob his brother, but to find clues regarding his guilt—or perhaps innocence—in a most damnable crime.

He opened the nightstand's bottom drawer and felt something inside it wrapped in cloth. Something oddly shaped and textured.

He pulled out the package and quickly unwrapped it, his wonder growing as he uncovered a crude statue, maybe eight inches high. Jon couldn't figure out what it was made from until he smelled it and realized it was dough of some odd consistency, baked hard as a rock. It was fashioned into a human form, roughly female, if the two lumps on its chest were any indication. Pins, or nails, were driven into the thing's chest between those breasts. Into its flat forehead. Into the juncture of its thighs.

A spell doll, Jon thought. He knew just enough about them to recognize one when he saw it. A female spell doll. That could possibly explain Trudi's extraordinary behavior of the last few days. Thomas had cast a spell on her. He *did* make her love him. Literally.

Anger burned through Jon. Any doubts as to his brother's innocence in this whole terrible crime suddenly vanished. Thomas was behind it all. Maybe he hadn't actually performed the killings with his own hands. Jon couldn't know. Maybe they'd been carried out by his hired thug from Five Points. But regardless of whoever had held the knife, Thomas was ultimately responsible for its use.

And Thomas, he vowed, would pay.

Jon clamped down on the anger that threatened to overwhelm him and push him to actions he'd regret. He had to get proof, which he could then lay out for Constable Pierce and Washington Irving. Surely they wouldn't be swayed by Thomas's charm or power as the new head of the Noirs. They would help bring him to justice.

He stood suddenly, the question now in his mind of what to do with the spell doll. He couldn't destroy it, or put it where it might be harmed. He had no idea what such an action might do to Trudi. If the doll made her love Thomas would its destruction result in her death? He didn't know. But Callie would. If he dared ask her. In the meantime, he could take it and hide it somewhere where it'd be safe from Thomas. Then he could figure out what to do with it.

He needed evidence, solid evidence to link Thomas to the crimes. He didn't know how much time he had left before Thomas would finish his bath. He would have to search the rest of the room quickly, as best as he could. He slipped the doll inside his shirt and turned to Thomas's wardrobe.

The seconds ticked off in his head as he searched wardrobe, trunk, and even among the cushions of Thomas's chairs. Nothing. Nothing tangible, let alone damning. He was jittery with frustration and the fear of being discovered, virtually hopping from foot to foot in his anxiety, when he thought of the bed. He flipped up

THE TWILIGHT ZONE

its soft mattress, exposing the taut hemp ropes beneath. And the wine-colored trousers that had been pressed between. The trousers with the suspicious dark stain on the upper thigh.

Work long enough on a farm and you can easily recognize a bloodstain on clothing. There was no doubting that this was one. Jon clamped his mouth shut so that he wouldn't shout in glee. He grabbed the trousers and balled them up in a tight a bundle as he could, letting the mattress fall back in place.

He went to the door, listening for a moment. He heard nothing. He slipped out the door, shutting it behind himself as suddenly a grumbling McCool reached the landing with yet another pair of buckets.

Jon went down the hall as unconcernedly as he could, his heart hammering in his chest.

"Good afternoon," he said.

"Afternoon, Your Honor," McCool replied.

John couldn't tell if there was suspicion in that cool Gaelic expression or not. He ducked into his room before the blush he felt rising on his features could betray him, and pulled the door shut.

He had, he was sure, his proof. All he had to do now was live to use it.

Thomas rubbed himself dry on his soft, freshly laundered towels, and shrugged into his robe. He went whistling to his room, planning the day's next activity. He'd better see to Irving. It'd have to be subtle, though, because he couldn't afford to offend a rich, famous author. A pillar of New York society who had the ear of the Brooklyn magistrate and lord knows how many other politicians and social functionaries. In fact, Irving would be a man to cultivate. If he played his cards right, Thomas thought, Irving could be his entree into the highest levels of New York society.

He opened the door and stopped, nonplused, at the sight of Tully McCool sitting in his best chair.

"What are you doing here?" Thomas said ominously. "I've told you never to enter this room without my specific request."

"Aye, that Your Honor did," McCool said in his calculated tones that put Thomas's teeth on edge. "But I'm only looking out for Your Honor's interests. Someone should be guarding your property against snoops and light-fingered thieves, I'm thinking."

"What in the world are you babbling about?" Thomas asked, entering the room and shutting the door behind him. He had the sudden feeling that he didn't want anyone listening to this conversation.

"Why, I saw your brother leaving this very room, didn't I? Not a few moments ago when I was bringing up the last buckets o' water. Tully, I says to myself—"

"My brother?" Thomas rumbled, his face starting to cloud with anger. "James?"

"James?" McCool repeated, and pondered for a moment. "Why no, sorr. Jon it was."

"Jon," Thomas said flatly. He sat down on the edge of his bed without even realizing it. It would have to be Jon. The one Noir not firmly under his control. The one Noir who had been his antagonist, all his life. "He didn't

THE TWILIGHT ZONE

have anything with him, did he?" Thomas asked suddenly.

"Well," McCool said, as if enjoying Thomas's sudden apprehension, "let me think." His expression slipped at the sudden change on Thomas's face, as if he decided he'd better come clean. "He had a cloth bundle of some kind, rolled up into a ball. Dull red in color."

The color went out of Thomas's face as if someone had pulled a drain plug. He jumped to his feet and suddenly flipped his mattress up, to see nothing underneath.

"Damnation and fire on his treacherous head," Thomas swore.

"Something missing?" McCool asked innocently.

Thomas shook his head. He hadn't told McCool about the bloodstained trousers, and he wasn't going to. He didn't trust him half enough to tell him about evidence incriminating him in the Captain's murder.

Damn that Jon! He—wait. Thomas suddenly sobered, suddenly cool and in control. If Jon had searched the room, perhaps he'd taken something else.

Thomas went right to the bottom drawer of the nightstand next to the bed. It was empty. He sat back down on the bed, too angry to show any expression at all on his features.

"What is it?" McCool asked, something between concern and curiosity in his voice.

"Nothing," Thomas said flatly. "Nothing you need to know of in detail. My dear brother Jon has taken...two items...from my room. Two items that I need back."

"And Your Honor wants me to get them back?"

"Yes. Search his room at the first opportunity. He may

be just enough of a dolt to try to hide them there. If they're not there, follow him. Keep your eyes on him. See if he's taken them somewhere else to hide."

"And if that doesn't work?"

Thomas looked at him. He could find any one of a dozen men to run the farm. Only Jon could tie him to the Captain's death and Trudi Schmidt's ensorcelment. The scale of his brother's fate slipped from Life to Death.

"Get him somewhere. Make him talk."

McCool nodded. Above all, he was a man who loved his work.

14.

"What's this?" Jon asked, holding the odd pin-cushioned doll before Callie's eyes.

She was silent for a long time, but her expression didn't change. It was as antique and unreadable as always. Jon felt affection towards her. He had all his life, though she had never demonstrated that her heart did anything but move blood around her body. But Jon's store of sentiment was running out. Being accommodating to others, being decent in his relations with those close and even distant to him, had gotten him nowhere. Perhaps it was time for him to change.

"Tell me," he repeated, gripping the doll harder and shaking it in her face, "what is this thing?"

"Be gentle with it," Callie said softly, without looking at him. "Do not harm it least you harm who it signifies."

"You mean Trudi."

Callie nodded.

"Did you help Thomas put the spell on her?"

For the first time she met his gaze and again he couldn't read her eyes. Perhaps because there was nothing in them to read, he suddenly realized. Perhaps because she was a shell, emptied over the years of all human feelings and emotion. His resolve to be hard, to be inexorable, if necessary, suddenly fled almost as quickly as it had come.

"Oh, Callie, why? Why did he have to have *everything*?"

"He—" For the first time that he could remember in his entire life there was uncertainty in her voice as she stumbled over her words. "He was the young master. Everything he wanted was to be his."

"Why?" Jon put almost twenty-one years of frustration into his whispered query, torn from his heart unwillingly, almost unconsciously.

Callie looked back at the fire, rocking slowly, as if the springs governing her ancient body were finally running down.

"Because he would not live beyond his twenty-first birthday."

Jon was struck to utter silence. His mind, for a long moment, could not encompass Callie's words.

"What are you telling me?" he finally asked in a voice that sounded as dead as his father's corpse now lying in the icehouse.

Callie stopped rocking. She sighed. When she looked at Jon she was just an old, old woman who had lived beyond everything she had ever loved or wanted.

"He was the thirteenth son. He was born to be the vessel for Captain Noir's spirit once the Captain had reached his old age. The Captain always planned to take over Thomas's body just before his twenty-first birthday. But the spell...failed...somehow. When the Captain tried to jump the transfer almost killed Thomas. Twice. That would have meant the Captain's death as well. The second time convinced the Captain that something was wrong...terribly wrong...Thomas was not the proper vessel."

"And Thomas knew all this?" Jon asked, too shocked,

THE TWILIGHT ZONE

to immediately comprehend the enormity of Callie's revelation. Later, he knew, it would keep him up for long hours into the night.

Callie closed her eyes, as if she could look at Jon no longer.

"Yes. He figured it after the Captain's second attempt."

"So, Thomas killed our father?"

"Yes," she said, her eyes still shut.

But—Thomas had put *his* murderous plan into effect days before learning of their father's plan.

Like Callie, Jon closed his eyes. He couldn't bear to see anything. To hear. To feel. A family of patricides and filicides. Suddenly Jon had to get out of the house. He had to be anywhere but Noir Manor. He ran outside. The air was fresh and clean but he couldn't stand the sight of the *uraeus* gleaming in the sun. He spotted the sun glinting on the windows of the Glass House and almost instinctively headed for it. It smelled like Death inside, but that smell no longer bothered him.

From where he stood by the door he could still see the Corpse Flower thrusting proudly into the air. Suddenly it seemed rather emblematic of his family. A sudden movement behind the Flower's tub caught his eye, and automatically he put the doll back inside his shirt as Constable Pierce popped up from where he'd been on the floor, examining the base of the Flower's container.

"Oh, hello, Jonathan," he said in his mild voice. "I was just looking around and discovered something rather interesting."

Jon realized that he could either turn around and walk out of the building, or respond to the Constable's comment. Somehow, just then, talking seemed the more effortless course.

"What's that?" he asked without interest.

"Come here. Take a look."

Jon approached the pot and looked to where Constable Pierce was pointing. There, hidden by the bell of the spathe was a disturbed patch of dirt. It was rather apparent when you noticed it, but Jon had not thought to look there. He'd not thought to examine the vicinity of the Corpse Flower for clues at all.

He gazed up at Constable Pierce, who had a thoughtful look on his face.

"What do you suppose we'll find if we dig there?" he asked mildly.

Jon glanced at a neighboring bench and found a hand trowel.

"Let's see," he said.

"All right," the constable said, watching Jon closely with his gentle blue eyes.

Jon carefully sunk the trowel into the earth. His movements were controlled, smooth, and calm. It didn't take long to turn up a small leather bag. Somehow he knew what was inside it, but he looked anyway. He closed the mouth of the bag after a long moment and shut his eyes and grasped the edge of the basin. Pierce's soft voice somehow penetrated his consciousness.

"I don't think a supernatural avenger would bury his victim's heart in the nearest flower pot, do you Jonathan?"

Jon opened his eyes and gazed at Pierce. The constable's expression was as mild as ever. His voice was soft and gentle. There was no accusation in his eyes as he looked at Jon, only questions.

"No," Jon said. "I don't think so."

"So," Pierce continued, "you'd agree that the murders were executed by a human agency?"

"Yes," Jon said. "I do."

Pierce nodded. "I do, too." He sighed unhappily. "I've been investigating murders for, oh my goodness, twenty-six years now and I've yet to see one committed by a ghost."

"You've never been to Geiststadt before," Jon said in a low voice.

"True," the constable said. "And I understand strange things happen here. Tell me something," he said in the same mild tones that a man might use to a beloved but somewhat domineering wife, "you were here, present in Geiststadt, during the time all these murders were committed."

"Yes."

"But your brother Thomas wasn't?"

Jon shook his head. "No. But his valet was."

"Good lord," Pierce said. "That's interesting." He looked at Jon silently for another moment. "There's nothing else you'd like to tell me?"

Jon thought of the bloodstained trousers he'd already hidden in a secure place in the barn. But somehow he couldn't bring himself to mention them to the constable. If he told Pierce about them, he'd have evidence tying Thomas to the murders. Now the constable had nothing more then suspicions. Strong suspicions, but no proof. With proof would come an arrest, and then trial. Thomas deserved to pay for his crimes, but Jon couldn't stand the thought of the whole sordid affair becoming public knowledge. Patricide. Mass slayings. Mutilation. Magic and madness. No, it would be unbearable. Thomas would have to pay, but in a far less public court. Jon vowed silently that he would see to that.

He shook his head.

"Ah well," Pierce said, unperturbed. "That's too bad."

"I do have a question, constable, if you don't mind."

"Certainly, son," Pierce said. "Ask away."

"You indicated earlier that you didn't think Schmidt had killed himself. Could you tell me why?"

"Of course," the pudgy little man said. "In my twenty-six years of investigations I'd encountered seventeen suicides by throat-cutting before this case. In all seventeen the suicides had brief, shallow cuts in the flesh antecedent to the killing cut. Even the strongest-willed man – and they were all men – hesitates as the knife starts to bite his flesh. Schmidt wasn't a strong-willed man, was he?"

Jon shook his head. "And there were no hesitation marks on his throat?"

Pierce shook his head. "Good gracious, no. None at all."

"I see," Jon said, and he did. That cleared up the last shred of doubt in his mind. Schmidt's name had to be added to the roll of murder victims. Thomas probably chose him to provide a stalking horse for the village, to confuse and misdirect any investigation. And to isolate Trudi as well. To make her even more susceptible to his charms. And spells.

THE TWILIGHT ZONE

"One thing," Jon said after a moment. "What do we do with my father's heart?"

Pierce looked down at it, considering.

"You could take it the icehouse. Bury it with the rest of the body. But if word got out, how it was buried in the pot, how we found it, that might upset folks."

"It would," Jon said. "My father cared a lot about this plant in his own way. I don't think he'd mind if we just reburied his heart here."

"All right," the constable said.

Jon nodded, and did that thing, gently and respectfully.

"Sorry," he said when he was done and had put the trowel away, "that I wasn't able to help you any more."

"You've helped considerably, son," Pierce said. He paused, as if uncertain, then decided to say more. "You take care of yourself. You look about done in. And – be careful. I'm not sure this awful sequence of events is over yet."

"Yes," Jon said, nodding. "I will."

"Good lad." For a moment the constable laid his hand amicably on Jon's upper arm. His grip was rather stronger than Jon thought it would be. The pudgy little man cocked his head and looked at the Corpse Flower. "Gracious, but that's an odd plant. We don't have anything like it in Brooklyn." His nose crinkled. "Just as well. It smells awful."

"Tea, my dear Washington?" Thomas asked as the author sank into Thomas's old chair in the study. Irving fixed him with a frosty glare. Thomas stared back with a glassy smile. Thomas rarely backed down, but Irving's practiced glare did the trick. "Er, Mr. Irving, that is?"

"Yes," Irving said. "Thank you." He glanced around the study. "What an extraordinary room."

"I think so." *The old bastard probably remembers my comment about not reading popular authors*, Thomas thought as he yanked on the bell pull to summon Callie. *I should have kept my mouth shut.* "I've spent many a long hour here in study with the Captain."

"Studying what?" Irving inquired.

"Oh, language. Philosophy. Other cultures. Things like that. The Captain was a learned man with a wide range of interests."

"Did you inherit those interests?"

"Quite," Thomas acknowledged, thinking, time to try flattery. On the whole authors were conceited buggers who liked nothing better than having their vanity stroked. "Perhaps there's something here to interest you. Something you can turn into one of your fascinating tales."

"Ummm." Irving was noncommittal, but obviously interested. While they waited for Callie he asked permission to examine the sarcophagus. Thomas granted it graciously, and the writer moved around the room looking at various bric-a-brac, while Thomas chatted him up as genially as he could. If things worked out right, Thomas thought, Irving could be his entree into New York, and even Continental, society. He would have to cultivate him as assiduously as the Captain had babied that horrible plant in the Glass House.

THE TWILIGHT ZONE

Callie arrived at the door laden with a silver tray piled high with tea and cakes.

"Ah, tea," Thomas said brightly as she tottered into the room, barely managing to set the heavy tray down on the Captain's—*Rather, my*, Thomas realized with smug delight—desk. "Thank you, Callie. I'll pour."

Thomas took the teapot and poured the dark brew into both cups.

"Milk?" he asked.

"Just black, thank you."

Callie took cup and saucer and offered it to Irving, who hastily crossed the room and met her near his chair. He resumed his seat and took a sip.

"Hope you like it," Thomas said. "It's a special blend."

Irving made an odd face and took another sip.

"It's a bit bitter, isn't it?" he asked.

"It might take some getting used to," Thomas admitted.

"Ummm," Irving said again, and his face suddenly went slack. Thomas bounced up to his feet, and caught the cup and saucer before it could slip from the writer's fingers.

"Your potion acts that quickly?" he asked Callie.

"To those susceptible."

Thomas hunkered down and looked into Irving's eyes. They were open and staring into infinity. He waved his hand in front of them, but elicited no reaction from the author.

"How long will this last?"

"Not long," Callie warned. "He couldn't have partaken of much of the potion. Ask your questions quickly."

Thomas nodded, and turned his attention back to Irving.

"Listen to me, Irving," he said intently. "Do you remember the color of the trousers I was wearing when you saw me on the porch yesterday afternoon?"

"Burgundy," Irving said in a distinct, if flat-toned voice.

"Was there anything usual about them?"

There was a brief silence, as if Irving had to ponder the question before answering.

"No."

"Any stains?"

"No." This time the answer came much more quickly.

"All right," Thomas said with a smile. He swapped his cup with Irving's, and retreated to his chair. He glanced at Callie. "Wait here until he comes out of it. Otherwise he might get suspicious."

She made no reply, not even a nod, but Thomas scarcely noticed. He was elated. He was in the clear. No evidence linked him to the killings. At least, none would once McCool discovered where Jon had hidden the trousers. Then, Jon dispensed with, he really would be totally free.

Two, maybe three minutes went by while Thomas contemplated the removal of his brother, and Irving sat upright, eyes staring but unfocused. Suddenly he started, as if he'd taken an abrupt but mild fright, and looked around.

"Did I—did I doze off?" Irving asked, confused.

"Not at all," Thomas said. "I thought you were simply enjoying your tea."

THE TWILIGHT ZONE

"Was I?" He looked down at the teacup on the small table next to his chair.

"Have another sip."

Irving did so. "Not bad," he said. "Could be a little warmer."

Thomas looked at Callie. "Freshen his cup, and then you may go. I have some questions for my friend Mr. Irving about the New York social season."

"Jon!"

Jon turned and saw Isaac waving strenuously at him. He waited as his friend caught up.

"Where you going, Jon?" Isaac asked.

"I'm not really sure," he admitted. "Just...walking...I don't know what to do." His voice was plaintive, as was the expression in his eyes as he looked up at his friend.

Isaac was plainly concerned. "You got to take it easy, Jon. The last few days have been terrible. Just terrible. You look like the walking dead."

Jon almost laughed, but it wasn't that funny. Not really. There wasn't anything funny about the dead walking, at all.

"Anyway, I hear Agatha Derlicht is wanting to see you."

"About what?"

Isaac shook his head. "I don't know. But talk to her, Jon. Talk to her then get some rest."

Jon could hear the concern in Isaac's voice. He didn't want to worry him any more, so he lied to him.

"I will. But listen, Isaac, you have to do something for me."

"Anything, Jon."

"This is important." He reached into his shirt and took out the cloth-wrapped doll. He peeled back the wrapping for a second, showing Isaac what it concealed, and thrust the bundle into his hands. "Take this. Hide it. But for God's sake, be careful with it."

Isaac's eyes were large with distress. "What is it?"

"It's a love doll Thomas used to cast a spell on Trudi."

Isaac nodded, believing him. "What're we gone do with it?"

"I don't know just yet. We can't destroy it. That would harm Trudi, too. But there's got to be some way we can neutralize it. Maybe I can get Callie to talk later. You hide the doll. I'll go see Agatha Derlicht. Then Callie."

Isaac nodded in agreement. "All right, Jon." He hesitated. "You be careful."

"I will." He paused, then he embraced Isaac, hugging him like a brother. Jon didn't know what made him do that, but he felt better once he had. He bobbed his head in a single, decisive nod, then headed off to Derlicht Haus.

His mind was filled with an unsettled haze. The sky had suddenly become grey and clouded. The breeze was distinctly chilly for the last day of spring, matching Jon's grim mood. It was up to him, he knew, to avenge his father's death. And Erich's. Rolf's Derlicht's. Even Johann Schmidt's, a man he'd only known for a day and didn't much care for. But he hadn't deserved his horrible death. None of them had. Except...maybe...his father. That's what hurt the most.

He looked up. He'd been walking north through

THE TWILIGHT ZONE

Geiststadt, and suddenly he found himself in the cooper's yard where only four days ago he'd met the girl he loved and already lost. There she was, sitting at the table under the oak tree, alone and lonely, hunched down against the cool breeze that blew steadily off HangedMan's Hill.

He shouldn't talk to her, he told himself. He should stay clear until he learned how to deal with the spell Thomas had put on her. But it was useless. He couldn't help himself. He had to see her. Speak to her. Hear her voice in return.

He found herself walking towards her. She heard him and looked up. There was no welcoming smile on her face, only dull acceptance of his presence.

"Hello, Trudi."

"Hello." It was difficult for her beauty to shine through her pain, but somehow it managed. He ached to reach out and hold her, but instead simply stood before her, feeling awkward and uneasy.

"Are you all right?" he finally managed.

"Yes. I guess so."

"Have you seen Thomas? Lately?"

She glanced in the direction of Noir Manor.

"No. But I'm sure he'll be by soon. He—he has problems, too." It was as if she suddenly remembered something. Her face became more animated and she blushed slightly. "I don't know what's wrong with me. You, too. I mean, I know you've lost—I'm so sorry, Jon, so sorry for your loss."

I know what's wrong with you, Jon thought. And I'll take care of it. Somehow. Soon. He nodded, feeling crushed by the awful responsibility to make everything right. It felt like the weight of the world on his shoulders. Now Agatha Derlicht. She, too, probably wanted something from him.

"I have to go see Frau Derlicht. But I'll be back soon. Let me know if you need anything. Just let me know."

"All right, Jon," Trudi reached out her hand tentatively, then withdrew it before he could move closer and take it. It seemed to Jon that she was fighting Thomas's insidious influence. Fighting it though she didn't even realize it existed. That was a good sign, he told himself as he nodded and took his leave.

Or, he thought, was he reduced to grasping at straws?

Thomas was sitting at the Captain's desk, enjoying himself and his new found mantle of authority when McCool barged into the study without knocking.

"Your Honor—" he began.

"What are you doing here?" Thomas barked at him before he could finish. "I told you to stick to Jon! To find out what he did—"

"I did, respecting Your Honor." He was so excited that he forgot to be disrespectful. "I saw him give something to that big darkie he goes around with, didn't I? A small bundle, like."

"The trousers?" Thomas asked eagerly.

McCool shook his head. "The packet was too small. Probably the figure your honor told me to look out for."

Thomas smiled. "Well, at least that's something. What did my brother's dark friend do with it?"

"He took it to the bunk house," McCool said, "and hid

THE TWILIGHT ZONE

it there. At least, when he came out he didn't have it no more, did he?"

"Good, very good," Thomas said. "And Jonathan?"

"It was hard to keep track of both, but last I seen your brother he was headed for the Derlicht's."

"Damn the Derlichts," Thomas said in sudden anger. "He's joining with them, sure as a serpent crawls on its belly. The traitor. He's leaguing with my enemies." He fell silent, thinking for a moment. "All right," he finally said to his henchman. "You make a diversion to attract everyone's attention. I'll go the bunkhouse. When I'm sure it's empty I'll go in and recover the, uh, figure."

"Diversion?" McCool asked. "What kind?"

"Do I have to tell you everything?" Thomas asked. "Something, something big. That will attract a lot of attention. Figure it out yourself. Now go, before I have to remind you how to breathe, as well."

McCool took the rebuke remarkably well. He bobbed and smiled and even put a hand to his forehead in a kind of quick salute. He was always more docile, Thomas thought, when he was on the job. It was best to keep him excited and busy. He'd turned out, after all, to be pretty handy to have around. Too bad, Thomas thought, he wouldn't be around much longer. Once they'd reclaimed the missing trousers Tully McCool would have to vanish with them. He knew too much. Too bad, but there it was. Besides, there were hundreds like him in Five Points. He'd be easy to replace.

McCool threw open the study door as he exited the room, stopped, bowed sketchily, and stepped aside.

"Pardon, Your Honors," he said, and scurried out after Seth and James entered the room.

"Well," Thomas said. He settled back behind the desk, just having risen to go wait for McCool's diversion near the bunkhouse. "To what do I owe the honor of this visit?" He smiled heartily and took his watch out of his vest pocket and made a show of checking the time. "Unfortunately, I have little time to spare. I'm due at, uh, my fiancé's in a few moments."

Seth smiled. But, un-Seth-like, there was an edge to it. He had a large ledger underneath his arm. James stood by his side, apparently sober, and every inch as grim.

"This won't take long," Seth said.

"We've come to say good-bye," James added.

"You have?" Thomas echoed, losing his wide, false smile.

"Yes," Seth said. "The thought of staying at Noir Manor under your...leadership...is not appealing. We've had a long-standing invitation to join our brother Daniel in business in Boston. We've decided to take him up on it. Immediately."

"You have?" Thomas echoed. He looked from brother to brother. "Even you, James?"

"Even me, Thomas," James said. "It's time I stood on my own two feet."

Thomas laughed. "*Can* you?"

"He can," Seth said. "Perhaps he'll need a little help at first, but he can lean on me for a while."

James looked at him gratefully, and Seth returned the look and nodded decisively.

Thomas laughed again. "Well, far be it for me to stand

in your way, dear, dear brothers. Have fun selling shoes in Boston, or whatever it is you will do."

"Daniel has a growing import-export business," Seth said, approaching Thomas's desk. "Shoes are only one of the many items he handles."

"What's this?" Thomas said, automatically taking the ledger as Seth extended it to him.

"The current book on the farm. I thought you'd better have a look at it."

"Of course." He opened the tome and started to thumb through it.

Seth laid his hand on James arm when they reached the study door and they stopped. Seth turned back to Thomas who was frowning over the columns of figures on the ledger's last page.

"I thought we should tell you," Seth said. "We're asking Jon to come with us, as well."

Thomas looked up at him and shrugged.

"It should be just as easy to replace a cowherd as it is to replace a bookkeeper and a drunk," he said.

Seth smiled. "Charming to the end, I see," he said, and he and James left the study.

Thomas frowned over the ledger for a few moments. He wasn't a trained accountant, but he could read figures. And what these figures told him was that Noir Manor was not, contrary to his belief, a richly remunerative enterprise. In fact, if he was reading them right, it was in debt. Deep debt to a Manhattan bank, and had been for several years. Thomas looked up, stunned, his mind blank and groping for explanations.

But there was no one left, he realized, who could tell

him anything. He was all alone in his new study and he was deep in debt.

15.

Jon felt confused, and angry at his confusion, as he headed for Derlicht Haus, so wrapped up in his inner turmoil that he didn't even realize that many villagers called out condolences or well-wishes as he passed by.

His life had changed so suddenly, so irrevocably. There was no possibility of going back to the way things were just four days ago. More so—Jon couldn't let the situation continue as it currently stood. Thomas couldn't remain in charge of the Noir fortunes. He had committed terrible crimes, and must pay for them. But how? Jon was repelled by the murders within the family. There had already been patricide and attempted filicide. Should he add fratricide to the list, as well?

Perhaps the best course open to him, after all, was to give his evidence to Constable Pierce, and let the law take its course. The resultant scandal would shame the name of Noir for all time, but perhaps that was the price they all had to pay.

He stopped at the door to Derlicht Haus, but it swung open before he could knock, as if someone had been waiting for his arrival. Pompey was at the door, a look of concern over lying his usual superciliousness.

"What is it?" Jon asked when he saw the expression on the butler's face.

"It's Madame Agatha, sir," the butler said. For the first time ever Jon saw age and doubt quivering on his features. "She's not well. She's taken to her bed. She...she's been asking for you, and you alone."

"Take me to her."

Pompey bobbed his head in a nervous nod.

"This way, sir."

Agatha Derlicht ill? Jon was stunned at the thought. What next? His father dead. Agatha Derlicht, ailing. The small, placid universe that was Geiststadt was being torn apart with no hope of repair. He wondered if this was part of Thomas's scheme. If, like the Trudi doll, he'd had an Agatha Derlicht doll upon which he'd laid a different kind of spell.

Jon pondered that as Pompey led him up the stairs to the second floor of the gloomy dwelling. He opened the door to Agatha Derlicht's bedroom quietly and Jon looked inside. It was all massive dark wood furniture and guttering candles with small windows heavily curtained to block the sunlight. There was a distinct, unhealthy chill to the air. Agatha Derlicht herself was a pale shadow reclining upon a cluster of pillows in a huge four poster bed. She looked wan and tired, more ghostly than her sister Katja.

Pompey gestured silently and Jon slowly entered the room as the door closed softly behind him.

Jon approached her bedside. "Frau Derlicht?"

Her head turned on her vast white pillow. She seemed to notice and recognize him. She lifted a hand. Some impulse made Jon reach out and gently take it. It was cold as if no blood at all ran through it. It shook constantly, but as Jon held it his warmth crept into the old woman's flesh and the shaking diminished.

THE TWILIGHT ZONE

"Jon," she said in a thin, tired voice. She spoke without her stutter, as if she lacked the energy for such unnecessary things. "Jon. I need to see Katja. I need to tell her—to say—say I'm sorry. Sorry for what happened between us. For what I did to her."

"She'd be happy to hear it."

"Can you take me to her?" Agatha Derlicht asked.

Jon looked at her, shaking his head.

"I don't think you'd be able to make the climb up HangedMan's Hill. Maybe if you got stronger, in a few days."

Agatha Derlicht smiled faintly. "My strength is draining from me like water through a broken dam. I don't know how many days I have left."

Jon held her hand more tightly.

"You can't mean that!" he said. "You can't fade now. You have to make Roderick into the new leader for the Derlicht family. You have to train him so he'll be able to stand up to Thomas. You said so yourself."

She shook her head. "I'm an old woman. I'm tired. I don't know if anyone can stand up to Thomas."

"I will," Jon said. "I'm going to put him away where he'll never be able to harm anyone again." He paused. "At least, I'm going to try. But if I fail—you have to be there. For Geiststadt. For all the good and decent people who depend on you."

Agatha Derlicht nodded, seeming to take strength from Jon's words. Her grip hardened. It seemed as if Jon could feel some of his vitality pass on to her. That was all right. Suddenly he felt strong as a mountain, steadfast and mighty. He had strength to spare.

"You couldn't make it up HangedMan's Hill," he said, struck by a sudden idea, "but perhaps you can make it up to the attic."

"The attic? Why?"

"Your sister was...imprisoned...there for many years. I-I have a feeling that if we called to her from that place, she might be able to respond. She spent so much time there—perhaps she could return."

"That sounds ungodly," Agatha Derlicht said. "But I don't know any more what's heaven-sent or demon-cursed. I only know that I have to see my sister again. I have to talk to her before I die. It's the only way I'll be able to find peace..."

Jon helped her sit up. She was dressed in a thick flannel nightgown. Her hair was a snowy cascade down her back and breast. She grasped his shoulder, swung her legs out of the bed, and stood shakily. Jon half supported her as she took small, trembling steps. They stopped to rest at the foot of the back staircase that led to the attic. Finally she nodded and they started the ascent.

The stair was dark and dusty. Jon was grateful that he'd thought to grab a candelabrum as they'd left the bedroom. The candles threw gloomy, fitful light ahead of them as they made their way up the narrow staircase and stopped to rest at the top. Jon unlatched the trapdoor to the attic and pushed it open.

He led Agatha into the dark that was but little dispelled by the guttering candles. They looked around. It was a large space, mostly empty. An old bed sagged against one wall. There were small round windows on all walls, north, south, east, and west, grilled and barred. For forty years they had been Katja Derlicht's only eyes onto the world.

Agatha Derlicht sighed as if in insupportable pain.

"What a terrible thing I did to her."

"That was in the past," Jon said. "If there's one thing I've learned from this whole appalling week, it's that redemption is possible. If the Hessian could find redemption after his awful deeds, you can as well. We all can."

Agatha Derlicht gripped his hands tightly. He could feel an awesome strength flow from him into her as she closed her eyes and whispered her sister's name, over and over again.

It didn't take long. After only a few moments a mist began to roil in one corner of the dusty attic. A swirling white fog seemed to come from nowhere, but steadily resolved itself into a human size and shape and slowly took on distinct features that settled into those of an old woman with a strong familial resemblance to Agatha Derlicht.

"Agatha," she said in a soft voice that nevertheless somehow penetrated to every corner of the room.

Agatha Derlicht opened her eyes, and shrunk against Jon at the sight of the apparition that stood across the room smiling at her.

"Don't be afraid," Jon said supportively. "There's nothing to fear."

"He's right, dear," Katja Derlicht said. "You've called to me and I've come."

"Is that..." Agatha Derlicht said hesitantly. "Is that all it takes?"

Katja nodded. "Oh, some years ago I would have been somewhat irate if you'd summoned me. I'm not a saint, you know. It took me some time to work off the anger of my life. But it peeled away from me during my years on the Hill. After all, it wasn't hate or fury that bound me to this earth. It was love."

"Oh K-K-Katja," Agatha Derlicht tottered away from Jon, reaching out for her sister. "Can you ever forgive me?"

"I forgave you years ago, sister."

"Is there nothing I can do for you?" Agatha Derlicht asked.

"There is, dear sister. All things come to end—and I think it is time I move from this earth. Bury my bones in the old cemetery. Bury me with my Hessian, who, thanks to Jon, is ready to move on as well."

"Thanks to me?" Jon asked. "What did I do?"

"You believed in his redemption. And your words helped convince Constable Pierce that his spirit was innocent of the terrible crimes laid at his feet."

"That was nothing," Jon said.

Katja smiled. "It was enough."

"But—the Hessian," Agatha Derlicht said. "No one knows where he lies—"

It was Jon's turn to smile. "His bones lie in a wooden casket hidden behind the stand of lime trees in the Glass House."

"How—?" Agatha began.

"I'll explain it all later," Jon said.

Agatha nodded. She went to her sister. They met and hugged one another. Katja had taken on a degree of

THE TWILIGHT ZONE

solidity, but Jon could still see her form sink partly into Agatha as they embraced. They held each other for a long minute, Agatha Derlicht softly weeping. Then her weeping stopped and her eyes closed and she slipped slowly to the floor, Katja supporting the weight of her as best she could, gently letting her down.

Jon looked on, dismayed. "Is she dead?"

Katja straightened, looked at him, and smiled.

"No, Jon Noir, only sleeping. Sleeping deeply and profoundly. Perhaps for the first time in years. Her greatest fear has been soothed, and now she's at peace."

Jon smiled. If only everything could work out so smoothly, so happily.

"Goodbye, Jon," Katja said. "Good fortune and happiness follow you, though I'm afraid your road will be long and hard."

Jon frowned. He didn't like the sound of that.

"What do you mean?" he asked.

But Katja was fading. With a final shake of her head and a smile, and a last fond look at her sister dead asleep on the floor, she broke up like morning mist in the summer sun. Like smoke on the wind—

Jon paused. Smoke? Why did he think of that? He took a deep, thoughtful breath and realized what had brought the word to his mind. He could smell smoke faintly on the thick, enclosed attic air.

"Well," a voice said behind him, "what's all this then?"

Jon whirled, to see Tully McCool standing by the open trapdoor. He had a smile on his face and a long-bladed dagger in his hand, and Jon couldn't say which looked worse.

"What are you doing?" Jon asked as the Irishman came towards him, smiling that too-bright and too-fixed smile.

"Killing two birds with one stone, Your Honor," he said. "Creating a diversion by firing Derlicht Haus. And finding out what you've done with my master's goods." He lifted his blade higher, as if by way of emphasis.

"I don't know what you mean," Jon said, backing away as McCool advanced.

"Jaysus," McCool said, "don't play the fool. We haven't the time, have we? The fire will be licking at our arses at any moment. You tell me where the item you took from my master's room is, I'll let you and the old lady go. That's all we need, isn't it?"

Jon glanced down at Agatha Derlicht, still lost in deep slumber. If he woke her—

"Agatha!"

She stirred, but didn't awaken. He tried to go by her side to shake her, but, McCool advanced and he had to back off.

"Leave the old bitch be," McCool said. "Do you tell me, or do I have to cut you?"

Jon circled around. If he could reach the staircase, he could get help. If there was time.

Jon was quick, but so was McCool. Jon lunged for the stairway, but McCool was between them. His hand flashed out, his knife cut Jon from cheek to earlobe.

"Ain't got time for this, you stupid sod," McCool said through clenched teeth. "The fire will be upon us. This old place will burn like a thatched cottage during the drought."

THE TWILIGHT ZONE

"Kill me and you'll never find the trousers," Jon ground out through gritted teeth.

"Trousers?" McCool shrugged. "Just as well, then. If no one ever finds them I'm sure the master will be happy."

He leaped at Jon, knife held low for an underhanded slashing blow. Jon met him chest to chest. He grabbed for McCool's throat with one hand and his knife wrist with the other, but the Irish tough was a wily, experienced fighter. He twisted his wrist and it came free. He struck and Jon felt a bite of cold pain as the blade slipped into his chest. It was like ice in his heart. Jon gasped. McCool smiled viciously, but Jon caught his wrist in an iron grip, preventing him from twisting the blade or thrusting it further as Jon's fingers bit like claws into McCool's throat.

Hang on, Jon told himself desperately. *Hang on. Strangle the bastard. It's your only hope.*

They surged about the floor, dancing a clumsy waltz. McCool's vicious grin turned into a fixed rictus as Jon cut off his air supply with one hand while striving to prevent the Irishman from gutting him by trapping his knife wrist with the other.

Jon was the stronger, McCool the more experienced hand-to-hand fighter. McCool threw himself from side to side, trying to break Jon's grip, but he couldn't. He brought up his knee, trying to slam it into Jon's groin, but somehow Jon managed to shift weight, blocking each thrust.

Time, though, was running out. Jon knew it. McCool's blade had just missed its target, barely grazing Jon's heart. Still, it hurt like the devil, and his heart, still pumping, was filling his chest cavity and soaking his shirt with blood. He didn't have much time or strength left.

McCool finally tore away and yanked his knife out of the wound. A gush of blood followed. Jon pressed his hand against his chest despite the pain. He choked on the smoke that was now roiling up the staircase into the attic and wove dizzily on his feet.

"Die, you bloody bastard!" McCool cried, advancing for the killing blow.

Jon stood there, wounded and angry, praying for one last chance, one last opportunity to overcome his murderous enemy.

McCool stopped, his eyes suddenly wide with inexpressible fear as he looked over Jon's shoulder, behind him.

What? Jon thought. He risked a glance behind and his own heaving heart almost stopped.

It was the Hessian, as if fresh from his own killing. His uniform was torn and rent, his chest was heartless and bloody, his face awful from the beating he'd taken. His eyes glared ferociously as he advanced, his dire gaze fixed on McCool.

McCool backed away as the specter advanced. The Irishman moaned in terrible fear and stuttered prayers to Jaysus, Joseph, and Mary, but no one answered. He turned to run at the last moment as the Hessian reached out for him with bloody, broken fingers, but he was teetering at the edge of the open trapdoor and with a terrified scream Tully McCool fell down the stairs directly into the dancing flames. He fell as if he were plummeting

THE TWILIGHT ZONE

into Hell and he never stopped screaming, even when he hit bottom and the flames surged around him and were sucked into his lungs.

Jon swayed and fell to his knees. His hand knotted in his blood soaked shirt pressed against the awful pain in his chest. The Hessian turned to him and suddenly he looked like a normal man, with a plain, stern, but very human-looking face.

He kneeled down next to Jon.

"I'm sorry," he said. "I can do no more. I don't have the strength to bring you and Frau Derlicht to safety."

Jon coughed when he tried to speak, bringing up blood. The blade had nicked one of his lungs when McCool had pulled it from his chest. He spat the blood from his mouth and tried again.

"Then the fire will kill us."

"No." The Hessian gripped his upper arm. It felt like the caress of a kitten's paw. "You have the power. You do. Use it. Summon water from the sky, from the ground, from anywhere, to douse the fire. Do it," the Hessian said. "Do it...do it...do it..." he repeated as he slowly faded away.

Power? Jon thought. *I've been helpless all my life to the whims of my father, and now my brother. My brother. I can't die. Agatha can't die. We can't let him get away with everything. With Trudi.*

Power? All right. Let's see.

Though he didn't believe, his anger pushed him to dig deep down inside himself and inside he found something that he fastened upon. Something ancient. Powerful.

Unyielding. He grinned, coughing blood. *I'll show them power*! he thought. *Like they've never seen before*!

Later, they all said it was a miracle. It was another tale to tell of Geiststadt, the spirit city, and the strange things that had happened there over the years.

Old Derlicht Haus had caught fire. Its ancient wooden structure burned like the devil himself had set the blaze. It seemed as doomed as those inside who couldn't escape, among them Agatha Derlicht, and, as Pompey reported, young Jon Noir.

But angry black clouds appeared suddenly out of the clear afternoon sky. Thunder boomed like the roll of ancient drums and lightning split the darkness. It began to rain torrentially, as if someone had opened a spigot in the sky, but only on the Derlicht estate, directly over the old burning house.

But that was not all. The wind swirled madly and a waterspout appeared over the millpond that, fed by Skumring Kill, stood usually so placidly between the Derlicht and Noir estates. The wind blew like a hurricane and flung the waterspout through the sky, hurling it against the burning building, dowsing the inferno. Later, dead fish and dried water plants were found throughout the wreckage.

Despite the miraculous rain, the building was nearly a total loss. Most of it was destroyed, from the second floor down to the cellar where a ruined clutter of burnt beams, flooring, and furniture made an impenetrable jumble of destruction. The devastation was complete.

Except, oddly enough, for part of the attic which still stood impossibly untouched in the shell of the house.

THE TWILIGHT ZONE

The villagers had to use ladders to reach it, because they heard weak cries for help once the fire had been so mysteriously extinguished.

Inside they found Agatha Derlicht. She was wet and cold and somewhat bewildered by events, but well enough to live for seven years after the odd events of that day, and die in bed with a smile on her face.

She was all right because Jon Noir had huddled over her and wrapped her in his arms to protect her from flame and falling debris. They found him with an expression of utmost concentration, some said anger even, on his usually placid features, dead from a deep chest wound that simply could not—should not—have existed, as there was no weapon in the attic nor anyone else present who could have made the wound.

Thomas sat in his study, relieved and puzzled at the same time. He couldn't quite understand what had happened. McCool, apparently, had set the fire that destroyed Derlicht Haus. Thomas smiled to himself. When the bog-trotter created a diversion, he really created a diversion. How the fire was extinguished was a mystery, but then mysteries abounded in Geiststadt, and always would. Thomas had had no trouble in getting his spell doll back from the bunkhouse. It now resided safely under lock and key in his study's desk.

The fate of the bloodstained trousers was more problematical, but with Jon dead, perhaps they would never turn up. As far as he'd been able to discern, Jon had never told anyone about them. Perhaps the secret of their hiding place had died with Jon. And, if indeed they did turn up in the weeks or months or years to come, Thomas would just deal with them as he had dealt with every obstacle that had so far been put in his path. Perhaps everything hadn't worked out exactly as he'd planned, but all in all he was in a good position. Better, at any rate, than Jon and the Captain, for example.

There came a sudden knock at the study door, and Thomas looked at it, annoyed.

"Come," he ordered, wondering who was disturbing him now. Suddenly, he thought that perhaps it was McCool, returned after laying low for a while after his spectacular pyrotechnic performance. He was disappointed to see that it was only the darkie, Isaac.

"Yes, what is it?" Thomas asked impatiently.

"Mister Irving and Constable Pierce want to speak to you," Isaac said in his soft, rumbling voice.

"All right. Show them in."

"Yes, sir."

A sudden thought struck Thomas. "Oh, and go down to Miss Schmidt's place and fetch her for me. I'd like to see her."

Isaac shook his head. "No, sir."

"What?" Thomas asked, sitting up straighter in his chair.

"No, sir. I'll tell the gentlemen to come in, but that's it. I ain't running your errands. I ain't working for you no more. Me and some of the men are going to go to work for the Derlichts. They need extra hands to build the house again and all."

Thomas was incensed. "Noir gold is not good enough for you any more?" he asked angrily.

"No, sir," Isaac said steadily. "Thomas Noir gold ain't."

THE TWILIGHT ZONE

He opened the study door, said, "Gentlemen," and stepped aside so Irving and Pierce could enter. Then he left Noir Manor, forever.

Thomas clamped down on his seething anger, promising to himself to see about Isaac later, and managed a smile as Irving and Pierce came up to his desk.

"Gentlemen," he said, fairly genially, "sit down."

"No thank you," Irving said stiffly. "We'd rather stand."

Thomas frowned. "All right."

"Let me come to the point," Irving said. "You're a murderer, sir, a cold-blooded vicious killer. Whether by hire or by your own hand, it's all the same."

"What?" Thomas felt the blood drain from his features.

"It's all true," Pierce said mildly. He pursed his lips. "Where's your man McCool?"

Thomas thought quickly. "No doubt halfway to Brooklyn by now. He left my employ early this morning." Thomas leaned forward. "I discovered he wasn't totally reliable."

"No doubt," Irving said thinly. "After careful consideration of the events of the past five days Constable Pierce and I have decided that you're the one responsible for the wave of death and violence that has washed over Geiststadt like an evil tide. No other human agency. Certainly no inhuman one."

"Well, I don't know about that," Thomas said. He was thinking furiously, a cold sensation in the pit of his stomach. "McCool might have been responsible for it, but not under my instigation."

"Whose, then?" Pierce asked mildly.

"Jon's," Thomas said in suddenly inspiration.

"Preposterous!" Irving said.

Thomas shook his head, growing more confident. "Oh, no. My brother was quite bitter about his status. He felt he'd worked long and hard for no effect. He felt much more was due him. Why, after hearing some of his wild claims and accusations I wouldn't be surprised if he'd hatched the scheme, killed, what's-his-name, the cowherd, killed his old enemy Rolf, even killed Johann Schmidt so he could be closer to his daughter, then killed the Captain for his money." Thomas smiled. "It all fits. He probably even started the fire at Derlicht Haus. Who else could have?"

"Tully McCool," said Pierce.

"But he wasn't here." Thomas shrugged, hoping that they'd never find the bog-trotter's burned bones in the wreckage where they most likely resided.

"Moonbeams and sunshine," Irving said. "You're the one behind it."

Thomas's smile remained steady. "Do you any proof of that?"

"Proof?" Pierce shook his head. "Unfortunately, none that would stand in a court of law. We do, however, have this."

His hand was a blur as it reached under his coat, then flashed downward in a throwing motion. McCool's long-bladed dagger vibrated, point first, in Thomas's desktop, right in front of him.

"That's not mine," Thomas said. His voice was a bit thinner than he had intended.

"No, sir," Pierce said. "But it belonged to your man McCool. He was seen starting the fire that consumed

Derlicht Haus. He was carrying that very blade. The flames prevented our witness from following him, but he was able to rouse the house so most of its occupants were able to escape. Later, our witness found that," he nodded at the dagger embedded in the desktop, "amidst the rubble of the burned-out building."

Isaac, Thomas thought. *That damned darkie.* He managed a smile that he hoped was believable.

"Interesting story." He pulled the dagger from the desktop and examined it briefly before dropping it aside. "But it has nothing to do with me. Even if what you say is true, there's no proof that I was involved with any of this chicanery."

"No proof," Irving said, "but moral certainty. We know *you*, sir. We knew your brother Jon. Even after our brief acquaintance we know which one of you was capable of these horrendous crimes."

Thomas laughed. Moral certainty! What did he care of that? They had no proof of his involvement that would stand up in a court of law. Not a shred of evidence of his guilt. "The people will believe me," he said, "because they like a good story. And because I'll be here to tell it."

"They may believe your lies in Geiststadt, sir," Irving said coldly. "But do not bring your vile tale to Manhattan. If you do, *I* will make sure which version of the affair is believed."

Thomas frowned. "Are you threatening me, sir?"

Washington Irving leaned forward, placing his hands on Thomas's desk.

"Yes," he said, distinctly. "I am. The events of the past

few days would make for an interesting story. Perhaps I shall write it. With the names changed, of course. Even so, the people who read it will know." He stood up. "Manhattan is a small island. We don't need your kind there. Even in Europe society runs in small circles, and I have entree to all. If you ever dare to show your face in decent society, I will ruin you. I will make sure men spit at your shadow and women run from your offered hand. That is all, sir."

Irving turned to leave.

"He threatened me!" Thomas shouted. "Constable Pierce! You heard him!"

The constable looked all around the study. "Gracious," he said. "This is an interesting room. We have nothing like it in Brooklyn." He followed Irving to the door, but stopped, and turned back toward Thomas, who was staring at them with naked hate twisting his features into a grotesque mask. "It's gloomy, though. I hope you'll enjoy it for a long, long time."

He pulled the door shut after him.

EPILOGUE

June 21st, 1842, dawned like many of the other first days of summer that had come to Geistadt, a small village nestled between hill-ridge and marsh in Kings County, New York, on the west end of Long Island. It was bright and sunny, pleasantly warm with the mildness of spring surrendering to the sultry promise of summer in the air.

Despite the beautiful weather, Noir Manor seemed cold and empty to its new master, Thomas Noir, a man who had never before cared about or for the people who surrounded him. As he walked slowly down the stairs from his bedroom to the kitchen, he ticked off the names in his head. Benjamin Noir, dead. Jonathan Noir, dead. James and Seth Noir, gone. Tully McCool, vanished, presumably dead. Isaac and most of the servants and farmhands, gone. Even Washington Irving and Constable Pierce, gone.

He reached the kitchen and managed a smile at Callie, good old loyal Callie, rocking in her chair before the fire.

"I guess that just leaves you and me, old woman," he said. But Thomas Noir was not a man to dwell on his problems. Though abandoned by nearly everyone on a bankrupt estate, his dream of a luxurious life among the capitals of the world vanished, he still had something to hold on to. "But not for long. Soon I'll bring Trudi here as my wife, and I'll start siring those thirteen sons."

There were problems, of course. But he had a long time

to work them out. A very long time, once he'd had a thirteenth son. Most financial problems could be solved if you had a head on your shoulders and a long time to solve them. He would yet see the capitals of the world. In forty or fifty years. In a practically brand new twenty-one-year-old body. He sat down at the kitchen table, smiling. Yes, it was all just a matter of perspective. Of patience. Of time.

"Callie, some tea."

She didn't reply, didn't even indicate that she was aware of his presence in the room. Annoyed, Thomas looked over at her. She was rocking away before the blazing fire on the sultry first day of summer, Thomas's twenty-first birthday. For the first time he noticed that she had a large bound volume open on her lap.

"What do you have there?" he called out.

"Captain's journal," she said softly, "with a copy of the spell of transference from a thirteenth son to a thirteenth son. I've been studying it these days. Studying it hard, to see where the Captain went wrong."

Thomas smiled. "Well, that's fine. I've been wanting to see it, and you've tracked it down already. Let me take a look."

For the first time Callie gazed at him, and he saw bitterness on her face. Bitterness and loss and sudden contempt that struck him like a blow.

"Why?" she asked, her voice scornful. "Won't do *you* no good."

"What do you mean?" He was taken aback by her strangely defiant tone.

"Says here how you number the sons," she said, her

THE TWILIGHT ZONE

tone mocking. "Abortions don't count. Stillbirths don't count. The babes have to take a breath of air before they can be reckoned."

Thomas frowned. "So? That just makes it easier to keep track, don't it?"

"Birth order don't count," she said in that same terrible voice.

"What? That's preposterous—"

"Order of conception. That's what counts." She laughed as Thomas sat there, looking at her. "Don't you see, boy? It was Jon! He was the thirteenth! *You're* the fourteenth. He was *conceived* before you, boy. He was the one who got his daddy's *heka*."

"Ridiculous!" Thomas said. He rose from the table and stalked over to Callie's spot by the fire. "Preposterous!"

Thomas felt his anger rising. He couldn't tell if the heat on his face was from the fireplace or his own internal rage. "*I* am the thirteenth son!"

"You ain't nothing, boy," Callie said. And she laughed at him again. It was the cruelest thing she could have done.

Thomas roared wordlessly in anger. He loomed over Callie like an avenging angel of death. His shaking hands reaching out to crush the life from her and he saw her eyes as, unafraid, she looked up at him from her chair. Her eyes were cold and hard and powerful. Their impact cooled his anger like water thrown on a red-hot poker. He swayed on his feet, suddenly weak and afraid. She had the *heka*, he suddenly knew. Far more than he. Thomas stood stone-faced, suddenly withered inside. She was right. He knew it now. All his life had been a lie. He was nothing.

All that planning. All that killing. All that blood. All for nothing. Nothing. Nothing. Nothing but endless days grubbing a pathetic, sordid living out of the dirt. Nothing but a step-by-step, day-by-day trip to the grave, with no way to avoid it and no means to cushion the years as they dripped slowly by.

Callie laughed and laughed. "Jon was the one! He had the power! He had the *heka!*" Her laughter turned to sobs that trickled to a whisper husky with the sound of coming death.

"And I tell you. I see it. I see it clear as yesterday. He'll come back, boy. And he'll be *mad.*"

Thomas Noir put his hands over his face, but nothing would come, not even tears of despair.

Agatha Derlicht visited Jon Noir's grave nearly every day of her remaining years. In the end, Isaac, the new butler of the new Derlicht Haus, had to carry her there in his strong arms. Often they were accompanied by Roderick Derlicht, his wife, and, as the years passed, their children.

Butterflies danced over the grave, drawn by the wildflowers blooming there in unbridled profusion from earliest spring to the last days of autumn. Roderick's and Trudi's children chased them, laughing, as they fluttered above the resting place of Jonathan Noir's mortal remains in intricate ephemeral patterns of perfection and grace.